2003

Conejos County Library

S0-AVQ-387

Conejos County Library
Antonito Branch

37566000034790

Conejos Library District
Maria De Herrera Branch

The Visitor

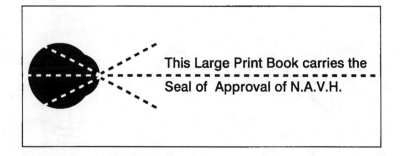

This Large Print Book carries the
Seal of Approval of N.A.V.H.

The Visitor

Lori Wick

Thorndike Press • Waterville, Maine

Copyright © 2003 by Lori Wick

All Scripture quotations are taken from the King James
Version of the Bible.

All rights reserved.

Published in 2003 by arrangement with
Harvest House Publishers.

Thorndike Press® Large Print Christian Romance.

The tree indicium is a trademark of Thorndike Press.

The text of this Large Print edition is unabridged.
Other aspects of the book may vary from the original edition.

Set in 16 pt. Plantin by Ramona Watson.

Printed in the United States on permanent paper.

Library of Congress Cataloging-in-Publication Data

Wick, Lori.
    The visitor / Lori Wick.
        p. cm. — (The English garden ; bk. 3)
      ISBN 0-7862-5641-9 (lg. print : hc : alk. paper)
      1. Accident victims — Fiction.   2. England — Fiction.
    3. Large type books. I. Title.
    PS3573.I237V57 2003b
    813'.54—dc21   2003052672

Conejos County Library
Antonito Branch
+ 796

To my readers . . .

Please do not think that I dedicate
this book to you lightly.
I don't.
At times you've been my harshest critics.
More often than not, you've
cheered the loudest.

I've asked you to believe in kingdoms
that don't exist.
You've gone with me through death
and triumph.
You've seen how the guy always gets
the girl, but never without pain.

Thank you for enjoying my books.
Thank you for the special people you are.
I pray for you.
Never forget you hold a special place
in my heart.

National Association for Visually Handicapped
---------------------- *serving the partially seeing*

As the Founder/CEO of NAVH, the only national health agency solely devoted to those who, although not totally blind, have an eye disease which could lead to serious visual impairment, I am pleased to recognize Thorndike Press★ as one of the leading publishers in the large print field.

Founded in 1954 in San Francisco to prepare large print textbooks for partially seeing children, NAVH became the pioneer and standard setting agency in the preparation of large type.

Today, those publishers who meet our standards carry the prestigious "Seal of Approval" indicating high quality large print. We are delighted that Thorndike Press is one of the publishers whose titles meet these standards. We are also pleased to recognize the significant contribution Thorndike Press is making in this important and growing field.

Lorraine H. Marchi, L.H.D.
Founder/CEO
NAVH

★ Thorndike Press encompasses the following imprints: Thorndike, Wheeler, Walker and Large Print Press.

Acknowledgments

It's hard to believe I'm finished with the third book in this series. I'm having a wonderful time writing about what I imagine life might have been like during this time in England's history. I couldn't do that unless my own world was full of people who challenge and encourage me. I need to thank . . .

- My brothers- and sisters-in-law, Jeff and Ann Wick, Darrell and Jane Kolstad, Chris and Margaret Arenas, and John and Cheryl Wick. Thank you for all of the love, support, and interest over the years. Thank you for the special friends you are. Holidays and birthdays would not be the same without you. I thank God for allowing me to be part of this family.

- The staff of Harvest House Publishers. Thanks for all your understanding. You're the first to know that plans don't always proceed without interruptions. Thank you for your patience and enthusiasm. You take such good care of Bob and me. Thank you for making us part of the family.

- Katie Barsness. Thank you for keeping your eyes on Christ when the darkness tried to crowd in. Thank you for heading to the Word for comfort and strength, knowing it was the only place for the real thing. You have been a great example and a help to me. I love both you and Dale.

- Pearl Hayes. Thanks, Mom, for your listening ear when we walk. I think this book came together so quickly because you cheered and laughed in all the right places. You are a treasure, as well as a dear friend.

- My Bob. Is there such a thing as professional husband-of-a-writer? If there is, you have certainly entered into the class. When a story falls apart, you're ready to hear the next idea. You know when to listen and when to ask for more details. You were the first to understand that obedience is more important than writing. Thank you for choosing to obey as often as you do. Have I told you lately that I love you? I hope so. I think it every day.

The English Garden
Collingbourne Families

Frank and Lydia Palmer
Children: Frank, Walt, Emma, Lizzy, and Oliver
Home: Tipton

William and Marianne Jennings (William Jennings is brother to Lydia Palmer)
Children: Thomas, James, Penny, and Catherine
Home: Thornton Hall

Robert and Anne Weston
Home: Brown Manor

Pastor Frederick and Judith Hurst
Children: Jeffrey, Jane, Margaret, and John
Home: the manse

James and Mary Walker (Marianne Jennings' parents)
Home: Blackburn Manor

The Steeles
Henry, Charlotte (married to John Barrington), Elizabeth, Edward, and Cassandra
Home: Newcomb Park

Alexander Tate (Harriet Thorpe is his aunt)
Home: Pembroke

Prologue

**London
Preston Manor
January 1812**

Dr Harvill stood patiently in the hallway outside of Alexander Tate's bedroom. Several maids entered the room, a manservant behind them, all of them seeing to their tasks and exiting one at a time. Tate's man, Hastings, as well as his business manager, Charles Pierrepont, were among the parade of people. Not accustomed in his line of work to being asked to wait, the good doctor remained silent to see what would happen.

"Mr Tate will see you now, Dr Harvil," Mrs Thorpe, Tate's aunt, finally appeared to say. She bid him enter. The doctor did so without comment.

"How are you today, Mr Tate?"

"I have a headache," the gentleman said quietly.

"I don't wonder," the doctor stated

11

mildly, but the comment was not lost on the injured man.

"What do you suggest I do?" Tate asked, his voice still quiet.

"I suggest you get out of London. It may be that you'll regain your sight if all you do is keep those patches in place, but if my vision were in question, I'd do everything I could to aid the healing."

"And what exactly will leaving London accomplish?"

"If done properly, it will give you peace and quiet. Make it clear to your staff that you're not to be disturbed. Leave all your business affairs behind, and rest without interruption or demands on your energy. Let your body heal without all this tension."

Such a thing had never occurred to Tate, and now the very thought of it caused him disquiet. That the fall from his horse had caused his vision to become dim and blurred was difficult enough, but now to give up all sense of a normal life? That was going to take some thought.

"How long?" he finally asked.

"No less than six months — possibly a year."

Six months? Tate's mind questioned as his hand came to his head. Had the ache intensified, or was he imagining it?

"I'll check your eyes now," the doctor said quietly as he went to work. Tate had not expected to find his vision clear when the patches were lifted, but the horrible blur of dark and gray, now six weeks old, was disheartening.

The painless yet thorough examination complete, the doctor stepped back, closed his bag, and pulled a chair close.

"We've known each other for years, Tate," the older man ventured with quiet respect. "I've long admired your family's faith, but even God needs a little help now and then."

Even with the eye patches, the doctor saw Tate's brows rise.

"Yes, yes, I might not have stated that well, but you know what I mean. You can't stay here in the name of faith in God and pretend that everything is fine. That fall could have killed you, and we both know it. Do yourself a favor and be reclusive for a time. Go away, and see if your eyesight doesn't return to you."

Tate couldn't argue. He was hoping for a miracle, but miracle or not, the doctor was right: He had done nothing to aid the healing process. Indeed, other than doing business from a comfortable chair in his

13

bedroom, he had not slowed down at all.

"I'll take your advice, Harvill. Will you be able to recommend a physician for me?"

"When you decide where you're going, let me know. I'll do whatever I can."

Thanking the man and shaking the hand that suddenly found his, Tate found himself alone a moment later. When the door opened after a few minutes, he was quite certain it was his aunt.

"Aunt Harriet?"

"Yes, Alex. What did the doctor say?"

In an abbreviated version, Tate explained the situation, his voice calm, not resigned or anxious.

"I don't expect you to trail after me," he finished, "but you're certainly welcome — not that I know where I'm headed."

"Are you open to suggestions?"

"You know I am."

When Harriet spoke again, he could hear the smile in her voice.

"I know just the place, my dear," she reassured him warmly. "Leave everything to me."

Chapter One

**Collingbourne, England
Newcomb Park
March 1812**

Elizabeth Steele, Lizzy to family and friends, worked her way through breakfast, correspondence around her. She had letters from both her sisters, her brother — whose last letter had said he was somewhere in Africa — and even one from an elderly relative in London.

The temptation to tear into her brother's letter was great, but she made herself save it for last. Even as she did this, a conversation came back to her, a conversation during a visit with Anne Weston in a Collingbourne shop just days after she'd arrived back in town.

"Anne, is that you?"

"Lizzy!" Anne exclaimed with delight as she rushed to hug the friend who had entered the aisle. "How are you?"

"I'm very well," Elizabeth Steele told her,

smiling in delight of their meeting. "How are you?"

"I'm married," Anne told her, her smile lighting her whole face. "I'm Mrs Robert Weston."

"Oh, Anne, I'm so pleased for you."

"But tell me, Lizzy!" Anne rushed on. "Are you visiting or have you moved back?"

"I'm back."

"How long have you been here?"

"Only a week."

"And what brought this about?"

"Several things, but mostly that my brother has left England to travel for a time."

Anne's brows rose in surprise. "Which brother?"

"Edward. He left in August, but it feels like forever. I told Henry that I wanted to return to Collingbourne, and surprisingly enough he wanted to move as well."

"And is it just Henry, or are all your siblings back?"

"Everyone save Edward," Elizabeth said with a smile. "A little peace and quiet at Newcomb Park would have been lovely, but we're all home."

"It's so wonderful to see you, Lizzy. Things are busy just now, but when the holidays are over, I want you to come and visit."

"*I want you to do the same. I must meet your Mr Weston.*"

"*And you shall. We'll be in church tomorrow.*"

"*I shall seek you out.*"

That conversation had been in November, four swift months earlier. In that time Lizzy's sister Charlotte had married John Barrington, and her sister Cassandra had accompanied a friend on a trip to northern England. Cassandra was scheduled to arrive in Collingbourne within a week, but when she would see the new Mrs Barrington or her brother Edward again was in question.

Thinking back on it, Lizzy wondered that Anne hadn't questioned why Edward's departure would precipitate her moving back to Newcomb Park, but right now she was very glad that part of her heart had remained a secret.

Henry, the oldest of the Steele family and by far the most reserved, arrived just then, helping to remove Lizzy's mind from the unread letter as well as her current thoughts.

"Breakfast, Henry?"

"Please."

Lizzy knew very well that if she didn't push the point, he would be happy to utter only that word to her all day. A man who simply did not need spoken words to live, Henry took his seat at the breakfast table, prayed, and calmly began to eat.

Lizzy knew she could draw him out with an effort, but at the moment she didn't have the energy. Her mind was on someone else, someone who had traveled with her brother, unaware that when he'd left England, he'd taken Lizzy's heart with him.

Collingbourne, England
Brown Manor

Robert Weston walked slowly along the garden path, his eyes scanning the lush greenery for signs of his wife. He knew she was out here — the early blooms were irresistible right now — but hadn't spotted her just yet. When he did, he stopped, just taking time to study her.

Anne Weston stood in profile to her husband, the breeze pressing her dress against her and giving full evidence of her condition. Weston watched as she placed a long-stemmed blossom in the basket that hung from her arm before reaching to snip another one. Not until she straightened did she spy her husband and smile.

"This looks fun," Weston commented as he joined her.

"It is, but I'm almost finished."

"Are you getting tired?"

"A little."

"Let Sally do the arranging and take a rest," Weston suggested.

"Actually, I was thinking I might play the piano for a time."

"Can you reach the keys these days?"

Anne couldn't stop her laugh.

"You are incorrigible."

Weston grinned. "I was hoping you would think so."

Weston took the basket, and the two walked toward the house. Work on the conservatory behind them continued at a good pace, but these things always took time. Married just nine months, Mr and Mrs Weston were both delighted that Anne was expecting their first child.

"Oh, that's right!" Anne stopped just as they neared the door. "I was going to gather some herbs from the kitchen garden."

"Sally can do that, or Cook."

Anne nodded in agreement, but her heart wasn't willing to give up one of her passions. Puttering in the garden was one of her favorite activities, and the spacious walled-in kitchen garden never ceased to delight her. Nevertheless, Weston held the door for his wife, and she entered the mansion they called home.

"Is this your luncheon day with Judith Hurst?" Weston asked just after he'd passed the flower basket to Sally.

"Yes. She's coming at noon."

"Will you rest before then?"

Anne, who had still been thinking about the herbs, finally looked at him.

"That's the second time you've mentioned resting."

"I just don't want you to overdo. And if my memory serves me correctly, the last time you had company, it wore you out."

Anne had forgotten about that.

"Do I look tired?" Anne now asked.

"Not tired, but a little flushed."

She saw the concern in his eyes and decided to take it easy.

"Good," Weston said when she told him. "You might actually fall asleep."

Anne, sure that she would do no such thing, only smiled and moved to the yellow salon to put her feet up and read for a while. When Weston checked on her some 30 minutes later, the book lay open in her lap, but her eyes were closed in sleep.

★ ★ ★

"I have news for you," Judith Hurst said the moment the two women were alone.

"Good news?"

"Very."

"Tell me."

"Your first child and my fifth will be in the nursery together."

"Oh, Judith," Anne said softly, moving to hug her friend. "That's wonderful. Is Pastor ecstatic?"

"Over the moon. You'd think it was our first!"

"How do you feel?"

"Usually fine. Morning can be a bit tense, but it's nothing that won't go away in a few more weeks."

"Have you let any of the church families know?"

Judith grinned. "We think it's more fun to let them find out for themselves."

Anne laughed at the look of conspiracy in her friend's eyes as the two enjoyed a lovely meal together. They also caught up on the latest news, something they usually didn't have time for on Sundays.

By the time Judith took her leave, Anne was weary, but her face held a smile. The Hursts' plan to let the congregation learn of the pregnancy on its own was a brilliant idea. Anne decided then and there not to tell Weston. She would wait until he heard the news and then have the delight of telling him she'd known all along.

Newcomb Park

Lizzy read Edward's letter again the next morning. Nothing had changed. She hadn't missed a thing, but her lonely heart somehow willed the words to be different. Laying her head back against the sofa in the small sitting room, her eyes slowly closing, Lizzy remembered the last time she'd seen Thomas Morland. It was a Sunday morning in Bath.

"I'm going to be gathering the last of my things tonight, Edward," Thomas said as soon as they exited the church building.

"All right. Shall I meet you at your house then?"

"Tuesday morning. I'll expect you at 8:00."

"I'll be there."

Lizzy stood quietly, as did her sister Cassandra. Henry had gone ahead to the coach to find some papers he'd promised Pastor Greville. For a moment it didn't look as though Morland would even remember to glance their way, but just before he turned away, his eyes found Lizzy's.

"Well, Lizzy and Cassie, I won't be seeing you again for a time, so I guess this is goodbye."

"Have a good trip, Morland," Cassandra bade him. "Take good care of yourself and our Edward."

"I shall. Goodbye."

"Goodbye," Lizzy put in as he turned, but he'd broken eye contact by then.

Lizzy wondered all the way home if her face showed how frozen her heart felt. It had all been so fast, and with no word on when they would see him again. She glanced at Edward, but clearly he was preoccupied with his own traveling plans. Cassandra was gazing out the window, so for the moment Lizzy felt free to let her eyes slide shut.

"Are you all right?"

Lizzy was stunned to hear her brother Henry quietly asking this. So stunned in fact, that for a moment she didn't answer.

"Yes, Henry. Thank you."

Henry's eyes remained on her for a few moments before shifting to the window. Lizzy's own gaze shifted as well. All she could wish for was her older sister, but Charlotte was visiting with her fiancé's family and would not be home for several more days.

Lizzy surfaced from the memory with a start, sitting upright in her seat. The scene was so painful in her mind that for a moment her breathing was labored.

"Do you need something, ma'am?"

Lizzy's personal maid had come to the room and found her mistress so pale that she interrupted her.

"No, Kitty, thank you," Lizzy said quietly, managing a smile. But the occurrence caused Lizzy to head for the mirror. After a brief look, she concluded that she looked awful and decided not to sit about and baby herself any longer. Calling for a basket and her small hand-clippers, she headed for the garden. Flowers were not her favorite pastime, but anything had to be better than sitting around and feeling sorry for herself.

Collingbourne, England
Pembroke

"Tate?" Harriet called as she knocked, opening the bedroom door just enough to be heard. "May I come in?"

"Yes."

Tate turned to the sound of his aunt entering as the door opened completely. He'd been standing in front of the open window, taking some air. The blackness was always there, surrounding him in every way. Most

24

of the time he could ignore it, but just then he'd smelled something pleasant through the open window. It might have been a flower, bush, or combination of both, but without going out to investigate, he was left wondering.

"How are you, dear?" his aunt asked, closing the door behind her.

"A bit cross, I must admit."

"Is there anything I can do?"

"Nothing comes to mind."

Harriet couldn't stop the smile that came to her mouth. Even in a poor mood, Alexander Tate was polite. He might be tempted to ask her to leave, but if he was, he was careful to keep such thoughts from showing on his face or in his voice. Certainly one could mask a great deal when eyes could not be seen, but Harriet was looking at her nephew's face, and there was not so much as a cross wrinkle to his brow or a single stern line to his relaxed mouth.

"You've a letter here from Banks," Harriet said, referring to the man who ran things in Tate's London home. "Would you like me to read it to you?"

"Not just now. Thank you, Aunt Harriet."

The smile dropped from Harriet's face.

Tate was doing an admirable job of hiding it, but his spirits were beginning to droop. The inactivity, darkness, and lack of companionship were starting to wear on him.

Harriet was on the verge of telling him her plans for the rest of the day, hoping to distract him, when someone knocked on the door. Harriet went to answer it, relief filling her when Hastings stood in the hallway and informed her that Dr Tilney had stopped by and wished to see Tate.

"Certainly, Hastings," Harriet told Tate's right-hand man. "Send him directly up."

Harriet didn't know if the doctor would have good news, but his visit alone would be a welcome interruption. The older woman left the men alone during the examination, but Harriet Thorpe wasted no time once Dr Tilney was through. She met him at the front door and walked him to his coach.

"How are his eyes?"

"There's improvement, but he needs to keep on as he is for several more months. That's when we'll know if all this darkness and rest have been worth it or not."

"Thank you, Dr Tilney."

"You're welcome," he said. He would have turned away, but Harriet wasn't done.

"I have something I want to ask you."

The doctor listened as Tate's aunt discussed an idea with him, one she felt desperate to try.

"I like your plan, Mrs Thorpe," the doctor said. "But it would have to be just the right person. Someone calm and undemanding. Someone who will know when to leave, a person who can read the signs that are not spoken."

Harriet nodded, glad that he had agreed.

"You're right, of course; not just anyone will do. But at least with your permission I can begin to keep my eyes and ears open."

The kind doctor put a comforting hand on her shoulder.

"Collingbourne is full of fine folk, Mrs Thorpe. No doubt the right person will come to you very soon."

Harriet thanked him without further comment, but there was plenty on her mind as the doctor's coach pulled away. *I'm sure Collingbourne does have many fine folk, Dr Tilney, but I won't be looking far and wide. I'll be concentrating my search within the church family.*

"Are you ever like Jonah?" Pastor Hurst asked the congregation in the closing minutes of his sermon on Sunday. "Four chapters in the Book have this prophet's name on them, and more than two of them are about his disobedience. Do more than half the things said about you concern your disobedience?

"Jonah's discontent was at a remarkable level. This prophet of God needed to be ashamed of himself in light of how swiftly wicked Nineveh repented. Jonah was given a job and ran. The citizens of Nineveh learned of their doom and fell to their knees in repentance. While we read about Jonah's repentant heart in the belly of the fish, it didn't take long for him to pout when God did things he disagreed with. When he was in trouble, he said God was His salvation, but when you look at chapter 4, verse 2, Jonah is disgusted with God for the salvation He offers to Nineveh."

Pastor Hurst smiled gently at the group gathered before him, his eyes warm.

"We're so like Jonah, aren't we? We have in our mind the way we think things should be done, and when they don't happen that way, we frown toward heaven and pout. But there's hope, isn't there? Jonah himself, even though he wasn't very happy, had to admit that God is a gracious God, merciful, slow to anger, and of great kindness. That's why there's hope. Not with us, but in the God who loves us.

"No matter how often we have failed, frowned, or followed our own path in the past, our gracious, kind, merciful, saving God is ready with forgiveness.

"We'll be talking about Jonah for several more weeks. There is much to be learned here about God's love and our discontent. If you have a chance, study the book of Jonah on your own. Ask God to teach you things that will change you forever."

Pastor Hurst then led them in a final prayer and dismissed the congregation.

Lizzy sat for a moment and thought about what she'd heard. She had been discontented since Thomas Morland left with Edward. She now realized what a waste of time that had been — her time and God's. It was time to confess her selfishness and agree with God no matter what His plan.

"Lizzy."

Lizzy looked up to see Mrs Walker calling to her from the end of the pew.

"Come and hug me," the older woman bade, "and tell me how you are."

Lizzy did as she was asked, glad for their friendship.

"I'm doing better after that sermon," Lizzy admitted as the women embraced.

"I'm glad to hear it. Can you and Henry join us for lunch today?"

"That sounds wonderful. I'll check with him."

Henry Steele enjoyed James Walker's company immensely. They might not have contact for months or even years at a time, but whenever they were together, their conversation picked up without faltering. With this in mind, Henry agreed to lunch at Blackburn Manor without hesitation.

Lizzy and Mrs Walker also enjoyed one another's company, but today there was an added bonus. After going home to check on Tate, Harriet Thorpe arrived for lunch as well.

"Mrs Thorpe," Lizzy greeted her warmly. "How are you?"

"I'm very well, Elizabeth." The two had met in January. "How are you?"

"I'm well. I was thinking about your nephew this morning when I saw you come in alone. Has there been any improvement?"

"Not yet. The doctor still wants him to take it very slowly."

Mrs Walker invited the women into the sitting room to get comfortable; the men were still in the study looking at elaborate plans for a plumbing system, something

Mr Walker had picked up at the town market.

"When does Cassandra arrive?" Mrs Walker asked Lizzy as soon as the women were settled.

"This week."

Lizzy went on to tell her hostess something about a recent letter, but Harriet barely heard her. As on the first occasion they had met, she couldn't remember the last time she'd spoken with such a beautiful young woman. She couldn't help but wonder if Tate had ever met her.

"I can't remember, Elizabeth," Harriet began when there was a lull. "Where were you moving from when you came to Collingbourne?"

"We have a home outside of Bath. We haven't lived or visited here for some time, but it's still like coming home."

"Tell her about Pembroke, Harriet," Mrs Walker put in. "It's such a fun story."

Harriet smiled. "Pembroke was built in 1755. It has a large ballroom, very ornate, and grounds of more than 600 acres. Twenty years after it was built, an observatory was added. Garden windows sit all along the first floor, and the sweeping view from the rear windows is nothing short of breathtaking."

Harriet smiled again before adding, "I honeymooned at Pembroke. When Thorpe and I were married, the house belonged to his father. We spent six months here, roaming about and falling deeper in love. When it was time to return to London, I cried. When my father-in-law died and everything came to Thorpe, I cried again, knowing we could visit whenever we wished. We didn't come nearly as often as I dreamed, but it was lovely knowing it waited here for us."

"How wonderful," Lizzy said, her voice betraying a tinge of envy.

"When Tate is feeling more the thing, you'll have to come to visit."

"I would enjoy that."

"Still no visitors?" Mrs Walker questioned her friend.

"No. Tate still needs to take things quite slowly. Dr Tilney and I have thought of something that might work, but it's a rather delicate matter. If you could pray that I'll have wisdom in the days and weeks to come, I would much appreciate it."

Harriet feared she might have said too much. She didn't wish to be questioned at this time, and she was relieved that the men joined them before the conversation could proceed further. The five acquaintances moved to the dining room to eat, and Harriet was able to keep her plan private.

She surreptitiously watched Lizzy Steele the rest of the afternoon, wondering in her heart if she might be the person Tate needed. Lizzy was certainly lovely enough — not that looks mattered at a time like this. Still, Harriet's heart was uncertain, so she kept her mouth shut. *It's one of two things, Harriet, old girl,* she said to herself. *Either the whole idea is an ill-fated one, or Elizabeth Steele is not the person needed at this time.*

For a moment, Harriet's gaze shifted to Henry Steele, only just realizing he'd been rather quiet during the meal. However, she didn't completely count him out, either. *It could be anyone, Lord, anyone at all. If the idea will work. You'll show me somehow. Help me to be wise and aware.*

Almost with a start, she realized she'd done little but think of Tate since arriving. Knowing enough was enough, Harriet settled in to enjoy the rest of lunch and her visit.

Chapter Two

Pembroke

Harriet wasted no time. She had checked on Tate before going to lunch but had then been gone for hours. The mansion was full of servants, and Tate was by no means helpless, but as soon as she arrived home she sought him out in order to check on him.

"How was lunch?" he asked kindly.

"It was lovely. Henry and Elizabeth Steele were there. Have you met Elizabeth, Tate?"

His brow furrowed. "Is she a blonde?"

"No, dark."

"Then I must have met Charlotte. A remarkably beautiful woman, I might add."

"As is Elizabeth. It isn't just her mahogany-colored hair; she also has spectacular green eyes. I couldn't stop staring at her."

"Did she notice?" Tate asked with a smile.

"I hope not." Harriet laughed a little.

"How are the Walkers?"

"They are both very well. They asked after you."

"That was kind of them. Do you have time to go over your sermon notes with me now?"

"I can do better than that. Pastor Hurst has begun writing a summary for you. If I read it to you each week, you'll be right up to date when you're up to going on your own. He even reiterated his offer to visit as soon as you would like."

"I'll have to dictate a thank-you note to him. Do you have time to read now?" Tate asked again, clearly ready for the day's sermon.

"Yes. I'll get the papers directly."

When Harriet returned, Tate made himself comfortable and concentrated on the words his aunt read. He asked God to heal his eyes. He asked God to help him with patience during the process. Then he thanked God for the fact that even if he never saw again, his ears would let him hear the Word.

Newcomb Park

On Monday morning after breakfast, Lizzy began a letter to Edward. She hadn't planned to write him so soon, but her heart woke with a lightness that came from peace with God, and she found herself wanting to talk to her younger brother about it.

"Cassandra will be back soon, and I'm very much looking forward to that," she wrote shortly after greeting him and asking about his health.

Henry is as ever, quiet and to himself, but genuinely kind. I am thankful for his presence. We lunched with Walkers yesterday. Henry very much enjoys Mr Walker. I think they could spend hours alone in the study with maps, plans, and such.

The sermon from the book of Jonah was challenging yesterday morning. I'm too like that stubborn prophet in the way I complain to God. It was a good reminder for me. I was in the midst of confessing my sin when Mrs Walker invited us to join them for lunch. I felt as though I'd been rescued because it helped take my mind from my selfish thoughts. Harriet Thorpe was also there, but her nephew, Tate, is still not well enough to be out.

My thoughts are often with you and Morland. I can only imagine a place as foreign as Africa, so you'll have to be more descriptive in your letters. How is the food and their tea? Do you eat your meals at the same times we do? And your bed? What are you sleeping in? As you can see, I'm full of wonder about the whole experience, even as I'm very glad to be in England.

Just yesterday I came to great peace about the two of you leaving, but out of curiosity, Edward, does Morland ever speak of me or ask after me? I know you won't say anything to him, and he can't see my red face from Africa, but I do wonder.

Have you word from Charlotte? I think she and Barrington will be stopping in Collingbourne at some point, but I'm not sure when. I asked her in my last letter, but because they're on the move, I'm not sure when she'll receive it.

Lizzy sat back and thought about how life had changed in the last few months. So often these days she was on her own. It had seemed to her that a bit of peace and quiet around Newcomb Park would be lovely, but she missed her siblings terribly — more than she had expected.

Write soon, Edward, and tell me if you are well. You know you are always in my prayers. Don't forget to send along any unusual maps or charts for Henry. His

37

birthday is coming soon, and you know how pleased he would be. Tell Morland I said hello, and please take care of yourself.

My love to you,
Lizzy

Lizzy addressed the letter and gave it to Kitty for the post. She realized when she was alone once again that her heart still yearned for Morland, but not with the angry ache that had been present for so many days.

I know I will fall again, Lord, but I ask You to help me. I ask for Your strength to go on, to be the woman You would have me be.

Lizzy didn't ask the Lord to send her a husband in His time. Her heart simply wasn't ready for that. Everything within her believed that she would never love anyone but Thomas Morland.

Pembroke

Tate's shin collided in an unforgiving manner with the drawer he'd left out, and for a moment the tall, blind man stood still and winced as pain radiated up and down his leg. He'd done the exact thing a week before on the other leg and wondered when he was going to learn.

38

Hastings heard the bump and wasn't long in checking on his employer.

"Did you need me, sir?"

Tate shut the drawer.

"Have I left anything else in my way, Hastings?"

"Yes. I'll just get this other drawer."

"Thank you."

"I think, sir," the faithful servant went on, shutting the dresser drawer and turning back to Tate, "if today is good for you, I'd like to trim your hair."

Tate's hand went to the back of his thick, dark hair. It was long at the nape and shaggy, even where the straps from his eye patches crossed the back of his head.

"Today will be fine. Right now even."

"Very good, sir. Would you like to sit outside this time?"

"Yes. I shall be down directly."

Hastings had helped him downstairs the first weeks they lived at Pembroke, but since the house and property were not entirely unfamiliar to Tate, it wasn't long before he was moving about on his own.

"Hastings?" Tate called to his man before he could leave. "Are you still here?"

"Yes, sir."

"Is my aunt nearby?" Tate asked, his voice dropping a bit.

39

"No. Shall I find her?"

"No," Tate stopped him, barely hiding his smile. "I have something I wish for you to do."

Hastings had a smile of his own by the time Tate finished describing his scheme, and only just in time. Harriet came looking for Tate's man a short while later with a question. When the three finally separated, Hastings and Tate for the haircut, and Aunt Harriet for town, Tate's plan was in place.

Tipton

The entire family was gathered at the Palmer home for dinner. Palmer and Lydia's brood of five were around the table, as were Jennings and Marianne's four children. Mr and Mrs Walker — grandparents to the Jennings children — had also joined the party. Seven-month-old Catherine was on her grandfather's knee, attempting to place the tablecloth in her mouth. Young Oliver Palmer, now nine months old, was in his sister's lap, happy to smile at anyone who caught his eye. Conversation flowed freely, and it took a moment for Palmer to gather everyone's attention so grace could be said.

"I think we'll pray now and get started,

although it doesn't seem as though anyone is lacking energy from not having eaten."

Those gathered about the table laughed at this light humor and then bowed their heads.

"We have much to thank You for, heavenly Father. Thank You for the food, the hands that prepared it, and all who have gathered here. Help us to be wise and mindful of You as we enjoy this time. I ask these things in Christ's holy name. Amen."

The conversation went back to full volume as food landed on every plate, and the feasting began.

"What do you hear about Tate?" Lydia asked the table. "Any word on his sight?"

"Harriet was over on Sunday," Mr Walker answered. "She said he still needs to take it easy and keep his eyes covered."

"How long has it been now?" Marianne asked.

"A while," put in Lydia.

"Since before Christmas," added Mrs Walker.

"Has it helped to be here in Collingbourne, taking things slower?" Jennings asked, having heard the reason for the move.

"They won't know for some time."

"He's so shut off from everything. How is he handling it?"

No one knew specific answers, so speculation abounded. Soon they moved on to the children's schooling. The older children were asked to report on what they'd been learning, the adults questioning them at some length. By the time this was accomplished, the children were finished eating and were dismissed.

The six adults enjoyed conversation of their own, and interestingly enough, the Hurst family came up. Palmer shocked everyone with his first statement.

"I think Judith might be expecting."

"Who told you that?" his wife wished to know, her mouth opening in surprise.

"No one. I just think it might be true."

There was no end of ribbing when he said this, and Palmer took it in stride. The group was right: He didn't know for certain. Nevertheless, he was quite sure in his heart, and when the topic changed to a possible trip to London, he did nothing to dissuade it. He told himself that they would all know soon enough.

Pembroke

"Aunt Harriet, is that you?" Tate called from the library. It had taken two more days to execute his plan, but he was now situated casually in one of the deep chairs, a side table next to him.

"Well, Tate," his aunt said with pleasure, "I don't think I've seen you in this room since we arrived."

Tate smiled to himself but said honestly, "I'd forgotten how good a library smells."

"It does at that," Harriet agreed softly, her eyes caressing the beautiful book-lined shelves.

"Are you in the mood to read for a time, Aunt Harriet?"

"Why, Tate," his aunt said with pleasure. "I'd love to read to you. What shall I read?"

"Oh, anything will do." His voice was a study in nonchalance. "I think there might be a book right here on the table."

"Wonderful."

Tate barely held his composure as Harriet took the book from his outstretched hand. He heard her settle in to read, turning the first few pages, but then everything stopped.

"Oh, Tate, this book is in French. My French is terrible."

"Oh, all right. No problem. I think there's another volume of some sort right here."

Tate took a second book from the table and held it out.

"Wonderful," Harriet said again, ready

to do some serious reading this time, but again, all movement stopped.

"Tate," she said, her voice growing suspicious. "This book is written in Italian. I don't know Italian."

"Don't you?" he asked, as though this were breaking news.

"Alexander Tate!" she explained sternly, even as laughter escaped. "Who helped you with this?"

Tate's head went back as he laughed, a full-bodied sound that Harriet hadn't heard in far too long. She went over to hug him, and he squeezed her tightly, very pleased with the success of his joke.

"You rascal!" she accused him, still laughing at his ploy. "Was Hastings in on this?"

"Of course."

Harriet sighed before asking, "*Would* you like me to read to you?"

"As a matter of fact, I'm happy just to sit here, but thank you."

"That was very naughty."

"Wasn't it?" Tate agreed, doing nothing to hide his smile.

Harriet began to rethink her plan. Maybe Tate didn't need anything else right now. Then again . . .

Tate was speaking to her, so Harriet attended as best she could, but her thoughts were running in a certain direction. It would be most intriguing to see what the future might bring.

Newcomb Park

"You're pacing," Henry said mildly, the second time he passed Lizzy in the large entryway. She turned to him, trying to look innocent but doing a dreadful job. Henry's serious eyes caused her shoulders to droop.

"I thought she would be here by now."

"As did I, but that doesn't mean something is wrong."

"I wonder why I always assume it does."

Henry didn't answer but did join her near the window, his own gaze going to the quiet driveway. He stood for several moments, his thoughts to himself, before touching Lizzy's shoulder and moving on his way.

Tempted as she was, Lizzy did not go back to pacing. Telling herself she would be too weary to enjoy Cassandra's first day back if she didn't settle down, she made herself stand still.

"Lizzy," Cassandra's rather husky voice came to her in the night, and Lizzy wished it was more than a dream.

"Wake up, Lizzy. I'm home."

"Cassie!" Lizzy gasped in surprise and delight when she realized her younger sister was sitting on the side of her bed, shaking her awake.

"It's terribly late. We had one delay after another. But I wanted you to know that I'd made it."

Lizzy hugged her for all she was worth.

"Are you all right?" Lizzy needed to know.

"I'm fine, and I'm so glad to be home. We'll have days to visit, but right now I've got to sleep."

Lizzy saw Cassandra to her room after she hugged Henry, who met them in the hallway, and then went back for her own sleep. She lay in the darkness a few moments, smiling up at the ceiling and thanking God for His protective hand that had brought her sister home.

Brown Manor

Anne did not know where her energy had gone. She had awakened that morning with such plans, but suddenly she had no will for any of them. Not even time in the garden sounded appealing.

Weston had gone to his study to get some work done. Anne knew he liked to have quiet, but right now she felt a need to be near him. She made her way toward the stairs, planning to apologize for being such a baby, even knowing he would understand.

Thankfully Weston had just left his desk to find Mansfield. He exited the study and saw his wife just as she reached the bottom of the stairs and collapsed into a small heap.

Anne was in Weston's arms just moments later, having missed his shouts for help and for a doctor, and when she awoke, his concerned face filled her gaze.

"I fainted, didn't I?"

"The doctor's on his way," Weston told her, his voice breathless with fright.

"Do you think I need a doctor?"

"Well, even if you don't, I do."

Anne smiled at his attempt to make her laugh, but she could see the distress in his gaze.

"Maybe I'd best go to bed."

Weston lifted her without a word. Praying that he would accept whatever God had for them, he nonetheless asked his heavenly Father to spare his precious wife.

Newcomb Park

Heedless of their late night, Cassandra was at the breakfast table with Lizzy bright

47

and early the next morning. Redheaded, brown-eyed, and covered with freckles, she was the baby of the family. Not that she acted as such, but the family did dote on her some.

This morning, feeling as though she'd been gone for years instead of months, she was filled with questions for her sister. For Lizzy, Cassandra was so much herself, warm and caring, that it was as though she'd never left.

"What do you hear from Morland and Edward, Lizzy?"

"A letter from Edward last week."

"Nothing from Morland?"

"No."

Cassandra stared at her.

"I didn't expect one, Cassie."

"Be that as it may, you were hoping."

Not having expected this, and not certain what to say, Lizzy stared rather helplessly at her.

Cassandra looked slightly amused as she asked, "Did you really think I didn't know?"

"That's precisely what I thought," Lizzy confessed. "I didn't think anyone knew. Did Charlotte tell you?"

"No, she didn't need to."

"Why didn't she need to?"

"Because I could see it in your eyes every time Morland was near you."

Lizzy felt slightly defeated. "Well, you must be the only one. Evidently Morland couldn't see a thing."

"Of course not." Cassandra's tone was matter-of-fact. "He's a man."

Laughter bubbled unexpectedly out of Lizzy's throat. Her sister's tone and expression were so utterly amusing that she couldn't help herself.

"Oh, there's Henry," Cassandra announced amid her sister's laughter and before slipping out of her chair and meeting him at the edge of the room. "Are you riding tomorrow morning, Henry?"

"Yes," he answered with a note of hesitation.

"May I accompany you?"

"Must you?" he asked, not bothering to hide his longsuffering sigh.

"Yes, but only if you don't hate it. If you only dislike it, I'll come. If you hate it, I won't."

Henry couldn't stop the smile that tugged up one corner of his mouth. There were few people who affected his heart more than his sister Cassandra.

Shorter than his other two sisters, she looked quite a ways up at him, her pansy-

49

brown eyes smiling, warm, and expectant.

"I don't hate it," he was forced to admit.

Cassandra's smile went into full bloom.

"What time shall I be ready?"

"Eight o'clock."

That matter settled, Cassandra declared that she had something in her room for both of them and sailed away to get it. Henry looked to Lizzy.

"Isn't it lovely that she's home?" his sister asked.

Henry couldn't stop the smile that stretched his mouth, as he admitted, "Indeed it is, Lizzy."

Brown Manor

"Oh, Lizzy," Anne said the moment that woman appeared in the doorway to her bedroom. "I'm so glad to see you."

"I came as soon as I got word." Lizzy moved close to the bed and took the prone woman's hand. "How are you?"

"Tired, all of a sudden. I don't know what went wrong, but I actually fainted, and now there's been some spotting. Dr Smith wants me to stay put until the baby comes."

"It's sounds as though it's for the best."

"I'm sure it is, but there was so much I wanted to get done."

Lizzy laughed a little.

"What's so funny?"

"We are — women in general. We're so busy planning, and usually with the best of intentions, but sometimes I think we get in God's way."

Anne laughed too.

"I'm not going to stay long and tire you out," Lizzy continued, "but Cassandra and I are going into town tomorrow. What can we bring you?"

"Cassandra's home?"

"Yes. She sends her love. Now, you'd best give me that list before someone comes along and shoos me out."

"You're right! Let me think a moment," Anne said, glad of the offer.

Lizzy remained quiet until Anne began a list. Taking mental notes, Mrs Weston's visitor waited only until she was done to give her a hug and then straighten to full height.

"If you think of anything more, just send word. We're not going before ten, and we shall simply stop on our way home. How does that sound?"

"Wonderful."

"Wonderful?" Weston asked as he entered the room. "You must be speaking of me."

Both women laughed. Weston checked on his wife and then offered to see Lizzy out.

Once on the drive, Lizzy asked directly, "Has she been told everything, Weston? Or is it graver than you've let on?"

"No," Weston shook his head firmly, "Dr Smith thinks she's overdone. If she stays quiet, there is no reason why she shouldn't deliver safely."

"Thank you for telling me. Anne's given me a list for town in the morning, so I'll be stopping again tomorrow when I'm finished."

"Thank you, Lizzy. You're a good friend."

Lizzy only smiled and took the hand he offered to climb into the carriage. She prayed for her friend all the way home, thinking about how good her color and spirits had been. It was nice to arrive home and be able to give Cassandra such a good report.

"What can we do to help?" her sister finally asked.

Lizzy was pleased to relate that Anne had given her a list, and outside of that, she was in Weston's and Dr Smith's capable hands.

Chapter Three

Their breath fogged the morning air as they rode from the stables out across the fields. Henry's mount was a larger animal but tame in his nature and steady in his gait. Cassandra's horse tended to be more skittish, but she was easy to control and liked Cassandra's light weight on her back.

Cassandra knew that Henry didn't care for superfluous conversation, so she kept her comments to a necessary minimum. She followed his lead, not wishing to interrupt his routine in any way, happy to do this until they came to the ridge. Not speaking or even expecting him to follow, Cassandra heeled Iris across the top of the ridge, giving her her head and hunching over the horse's back as they flew through the early dew.

Henry stayed with her, his own horse ready for the chase, until she pulled up and turned to him with a huge smile.

"It's official now, Henry," she breathlessly exclaimed as she slapped Iris' shoulder in reassurance, "I'm home."

Henry gave his lopsided grin. "Does it take riding the ridge to do that?"

"Among other things," she said with a laugh. "I'll let you know as I go."

"I can hardly wait," Henry teased, and then said not another word for the rest of their ride.

"Do you have a list of your own, Lizzy, or are you browsing today?"

"No, I have a list. Some of the crockery is beginning to wear, and I thought I might see what Benwick has."

"What's on Anne's list? Will Benwick have most of it?"

"Yes, I'm certain. Do you have a list?"

"A small one. My main concern is something for Henry's birthday. I shopped all the time I was away but found nothing. If we'd come back to London as we talked about, I know I would have found something, but plans changed."

"Why was that, Cassie? I don't think you said."

"Emma didn't tell me when we left for her uncle's that she was in an argument with her intended. She doesn't think him attentive enough and hoped that by leaving Bath he would pine for her. That was utter nonsense of course, but as I said, I didn't know about her plan until we were miles north."

"What does that have to do with London?"

"Well, only that Emma was the one who did all the pining, so rather than go with the original plan of shopping in London before we parted company, she wanted to go directly back to Bath."

"And of course, you'll never be that silly when you're in love," Lizzy teased her.

Cassandra only grinned. "I'll let you know as soon as I'm in love."

The women got down to some serious shopping as soon as the coach arrived in town. They started in Benwick's and began on Anne's baby list. As though shopping for their own child, they delighted over some of the things they found and even added purchases Anne hadn't listed.

They were in the midst of this endeavor when Harriet Thorpe came down the aisle toward them, an odd look on her face.

"Well, Mrs Thorpe," Lizzy began. "How are you?"

"I'm very well, Lizzy," she said softly, her gaze straying to Cassandra. "I heard your voices and assumed your sister had arrived. Am I correct?"

"Indeed, you are. Mrs Thorpe, please meet Cassandra, the youngest of the Steele clan."

"It's a pleasure to meet you, Cassandra."

"How do you do, Mrs Thorpe?"

"I'm well, thank you. Did you have a good trip?"

"It was very nice." Cassandra dimpled at her. "Almost as nice as coming home."

Harriet Thorpe smiled. *I like her. I like her very much, and I think she's just who I need right now.*

"You're going to find me absurd, Cassandra, but I actually have a favor to ask of you."

"All right," Cassandra said willingly, knowing that hearing her out wouldn't mean she had to agree.

"Could I possibly impose upon your time to explain in, say, an hour?"

"That would be fine. Where would you like to meet?"

"Gray's?"

"Gray's it is. I shall be there."

Harriet smiled at both younger women, bid them good shopping, and moved on her way. Lizzy looked at her sister.

"Cassie dear, I do believe I've been bored without you here and didn't even know it."

This sent Cassandra into gales of laughter that she was forced to stifle or be guilty of making a scene in the store.

Both women worked to control themselves and get back to the task at hand, Cassandra with a reminder to herself that she had to be at Gray's in an hour.

Brown Manor

"Oh, it's all so lovely," Anne exclaimed as Lizzy and Cassandra held up each tiny item. The bed was strewn with small caps and buntings, blankets and soft fabric for nappies and bath times.

"We got a bit of everything in all colors, even though we both think you'll have a boy."

"Is this based on science, or are you prescient?" Anne wished to know.

"Well, I hadn't seen you yet, so I guess that makes me prescient," Cassandra decided, but Lizzy had to admit to opinion only.

"We can't stay, Anne," Lizzy told her after a very short time. "We would love to, but we mustn't tax your strength at all."

"I understand. Judith was here this morning and said the same thing. Do tell me you'll come back, however."

"We certainly will."

The Steele women did a swift cleanup job, embraced Anne before they exited, and met Weston in the hall.

"I could tell she was pleased," he said without hesitation. "Thank you so much."

"It's our pleasure, Weston. Just send word if we can do anything else."

"We will probably be fine, but I won't forget your offer."

Weston saw them down to their coach and waved as the horses pulled away. Lizzy turned to her sister the moment the coach was in motion and stared for several seconds.

"Tell me again what Mrs Thorpe asked you to do."

Cassandra laughed and willingly obliged, causing Lizzy to shake her head in wonder all over again.

Pembroke

It couldn't have been more perfect. Harriet had all she could do not to dance when she realized that Tate had gone back to sit in the library just before Cassandra arrived on Saturday afternoon.

"Is this a good time?" Cassandra asked.

"This is perfect. I'll just bring you into the room and let you take it from there."

Cassandra smiled at the delight in the other woman's eyes, trusting her to know what was best for her nephew.

"Tate," Harriet began as she stepped into the library, "you have a visitor."

"A visitor?" he asked quietly.

"Yes."

Tate listened as his aunt walked from the room. The moment her footsteps died away, a woman's husky voice spoke.

"Hello, Mr Tate. I'm Cassandra. Your aunt asked me to come and read to you."

"Did she now?" he asked with a bit of humor in his voice, needing no time to catch on.

"Yes. Is there something in particular you'd like me to read?"

"Why, thank you for asking. Why don't we start with this book right here?"

"Very well."

Tate felt the book leave his hand, not entirely certain his aunt hadn't tiptoed back to watch. If she had, she'd know soon enough that he was about to turn the joke back to her.

It was with a great deal of admiration and some chagrin that he heard this Cassandra woman begin reading to him in per-

59

fectly accented French. Some of his thoughts must have shown on his face, as she stopped after just a few paragraphs.

"Is this where you were in the story, Mr Tate? I found a slip of paper and assumed."

Willing to listen for a time, and hoping that his aunt was in fact nearby, he responded, "That's fine."

Cassandra didn't know if Mrs Thorpe had remained in the vicinity or not. She had been given instructions and was just doing as she was told. She was to stay for less than an hour and to leave sooner if she was asked.

"Excuse me," Tate cut in after only five pages. "Would you mind terribly if we changed books?"

"Not at all."

Tate had all he could do not to snap his fingers in defeat when her Italian was as well versed as her French. He would never have dreamed he would need more languages, or he'd have put Hastings to work.

And then to his surprise, somewhere in the story, the joke faded away. Tate found himself relaxing, his mind willingly following the plot and her deep, soothing voice. She corrected a few of her pronunciations from time to time, but it wasn't distracting in the least. Tate was nothing short of amazed when she stopped and closed the book.

"Well, Mr Tate. We made it through the first four chapters, but now I must be off."

"Thank you," Tate said automatically, realizing she was moving out of the room before he could frame any more of a reply. Not long after, he heard a door close and knew she had gone. He wasted no time coming to his feet. He found the door out of the library and hollered like a fishwife.

"Harriet Thorpe, where are you? Harriet Thorpe, you come here this instant!"

Her laughter gave her away as she came from the foyer, so satisfied with herself that she danced a little jig.

"Come here," Tate commanded, holding his arms out to hug her.

Harriet went into his embrace and hugged him right back, both of them laughing until they felt weak.

Still holding his aunt close, Tate's voice became serious. "Have I told you how much I appreciate all you've done?"

"I think you just did."

Tate found her forehead and kissed it. Harriet, still very pleased with herself, told him that tea would be in an hour and that she was going to change.

★ ★ ★

Tate sat in his bedroom on Sunday morning — although the whole house was quiet — to pray and think on the Word. He had been studying the life of Moses when the accident occurred, and he worked every day to recall what he'd learned about that man and God's work in his life, asking Hastings or his aunt to read to him about things he couldn't remember.

This morning, however, he just wished to pray. Prayer had become an integral part of his life since the accident. He'd always wanted to be stronger in that area, and having been plunged into darkness had certainly accomplished that.

Please bless Pastor Hurst and all those listening to him today. Prepare hearts and change lives, Lord. Thank You that Harriet could meet with the church family this morning. Thank You for her love for You. Bless her, Lord. Help her ears to be open to Your Word this morning and to listen keenly for things she needs to learn. And please help her, Lord, to be aware of others around her.

Tate stopped. This was not so much a prayer request for his aunt but one that he would be praying for himself should he ever see again. He had not been an uncaring man, just a busy one.

"Of course," he said quietly in his room, "that's probably the same thing."

Tate spent the next two hours in his room. At times his heart was quiet, just thinking about the great God who loved him. At other moments, he lifted up all he could think of, friends and family alike, asking God to protect and save.

Not until it was almost time for Harriet to return did Tate remember Cassandra. She had such a nice voice — deep and soothing. He wondered if she was going to come again.

"I'm fascinated with Jonah," Pastor Hurst admitted during his sermon. "I think I would choose to do better. I think in the same situation I would act differently, but then something comes up in my life that reminds me I am not thinking as God thinks, and I have to suspect that I would have done no better than Jonah.

"He's doing the right thing one minute and completely rebelling the next. Can you imagine being one of the sailors on that ship? They begged God not to hold them accountable for the murder of Jonah, but what else could they do but throw him overboard? The ship was being torn to pieces. Murder or not, they had to try it or all drown.

"Rebelling against God is exhausting work. The sea and wind are about to break this ship to pieces, but Jonah is sleeping somewhere below deck. I personally would be so seasick that I would wish for death, but he's run from God and is now worn out.

"Do you ever run from God? I don't mean literally, although that might be the case. I'm talking about the times you ignore what you're supposed to do. That's a form of running from God. How about the sin you know it's time to give up? Guarding that sin and pretending you're not is running from God.

"But as we talked about last week, in God there is always hope. Even when we run, God is planning for our return. Even Jonah understood this. He's been cast into the sea and swallowed whole, but look at what he says in chapter 2, verse 4. 'I am cast out of thy sight; yet I will look again toward thy holy temple.' Verse 7 goes on to say, 'When my soul fainted within me, I remembered the Lord; and my prayer came in unto thee, into thine holy temple.'

"Hope, my friends. It's a precious thing. The hope we can have in our saving God is huge. There is no sin that He can't forgive. There is no need that He can't supply. Even if you've run. Even if you're running right now. Our saving God is waiting for you to turn to Him."

Cassandra felt tears in her eyes. She hadn't run from God in sin, but she'd been gone so long. She had let Emma talk her into staying away much longer than she had wished. It was simply wonderful to be back with Henry and Lizzy in her home church.

The sermon ended a short time later. Cassandra always managed to miss notes, but she still sang out with all her heart, giving praise to the God who had brought her to this place.

When they exited the church, Henry ended up beside her in the aisle. She turned to him, her eyes still a bit wet, and waited for him to look down.

"It's definitely official, Henry. I'm home."

Henry smiled his kind smile, the one he usually had for her, the one that didn't need words.

"How is Anne today, Weston?" Lydia Palmer asked, snagging Weston as he walked from church.

"She's doing well but wishing she could be here."

"I can well imagine. Please tell her that I'm going to visit this week. Is any day not good for you?"

"Judith is coming Tuesday. Will another day work?"

"Yes, I'll come Thursday. Send word if that isn't convenient. Is morning or afternoon best?"

"She tends to sleep off and on. Come whenever you like."

"All right. I have something for the baby that I was going to give to her later, but perhaps it will cheer her up."

Weston smiled. "Thank you, Lydia. I know she'll appreciate your visit."

Lydia had no more than finished when several other people stopped to ask after Anne. That she was loved by the church family was more than evident. Weston smiled as he rode home, knowing such a report would do her heart a world of good.

Pembroke

"I have new notes for you."

"More on Jonah?"

"Yes."

"Good. I'm looking forward to hearing them."

"And Anne Weston has been put on bed

rest," Harriet said. Home from church and sitting down to lunch, she was filling Tate in on all the news. "I don't think you've met the Westons, but things have suddenly gotten a bit rocky with Anne's first pregnancy."

"Is Weston's first name Robert?"

"I believe it is, yes."

"I think I know him from London."

"Now that you mention it," Harriet's brow creased with thought, "I think he said that very thing to me when we met."

"I didn't know he had married."

"I believe it's recent — just last year."

Tate brought his glass to his lips, having become practiced with the effort, and took a drink. When he set his glass back down, careful to miss the edge of his plate, he had a question for his aunt. This time there was no joke in his mind.

"Is Cassandra coming back tomorrow?"

"Coming back?"

"Yes, to read to me."

In her surprise, Harriet took a moment to say, "I didn't know you wanted her to."

"I thought that might be the plan."

"Not exactly, Tate," Harriet began, her mind scrambling with how to explain. "You seemed to be getting down, Tate. I began to worry. I even talked to Dr Tilney about having someone come in each day and read to you."

"And what did he say?"

"He said if we could find the right person, one who wouldn't overtax you, then it might be helpful. But then you played that joke on me, and I decided to tease you back, thinking you didn't really need a daily diversion after all."

"That all makes perfect sense, but I ended up enjoying Cassandra's reading, Aunt Harriet. I wish her to come back."

"And what of your rest?"

"She's very restful. When I got over the joke, I simply listened to her read and found it most soothing."

Harriet was stunned. Her silence told Tate as much, but he was quite serious.

"Will you ask her, or should I dictate a note to Hastings?"

"I'll certainly ask her for you, but I don't know what she'll say."

"Well, that's up to her," Tate responded pragmatically. "At least you'll be able to say you tried."

Still a little shocked by this turn of events, Harriet was quiet for a time, but then she remembered how much she liked Cassandra Steele and how willing the young woman had been to help out and go along with the joke.

Maybe she's what we all need right now, Lord. I asked You to help me know, and Tate is now requesting her return. I don't think You can make it any clearer than that.

Newcomb Park

"Why, Mrs Thorpe," Lizzy said with pleasure on seeing her. "Please come in."

"I'm sorry to come unannounced, Elizabeth. It's most rude of me."

"Not at all. Cassie and I were about to enjoy a mid-morning cup of tea. Can you join us?"

"That would be lovely. Thank you. Hello, Cassandra."

"Hello, Mrs Thorpe," the younger Steele sister greeted her as she entered the room. "Are you joining us for tea?"

"Your sister just invited me, yes."

"I'm glad. You can tell us how your joke worked."

"A little too well," Mrs Thorpe said with a laugh while the three made themselves comfortable. "Mr Tate wants you to come back."

The looks on Cassandra's and Lizzy's faces were comical. Harriet laughed a little and waited while they exchanged a look.

"Do tell, Mrs Thorpe," Lizzy put in. "We beg of you."

Harriet gave them every detail, and they laughed at how well she pulled it off.

"But then," she went on, "Tate asked in complete seriousness if Cassandra was going to keep coming. I worried that it might be too much for him, but he said he found it very soothing." The older woman shrugged, looking as helpless as she felt. "I told him I would ask."

"Well, of course I will, Mrs Thorpe. I don't think I can come every day, but I would be happy to help in any way possible."

Harriet stared at her, gratitude in every line of her being. "I liked you the moment I met you, Cassandra Steele. I can't thank you enough for this. Tate has done remarkably well, but it will be weeks before the doctor allows the patches off. I fear he feels completely cut off from everything."

"He was very kind," Cassandra said, thinking back. "I could tell he was amused, but he handled himself very well. Not an easy task when you can't see."

"So you'll come?"

"Certainly. Is tomorrow soon enough to start?"

"Tomorrow is wonderful."

The Steele sisters smiled at her. Harrie had done nothing to disguise the relief in her voice, and both Lizzy and Cassandra found this highly amusing.

The three of them enjoyed a cup of tea together and talked about the different people they knew in common. Before Harriet left, however, she made sure that Cassandra understood what she'd first told her about Tate's need for rest.

"He's been very careful, but should you ever sense that Tate has overtaxed himself with your presence, err to the side of caution and leave."

"I'll plan on that."

"I can't thank you enough, Cassandra."

The youngest Steele smiled sweetly, not needing to be thanked again.

"I'll see you tomorrow."

"Yes, tomorrow."

Harriet took her leave a short time later, and when the two sisters were alone, they both speculated as to what Cassandra might have gotten herself into.

Chapter Four

The Manse

"How are you this morning?"

Judith Hurst's eyes had only just opened, but Frederick Hurst was very close by. For two hours he had been waiting to ask the question, but knowing what a rough night she'd had, he'd kept quiet until she stirred.

"I think I'm better," she answered slowly, her hand going to her aching stomach. She had been terribly ill in the night and now felt drained and weak, but not nauseous.

"Do you want anything, dear?" Frederick asked.

"Maybe a bit of tea."

Phoebe, the housekeeper at the manse, had anticipated this and kept the pot fresh. Frederick was able to pour her some immediately. Judith was taking her first sips when the door creaked open a bit. Jane peeked in, her face anxious.

"Come in, Jane," Pastor Hurst called to

his oldest daughter and then chuckled to see that all four of the children were waiting to see their mother. They gathered close to the edge of the bed, all eyes staring at their mother in wonder. She was rarely ill, and *never* bedridden. It was a new experience for all.

"What day is it, Frederick?" Judith asked, once she'd assured the children that she was not dying.

"Tuesday."

"Oh, no." Her voice was weak, but her eyes showed her dismay. "Will you please get word to Anne that I won't make it?"

"Of course I will, and you know she'll understand, Judith."

"I'm sure you're right, but I do wish I could go."

"Ask someone else, Mother," Margaret suggested. "Maybe Jane and I could go."

"That's lovely of you to offer, Margaret, but not this time. I do like your idea, however, of asking someone else. Maybe I'll send word to Lydia Palmer or Elizabeth Steele."

This was precisely what Judith, with her husband's help, ended up doing. First they sent word to Anne, letting her know Judith was ill. They then let Lizzy know of the situation, in hopes that she could pay a visit instead. Beyond sending word, Judith knew she could do little else. In fact, right now she was too weak to care.

Pembroke

"This home is beautiful," Cassandra told Harriet the moment she arrived mid-morning, Tuesday.

"Thank you, Cassandra. It's been in the Thorpe family for years."

Cassandra would have loved a tour but knew that now was not the time. Indeed, there might never be a time. She had to be careful not to get too personally involved in this situation. That was the safest way to proceed. She had arrived with low expectations, so she wouldn't be disappointed. She didn't expect a tour now, nor would she ever.

"Tate," Harriet called from the entrance of the library, just as she had before. "You have a visitor."

"Hello, Mr Tate," Cassandra said as soon as her hostess walked away and she was fully in the room.

"Hello, Cassandra. Thank you for coming."

"You're very welcome. Do you have a particular book in mind for today?"

"I do, yes." He handed her the Italian volume. "If you'll go on in this."

"Certainly."

Taking the sofa that was nearest Tate's chair, Cassandra carried on with ease, reading in her usual style, with a certain amount of inflection, but not trying to imitate anyone's voice in dialog.

She read for more than an hour, her listener seeming to be as relaxed as a cat in the sunshine. Glancing ahead to the end of the chapter, she thought she might get in the next chapter as well before she had to go.

At any moment she expected to find Mr Tate sleeping or interrupting, but neither happened. Cassandra's voice began to tire before he showed any signs of doing so, and it was she who shut the book and called an end to the day's session.

"If it's all right with you, Mr Tate, I'll be finished for today."

"That's fine. Thank you for coming."

Cassandra came to her feet but hesitated just a moment longer.

"May I ask you something, Mr Tate?"

"Yes."

"You didn't think your visitor could read French or Italian, did you?"

Tate's smile was huge as he admitted,

"Guilty. I thought my aunt might be nearby and wanted her to know I was on to her scheme."

Tate listened to her laughter, liking the sound.

"Are you returning tomorrow?" he asked when he heard her feet on the carpet.

Cassandra stopped. "If I can come in the afternoon."

"That would be fine."

"Very well. I'll see you then."

Tate didn't answer, and Cassandra wondered at her choice of words. It was so natural to tell someone you would see him later, but of course Tate would not have returned that farewell.

Hastings saw her out — Harriet was nowhere around — and all the way home Cassandra asked herself if she'd been utterly insensitive to Mr Tate's plight.

Newcomb Park

"Henry?" Cassandra sought him out in his study. "I'm having some lunch. Would you care to join me?"

Henry looked up from the account book he was studying but didn't answer.

"Are you not hungry?"

Now that she had mentioned it, Henry

76

thought he might be quite hungry, but his mind was still on the business in front of him.

"Shall I have something delivered to you?"

"Please," Henry answered automatically, regretting it when Cassandra looked a bit disappointed. He sat back in his chair, thinking through a different reply, but a moment later the door closed and his sister was gone. Henry sat and debated what to do, but he soon found he'd waited too long again. When Mrs Jasper delivered a lunch tray to his office, he asked after Cassandra and was told by the housekeeper that Miss Cassandra had decided to go riding.

Brown Manor

"Did you actually speak with Judith or just receive word?"

"Only word, but I assume it was a nasty illness to keep Judith from going out."

"I think you must be right."

Anne took a sip of her tea and asked more questions of Lizzy. She felt very cut off and craved news of the church family.

"What is Cassie doing today?"

"She went this morning and read to Mr Tate."

"Did she? How did that come about?"

Lizzy explained the story, which Anne found quite interesting.

"Is Tate improving?"

"The doctor wants the patches to remain in place at all times, so it's rather hard to say."

"Well, I keep praying for him. That's been a great advantage to being in this bed," Anne explained. "One has so much more time to pray, and in the midst of that, I've thought about how special it is to be able to pray for Mrs Thorpe and her nephew, even though I've never met him. It's wonderful having a God like ours, isn't it, Lizzy?"

"It is indeed, Anne."

"But now I also must tell you, before we keep talking about Collingbourne and the church family, that I've been asking God to bring you a husband."

Lizzy couldn't stop her laugh.

"Is that so? Have you had an answer?"

"Of sorts, yes."

Lizzy laughed again. "I can hardly wait to hear this."

"Well, it occurred to me," Anne continued, clearly enjoying herself, "that a woman as lovely as you must be catching someone's eye, but you must not be interested back. Then it occurred to me that you're interested in someone who must have overlooked you. How close am I?"

"I think you've been spending much too much time on your own," Lizzy teased her in an effort to avoid the facts.

"That's probably true," Anne agreed with a sigh and a small laugh of her own, her eyes looking to the ceiling. "You're going to think me fanciful, but I've always thought you should marry Thomas Morland."

Tears sprang so swiftly to Lizzy's eyes that she couldn't camouflage them. Anne would have been blind to miss them.

"Oh, Lizzy." Anne's voice filled with compassion. "What did I say?"

"It's all right, Anne. We won't speak of it. You need your rest."

Anne knew her friend was right. Just the pain she felt at seeing those tears told her it would be very easy to become emotionally involved. Weston was counting on her to rest, as was her baby. She knew she could not follow her heart right now.

"Know this, Elizabeth Steele" — Anne had to whisper just this much — "I'll still be praying. Know that I will."

Lizzy took the outstretched hand that Anne offered her and with her free hand attempted to dry her face.

When the conversation finally picked back up, neither woman mentioned marriage or Thomas Morland.

Collingbourne

Cassandra could have pinched herself. Back in Collingbourne so soon, and all because she couldn't concentrate. She had been so preoccupied by Harriet Thorpe's favor the week before that she completely forgot to shop for Henry. Now she was back at Benwick's hoping something would appeal to her as an appropriate gift for her sedate brother.

When Lizzy had arrived home from Anne's the day before, she had mentioned that Weston was a lover of clocks. They were all over Brown Manor, small and large alike, some made locally, but many from all over the world.

Cassandra now stood in front of a shelf that held a rococo bronze clock. The small tag indicated that it was English-made, and she wondered if such a thing could possibly interest her brother.

Benwick was suddenly beside her. "May I help you find something today, Miss Steele?"

"I don't know, Benwick. Henry's birthday is near, and he's difficult to shop for."

"Were you looking at the clock?"

"Yes, but I don't think he has any interest."

"If I recall, his tastes run to sailing charts and maps."

"That's correct." Cassandra looked at him beseechingly. "Have you anything that might interest him?"

"Well, to be honest, Miss Steele, he's seen everything I have. But I did get something in on Monday. It's unusual and secondhand."

Feeling desperate, Cassandra asked, "May I see it?"

Benwick wasted no time in telling his son he would be in the back room before taking Cassandra that way. What he produced was a volume of maps — a large book — exquisite in detail and color.

"Oh, my," was all Cassandra could say as she paged through it. "Where did you get this?"

"A local family had a death, and some things were sold. You don't often see a book of maps like this, and I thought it might go for something."

Cassandra studied the cover.

"I've heard of Frederick de Witt. He's Dutch, isn't he?"

"Yes. I have to quote rather a stiff price, I'm afraid."

Cassandra inquired and discovered that Benwick had not been joking. He wanted more than she usually spent, but knowing how much Henry would enjoy it, she asked him to hold it for her.

"I'll give you some of the money now and be back for it, probably at the end of the week."

"I wouldn't think of it, Miss Steele. You take the maps now, and bring the rest of the money when you're next in town."

"Thank you, Benwick. If Henry comes in, you'll not say you've seen me, all right?"

"Seen who, Miss Steele?"

Cassandra smiled at him in a way that melted his heart a little before he took the volume to wrap it for safe travel.

Cassandra was on her way out of Collingbourne a short time later, the book stored in the rear of the carriage. Henry never got overly excited about anything, but she thought this birthday present might be just the thing to bring a smile to his face.

Pembroke

On Wednesday afternoon Cassandra was met at the door by Hastings, not Mrs Thorpe.

"Good afternoon, Miss Steele. Mr Tate

is in the library. Shall I show you in?"

"Oh, I can find my way," she told him kindly and proceeded in that direction. She didn't hurry and enjoyed taking in the fine lines and furnishings of the foyer and hallway that led to the spacious library.

Once at the open library door, she knocked, not wishing to surprise her host, and spoke from the doorway.

"Mr Tate?"

"Come in, Cassandra. Did my Aunt Harriet not meet you at the door today?"

"No, not today. And I told Hastings I could find my way."

"Very good. Are you up to a little more Italian?"

"Yes, that would be fine."

Cassandra began, her voice weaving its spell over Tate's mind. He wasn't anxious before she arrived or after she left, but the relaxation he felt in having her read to him was unparalleled to anything since he'd been blinded. Nevertheless, today his mind strayed a bit, and he began to wonder about the woman herself, a woman who would come in as part of a joke and return with such selflessness.

Cassandra sensed none of this as she read page after page, but she had only been working her way through the book for ten minutes when Tate interrupted her.

"Cassandra," he said quietly.

"Yes?"

"What is your last name?"

"Steele."

Tate's brows rose over the patches. "Is your brother named Henry?"

"Yes."

"Ah," his voice softened with recognition. "I'm being read to by one of the beautiful Steele sisters."

Charlotte and Elizabeth's perfect faces sprang into her mind as Cassandra felt her own face flame, tremendously thankful that her host could not see her.

"Do you wish me to go on?" she finally managed.

"Please," Tate replied softly, wishing he'd kept his thoughts to himself. Clearly he'd taken her by surprise and made her uncomfortable, something he never meant to do. Missing part of the story, he debated whether or not to speak any more on the subject. He felt himself tensing and realized that was defeating the whole purpose.

Forcing his mind back to the story, Tate relaxed once more. He might give some thought and energy to the matter later on, but not now. Now he would just relax and listen to her read.

Brown Manor

"Is anyone ill at your house?" Anne asked Lydia almost as soon as she arrived on Thursday, her scheduled day to visit.

"No, but I heard about Judith, and I believe Cassandra Steele has caught it."

"It doesn't sound very fun."

"No, it doesn't. I don't want you to catch it."

The women looked at each other, both wanting Anne's baby to be all right.

"I have something for you," Lydia finally said, bringing out the gift she had carefully bundled along.

"Oh, Liddy," Anne said when she saw the framed painting. "It's beautiful. Wherever did you find it?"

"I bought it the last time Palmer and I were in London. I knew someday God would give you children, and this would be perfect."

Anne looked at the painting. Six young children played in a yard, four boys and two girls, and in the background was a home that greatly resembled Brown Manor.

"We shall put this on the nursery wall," Anne said with a smile, "and tell our baby that it's from our good friends the Palmers."

Lydia smiled at her, just holding tears. "We'll have none of that," Anne teased her. "You're here to cheer me up."

Lydia laughed a little, lightening the mood as she proceeded to do as Anne requested, telling stories about her own children, what they thought of the painting, and what fine parents she knew Weston and Anne would be.

Newcomb Park

"You'll have to send word to Pembroke," a miserable Cassandra told her older sister. "I can't possibly go to read."

"I did that first thing this morning," Lizzy consoled her, "when you woke up so ill."

"Thank you."

"Try to sleep for a time, dear."

Cassandra gave a small nod and did try, but it wasn't long before her stomach woke her, making demands in a most uncomfortable way.

Pembroke

"Word has come from Newcomb Park, sir," Hastings told Tate as soon as he awoke. "Do you wish to hear it now?"

"Please, Hastings."

" 'Mr Tate, my sister is unable to come today. She is ill. Elizabeth Steele.' "

"She doesn't say if it's that flu?"

"No, sir."

"Please send word back to her from me."

"Very well, sir." Hastings was prepared as usual, and pulled out the needed paper.

Tate dictated this message: "Cassandra, I hope this finds you improving. Please take care of yourself. I'll be praying for your full recovery. If you care to return to Pembroke when you are well, I would welcome your visit. God bless you, Cassandra. Tate."

"Would you like this sent out right away, sir?"

"Please, and let me know immediately if there is any type of reply."

Tate was glad to be alone with his thoughts a moment later. He hadn't checked with Cassandra about his comment the last time, thinking that it was best to leave it alone, but now she was ill. Or was she? He didn't think she would play games with him, but what did he really know of her? It was a question that plagued the blind man the rest of the day, even as he reminded himself that he was supposed to be resting.

Newcomb Park

Cassandra was feeling better by late afternoon, not so sick to the stomach but still terribly weak. The staff had come and gone all day, seeing to her comfort, and Lizzy had been around much of the time, checking on her and doing small things to ease her pain.

"Lizzy," Cassandra called to her when they were on their own.

"Yes, dear."

"Is Henry a believer?"

Lizzy had prayed about that very thing and asked herself that question many times, but she had never voiced it out loud.

"Why do you ask?" the older sister inquired, sounding calmer than she felt.

"It makes no sense to me that Henry can be as selfish as he is if Christ lives inside of him."

"That's a very profound observation," Lizzy said, moving a soft, cool cloth to Cassandra's brow.

"Have you ever talked with Henry about the matter?"

"No, have you?"

"No," Cassandra was forced to admit. "What do you think Henry would say about his salvation?"

Lizzy looked pained and skeptical. "Probably that he's reserved but in church every Sunday, and what more does God expect?"

"But, Lizzy, how can he feel that way when he hears the truth each week? When Pastor Hurst and Pastor Greville are so good about explaining how God's plan works?"

"You forget, Cassie, that I answered for him. He hasn't actually said that. Maybe that wouldn't be his response at all."

Cassandra nodded in agreement. It really wasn't fair to put someone else's answer on him, but his life did cause one to wonder.

"What brought this to mind?" Lizzy asked.

"Oh, just the fact that he hasn't even checked on me today. I wouldn't want him to catch anything, but it wouldn't hurt to poke his head in and say hello."

"Maybe he did that while you were sleeping."

Cassandra's head full of dark red curls moved against the pillow.

"No, he didn't. I asked Mrs Jasper, and she said he's been in his study all day."

"Well, there are several hours left in the day; maybe he's still coming."

For a moment there was silence in the room.

"You've forgotten again."

Lizzy looked confused, her beautiful blue eyes looking down at the woman in the bed.

"Forgotten what?"

"That I'm not a five-year-old waiting for Father to come home."

Lizzy looked stunned this time.

"How often do I do that?" she asked when she could find her voice.

Cassandra only smiled, and Lizzy's sigh held more than a little weight.

"I guess I've a need to baby someone, Cassie, and you're it."

"I didn't mean it as a rebuke, Lizzy, but clearly you've had some of the same thoughts about Henry as I have. Maybe if you didn't see me as the baby we could have spoken of it before. It would have done my heart a lot of good."

Her sister was so right that Lizzy could only stare at her tired, pale face. She did see her as the little one, the one who needed to be protected, when in fact she'd proven over and over that she was a smart, capable woman in her own right, not just the baby of the Steele family.

"Don't give up on me, Cassie. Please."

The youngest Steele smiled warmly, albeit weakly.

"Never, Lizzy. Never."

Chapter Five

Pembroke

"You have a visitor," Harriet announced — as she enjoyed doing — to her nephew when Cassandra arrived on Saturday morning, causing Tate to smile and wait for Cassandra's usual greeting.

"Hello, Mr Tate."

"Hello, Cassandra. How are you?" Tate asked, truly wishing to know.

It had taken her a few days to get back on her feet — she was still pale and a bit thin but definitely on the mend and most anxious to be out.

"I'm very well, thank you," Cassandra answered and then added, "you won't catch anything."

"That," he said firmly, "is the least of my worries. Are you certain you're up to this?"

"Yes, I'm fine. Shall we go ahead with *DeMitri's Pomario*?"

"Please."

It was much as it had been on other

days, Cassandra reading and Tate relaxing, but that lasted for only 30 minutes.

"Cassandra?" he interrupted her.

"Yes?"

"Are you enjoying this book? We can pick another if you like."

"No, I quite like it, but thank you for asking." Cassandra began to go back to the page she had opened but stopped. "Do you like it, Mr Tate? Do you wish to change?"

"No, I'm enjoying it very much. It's an interesting story, isn't it?"

"Yes. At first I didn't like Antonia, but she's beginning to grow on me."

"What didn't you like about her?" Tate asked.

"Her expectation that nothing would go amiss in her life, almost as if a calm, well-placed life was her due. That's utter foolishness, and she was naive to expect it."

"But what of her station? Wouldn't she naturally expect such a life with her father's position?"

"As a child maybe, but when she was old enough to face the realities of life, surely she should have been able to see that things don't always go as we assume, and that all the money in the world can't bring back someone or something you love."

Tate had such a thoughtful look on his

face that Cassandra halted. Had she insulted him? Had she spoken out of turn? She determined then and there to find out.

"Do I need to apologize for something, Mr Tate?"

"No, I quite agree with you. Antonia has taken a long time to grow up."

"Indeed. It was nice to even hear her admit it."

"When did she do that?" Tate sat up a bit straighter.

"In the music room with her old nanny."

"I missed that part."

Tate listened as the pages turned and then Cassandra read from that scene.

"I must have faded off on those pages."

"Are you tiring?"

"Not right now."

"Shall I go on?"

"Please."

Cassandra did without further delay. Several times she caught herself forgetting that anyone else was in the room. She sank into the pages of the story, and seemingly in an instant, more than an hour had passed.

"I should go," Cassandra said, having glanced at the clock but for the first time not wanting to leave.

"Are you able to return on Monday?"

"Yes, I shall plan on it."

"Don't come if you don't feel up to it," Tate remembered to put in, wishing for the first time that he could see her in order to gauge for himself how she might be feeling.

"All right. Goodbye, Mr Tate."

"Goodbye, Cassandra. Thank you."

Not until Cassandra made her way from the room and climbed into the coach for home did she notice her fatigue. Wanting to be fresh for church in the morning, she decided to rest for the remainder of the day. A portion of her heart, however, lingered on Mr Tate. She wasn't sure why he was on her mind, and that only caused her to wonder all the more.

Newcomb Park

"This week went by so swiftly," Cassandra commented almost a week later as she and Lizzy took birthday gifts for Henry to the parlor.

"It rained all week, Cassie," Lizzy reminded her. "I felt it dragged a bit."

Cassandra looked surprised.

"I think it might have something to do with the fact that you go to Pembroke every day. I noticed that you even stayed longer a few times."

"It must be the book," Cassandra concluded. "We find it rather fascinating and can't put it down. We're almost done with it. I'm not sure what we'll read next."

Lizzy stared at her sister, but she didn't notice. She couldn't help but ask herself whether Cassandra had noticed how often she referred to herself and Mr Tate as *we*.

"So do you think you'll keep going back?"

"I think so. The whole point is for relaxation, and it seems Mr Tate is getting plenty of that."

"And are you enjoying it?" Lizzy asked, but this time Cassandra heard something in her voice.

"What are you up to, Lizzy?"

"I'm not up to anything."

Cassandra looked skeptical, especially when Lizzy turned to the glass above the mantel and checked her hair.

"I just can't help but wonder," Lizzy admitted, her back still to her sister, "if things might not get a bit personal between you and Mr Tate."

Cassandra blinked.

"Lizzy, he can't even see me."

Lizzy turned to face her. "What does that matter?"

Cassandra opened her mouth to reply,

but no words formed, at least not for several seconds.

"It just does!"

Lizzy laughed. "That was an interesting conclusion."

"Come now, Lizzy, don't be planting ideas in my head. You'll make me uncomfortable in the poor man's presence."

"All right. I won't tease you."

Cassandra looked at her. "But you'll be thinking it, won't you?"

"Only what I've said to you; nothing more."

Cassandra nodded. That was a fair enough answer, and it brought the conversation to a good close. And only just in time. Dinner was about to be served, and after that — the gifts. Both women were excited about the presents they had to give.

"Thank you, Lizzy," Henry told her sincerely, looking again at the leather notebook. It was the type he always liked, and this time the leather had been dyed a dark green, just the color of his study.

"I have another gift to present to you," Lizzy said, passing a small, unwrapped box in his direction.

Henry took it wordlessly, his brows rising when he saw the contents. Both women laughed when he brought out a bug — a huge, dead beetle to be exact — lying on a bed of straw.

"Edward sent it," Lizzy put in, "and it wouldn't hurt my feelings in the least if it stayed in your office."

"I rather like it," Cassandra offered, leaning close to have a look. It was the largest insect she'd ever seen, very black and thick.

Henry bumped the straw just then, and the bug appeared to move. Cassandra sat back in a hurry.

"Are you sure it's dead?"

"Very," Henry told her, but it was obvious he was amused.

"I think Lizzy might be right, Henry. I can see it gracing the shelves of your study."

This actually wrung a smile from Henry, and after seeing it, Cassandra went for her gift. It was a bit cumbersome, but she didn't ask for help as she set it near his feet.

"This one is from me."

Henry tore back the wrapping, saw the name "de Witt," and froze.

"What have you done, Cassie?"

"Benwick had just gotten it in. Are you pleased?"

Henry was silent as the rest of the wrap gave way, but every part of his being radiated pleasure. He opened the book slowly, as though it was already a prized possession, studying the detail and touching the pages with reverence.

Cassandra didn't expect him to say very much, but she would have appreciated something. She looked over at Lizzy, who had just glanced her direction. Both women shrugged a little.

"Henry?" Cassandra finally tried.

He looked up to find his youngest sister smiling at him.

"Thank you, Cassie," he said simply, smiling back at her and returning to the colorful pages that showed maps of the world.

Cassandra tried not to be disappointed. She worked at not carrying her heart on her sleeve but couldn't quite pull it off this time. She had to ask herself at that moment whether she hadn't come with more expectations than she should have. She was also forced to ask herself whether a small part of her heart had been trying to buy Henry's love, or at the very least, his attention.

Pembroke

"Much as I'm enjoying the book, Cassandra," Tate said when she arrived on Saturday morning, "would you mind terribly if we did something different this morning?"

"Not at all."

Tate reached to the table beside him and found his Bible. He handed it to Cassandra.

"I would like to recite to you from Psalm 113. I'd like you to correct me if I get words wrong — but if I hesitate, give me a moment to find my place."

"Is your Bible in English?" Cassandra asked as she began to turn to the book of Psalms. She was rewarded by the sound of Tate's full laughter.

Cassandra smiled hugely as she watched him. That he'd found the question highly amusing was clear.

Harriet suddenly appeared at the door, having heard the noise. "Is everything all right?"

"Yes," Tate answered, although his voice was still full of laughter. "The joke continues. I'll tell you about it later."

Harriet gave Cassandra a smiling, wide-eyed look before agreeing and going on her way. Tate got down to business moments later.

" 'Praise ye the LORD. Praise, O ye servants of the LORD, praise the name of the LORD. Blessed be the name of the LORD from this time forth and forever.' "

" 'For evermore,' " Cassandra corrected quietly.

" 'For evermore,' " Tate repeated and picked up where he was. " 'From the rising of the sun unto the going down of the same the LORD's name is to be praised. The LORD is high above all nations, and his glory above the heavens.' "

Tate took a moment to think, and then went on, needing no help at all. " 'Who is like unto the LORD our God, who dwelleth on high, who humbleth himself to behold the things that are in heaven, and in the earth! He raiseth up the poor out of the dust, and lifteth the needy out of the dung-hill; that he may set him with princes, even with the princes of his people.' "

Tate paused for this last verse, his mind searching. "Is it, 'He maketh the barren woman . . .' ?"

"Yes."

Tate nodded and finished: " 'He maketh the barren woman to keep house, and to be a joyful mother of children. Praise ye the LORD.' How did I do?"

"Very well. I'm extremely impressed. I fudge on words all the time. Yours were nearly perfect."

"Thank you," Tate said humbly, but he

was ready to go on. "If you don't mind, I'd like for you to choose another psalm for me to memorize. Not too long."

"All right," Cassandra said, wishing to go easy on him. "How about 117?"

Tate smiled. "That has only two verses in it."

"You already know that one?" Cassandra sounded chagrined.

"Yes, and it sounds as though I should teach it to you."

"Oh, I don't know," she said, sounding embarrassed.

"Well, let's try."

"You don't have to do that, Mr Tate."

"That's good to know. Repeat after me," he said, ignoring her. " 'O praise the Lord, all ye nations.' "

Cassandra saw no help for it. She was there to help him relax, and if this was going to work, then she would do it. She repeated the words back to him, over and over again, and then Tate told her to try both verses on her own.

" 'O praise the Lord, all ye nations; praise him, all ye people. For his merciful kindness is great toward us; and the truth of the Lord endureth for ever. Praise ye the Lord.' "

"Cassandra Steele, you close that Bible this instant!"

Cassandra's laughter filled the room.

"How did you know?"

"I could tell that your head was bent, the way it is when you read."

"I told you I would fudge."

"That wasn't fudging; it was cheating," he told her, trying to sound firm but unable to stop smiling. "Here we go now, this time without the Bible."

Cassandra did as she was told, and by the time she was ready to leave, she knew Psalm 117 by heart, every word perfect.

"Thank you for coming," Tate said as she made to exit.

"No, Mr Tate, thank you for teaching me those verses. I didn't think I could do it word perfect."

Tate smiled. He was still smiling when his aunt came to check on him almost an hour later.

"Cassandra," Harriet called to her the moment church was over; she hadn't even had time to move from the pew.

"Good morning, Mrs Thorpe. How are you?"

"I'm very well, and I wanted to catch you before you left." Harriet sat next to her, turning so she could see her face. "Is it still working for you to come each day, or have we completely ruined your schedule?"

"Not at all. I can always fit it in, and on those days when it is impossible, Mr Tate has been very understanding."

Harriet took the younger woman's hand.

"I can't thank you enough, Cassandra. He so enjoys your visits. They give him something to look forward to."

"I'm pleased to hear that, but you must believe me when I tell you that I no longer come just for Mr Tate. I enjoy the visits too."

"I'm glad, my dear. I would love to invite you to dinner and tea, and offer you our hospitality, but I must give Tate as much time as he needs."

Cassandra squeezed the older hand, which was still nearby.

"Don't give it another thought. I don't expect such things. We want Mr Tate to heal. That's all that matters right now."

Harriet hugged her. She couldn't help herself. Cassandra gladly returned the embrace, thinking she had made a lovely friend.

Lizzy, watching them from a little ways off, smiled as well, but for an entirely different reason.

Brown Manor

"Hello, love," Weston said softly, sitting down on his own bed and watching his wife's eyes open. He leaned to kiss her before asking, "How did you end up in here?"

"I was tired of my room, so after my bath, I told Jenny I wanted to move. Do you mind?"

Weston's smile was intimate. "Since when do I mind finding you in my bed?"

Anne smiled back at him.

"How was church?"

"Excellent. We're still in Jonah, and I shall tell you all about it after we've eaten."

"I would like that."

"Oh! Before I forget, Marianne Jennings will be coming tomorrow."

"Good. Will she bring any of the children?"

"I don't know. She might assume, just as Judith and Lydia have, that one visitor at a time is enough."

"But we could send word, so she'll know the children would be welcome."

Weston hesitated. Much as he loved the children in question, he wasn't certain that Anne needed them to visit just yet.

"You're not saying anything."

"I'm just thinking."

Anne didn't need to ask the subject of his thoughts. Everything he did these days was with her health and the baby's delivery in mind. She didn't want to do anything to make it harder for him, but she thought that visiting with Penny Jennings or seeing baby Catherine would do her a world of good. It was only her husband's concerned face that kept her quiet.

She would work the rest of the day to be thankful that at least Marianne was going to come.

Thornton Hall

Jennings heard the cry the moment it sounded. He knew his wife, Marianne, as well as the nanny, were in with their youngest, so he didn't rush, but by the time he arrived in the nursery, Catherine was at full volume.

"She bumped her head," Marianne explained when the door opened.

Jennings had to hide a smile. Their daughter's round, pink face was buried in her mother's shoulder, as she felt most sorry for herself. Catherine's head came up. Her tears began to abate, and her lids began to droop.

Her thumb found its way into her now-quiet mouth, and within a minute she had fallen asleep in her mother's arms.

With Catherine tucked into the cradle and the nanny nearby, the couple made their way from the room, only to find James just coming down the hall, clearly intending to rescue.

"Was Catherine crying?"

"She was, James, but she's sleeping now."

"What happened?"

Marianne explained the way she'd been crawling and had charged directly into the leg of a table.

"It wasn't a hard bump," Marianne assured him. "But she's tired from church this morning."

"Maybe I should at least peek in on her."

"Sophie is with her."

James' shoulders relaxed. Sophie was a lovely young woman from the village. She adored babies, and the Jennings family felt she was a godsend.

"I believe it might be time for lunch, James," Jennings now suggested, seeing that might do the trick. About the only thing that could distract James from his baby sister was his stomach.

Jennings and Marianne exchanged a smile when James lit up like a candle and volunteered to check.

★ ★ ★

Cassandra had spoken with James Walker on Sunday just before leaving church with her siblings. He had shown not the slightest bit of surprise that she asked for some of his time, and to her great relief, she learned that he was free the next morning.

The coach pulled up in front of Blackburn Manor, one of the most beautiful homes in the area, but its spectacular architecture was lost on the woman who had come to call.

Mrs Walker was on hand to greet her, but Mr Walker was nearby, his expression calm and inviting. The two of them went into one of the small parlors where refreshments were waiting, but Cassandra couldn't eat a thing.

James Walker looked at the young woman who could have been his daughter and felt his heart wring with compassion. He didn't know what she needed, but he knew that if it was in his power to help, he would do just that.

"Thank you for your time, Mr Walker," she began as soon as she'd taken a seat. "It's most generous of you."

"Not at all, Cassandra. It's a pleasure to have you. Are you sure you wouldn't like some tea?"

"I'm sure. I won't beat about the bush, Mr Walker. I've come about my brother."

"Henry or Edward?"

"Henry. He seems to enjoy you so, and I was most curious as to whether or not the two of you have ever ventured into discussions of a spiritual nature. Lizzy and I can't seem to read Henry or get very close to him, and so I thought I would ask you if you have any sense of what Henry believes."

Walker had not been expecting this, but neither was he surprised. Henry Steele had often been on his mind, and he'd asked himself some of the same questions.

"May I ask you some questions, Cassandra?"

"Of course."

"Did something happen that caused you to suddenly think about this, or have you wondered for a long time?"

"It has been a long time, but just recently it's become so clear to me that Henry desires things over people. Would a man who considers himself to be a follower of God's Son really be so self-centered and involved in his own interests?"

Walker nodded thoughtfully.

"Have you or Lizzy ever asked him about this?"

"No. We wish to be respectful, and beyond that, he just never invites any type of personal interaction. I've never known a person who needed so few words to live. I honestly think he could be happy alone for the rest of his life."

Walker encouraged Cassandra to share what life was like at Newcomb Park, and when she did, Walker knew he was going to have to get involved. Henry Steele was a reserved man at church, but not when he was with James Walker. Walker, now understanding that Henry was not talkative and caring at home — to the point that his sisters doubted his salvation — knew it was time to check into things.

"I'm glad you came to me, Cassandra. I'll be setting up an appointment to talk with Henry very soon."

Cassandra looked a bit panicked about this, even coming to her feet.

"What if he's angry with me? What if he feels betrayed because I've never gone to him? What do I do then, Mr Walker?"

"It's all right, Cassandra," he comforted her, his face and voice full of compassion and understanding. "I'm not saying you can't talk to him, but I do plan to get involved. I won't even mention your visit unless he's open to talking to me about personal matters. But we can't just let this go. I've known your family for years, Cassandra. I don't believe Henry will feel threatened by me. I think he'll see how much I care, and if your visit comes up, I think he'll see the same thing about you."

Cassandra nodded. Mr Walker was right. Henry was not the type to anger easily or lash out. Indeed, he was remarkably mild. And Mr Walker was right about another thing: It wasn't right that things go on as they were. Even if Henry's view of her changed forever, a person of integrity couldn't go on pretending that all was well when it clearly was not.

Chapter Six

Brown Manor

When Marianne Jennings, accompanied by her baby daughter and nanny, arrived at Brown Manor, Weston met them on the drive, feeling a mixture of pleasure and chagrin.

"Hello, Weston," she greeted him kindly. "How is Anne today?"

"Very ready for your visit. We're so glad you could come."

"I need to tell you, Weston," Marianne began, "Sophie can take Catherine outside or play with her downstairs if you think it will be too much to have her upstairs."

"To be honest with you, Marianne, Anne hoped to see the children. I know she will enjoy it."

"We'll keep it brief," Marianne suggested wisely. "I'll send Sophie and Catherine down after just a bit."

"Thank you," Weston said to Marianne, but also to his heavenly Father. He had desperately wanted to give his wife this type of visit but didn't know how to go about it in a way that would not offend someone or tax his bedridden spouse.

Weston trailed his guests up the stairs for one reason: to hear his wife's reaction. It was just as he expected.

"Oh, Mari, you brought the baby! Look how big she is! And so lovely."

Marianne sat proudly near the bed, Catherine on her lap.

"Do you want to try to hold her, Anne?"

"I'm not supposed to lift at all," Anne answered, denying her own heart. "I'll just lie here and talk to her. Hello, Catherine. Your dress is so pretty."

The baby smiled when Anne smiled at her, melting the expectant mother's heart into a puddle.

"She's a good baby, isn't she?"

"Very. As soon as you're able, you need to come and see her interact with Thomas, James, and Penny. She adores them and can charm any of them into holding her and carting her around."

"And they love it."

"Yes. If she cries, it breaks their hearts. Even if she's been told no about touching something or dropping food on the floor, they can't stand for her to be sad."

Anne put her hand out, but Catherine's attention had gone to her mother's locket, and she didn't notice. Delighting in the soft button nose and baby chin, Anne studied that small profile and found herself asking God if she would ever hold her baby in such a way.

"I'm going to send Catherine out with Sophie now so we can visit."

"Thank you for bringing her, Mari. It's done my heart such good."

Marianne wasted no time in handing the baby off to her nanny and returning to give Anne her undivided attention. She watched Anne's gaze as it followed the baby all the way out the door, her own heart asking God to give Anne and Weston a child of their own.

Pembroke

Cassandra arrived to read in the afternoon. She and Mr Tate had finished *DeMitri's Pomario,* and were now taking time each day to read the newspaper, something they both enjoyed. She walked to the library in the usual way and began at once. Tate, however, stopped her in less then five minutes.

"Are you feeling all right today, Cassandra?"

"Yes, thank you. Are you all right?"

"Are you certain?" he asked, ignoring the question she had posed to him.

"Yes."

Tate sat quietly, his head turned in the usual way, his right ear toward her.

"Shall I go on?"

"No."

Cassandra didn't expect this and for a moment wasn't sure what to do.

"I think maybe I should leave," she concluded and began to stand.

"Has something happened? Are you troubled about something?"

Cassandra sat back. "How did you know I was troubled?"

"Your voice."

"What does it sound like?"

"It's deeper than usual."

Cassandra said nothing to this, so Tate went on.

"I get the impression you've been crying."

Cassandra drew in a sharp breath.

"Cassandra, what is it?"

"I can't do this." Her voice had taken on a breathless quality. "You need to be resting. This is not why I come."

Tate could tell she was on her feet.

"Please don't go," he begged her, scooting forward in his seat, wishing he could see where she was. "Please stay, Cassandra. We won't speak of it if you don't care to."

Tate heard her sniff, glad she was still in the room.

"Are you there?" he asked gently.

"Yes."

"Come and sit down." Tate sat back in his chair. "We'll just sit for a time."

Cassandra thought how unfair it would be to leave when she was upset. That would not be restful for either of them and would make for awkwardness the next time she came. She returned to her seat but did not reach for the paper.

"Do you think you remember the two verses from Psalm 117?"

"I think so."

"Good. Sometimes when the darkness crowds close to me in a way that's almost frightening, I start reciting verses to myself. It's a huge help to remember how big my God is."

"I can see how that would be. I do remember verses, just not as perfectly as you do."

"I think anything that reminds us of what God has to say on a matter is helpful. What do you think?"

"I think I need to remember that today."

Tate was quiet for a moment.

"I need to say something, Cassandra, and I hope you'll hear me out."

"I will, yes."

"If I've done something to upset you, I can't rest. No matter what effect it has on my health, you need to confront me. But even if I haven't caused an upset for you, you may speak to me. I'm not that fragile." Tate smiled a little. "I won't even be able to see if you blush."

Cassandra laughed a bit and felt herself relaxing.

"I had to meet with someone today concerning a situation that's painful for me. Had I known that it would have showed in my voice, I would not have come and put that burden on you."

"Was there resolution in the matter?"

"No. Steps will now be taken, but the outcome is a mystery."

"And your heart is involved."

"Yes."

"That's the most painful type, isn't it?"

"That's certainly true."

"Is the situation something that you must resolve, or did you have to leave that to someone else?"

Harriet chose that moment to walk past the library door. She glanced in but came to a complete halt when she saw that Cassandra wasn't reading.

"Cassandra?" Tate tried when he heard steps on the carpet, assuming she'd moved.

"Hello, Mrs Thorpe," Cassandra said quietly, able to see the upset in her eyes.

"Well, Aunt Harriet. I didn't know you'd come in."

"What are you doing, Tate?"

"I'm talking to Cassandra."

"Is that wise, Tate? I thought the reading was all you needed."

Tate sat up very straight, his voice changing a bit. Had his aunt any idea how rude she'd just sounded?

"Find a seat, Aunt Harriet. I need to speak with you."

"I'll go," Cassandra began.

"Please don't. I need to talk to both of you."

Tate waited until he'd heard them settle and then began.

"Aunt Harriet, you need to stop worrying so much, as does Cassandra, who's a little too afraid of upsetting me. Being babied can be stressful too. I don't know if all of this rest is helping my vision or not — we'll have to wait and see about that — but you need to trust me to know whether I've overtaxed myself. There's going to be a certain amount of burden for those seeing to me, but you'll

117

have to leave it up to me to admit when I've had enough. If I overdo and don't gain my sight back, that's something I'll have to live with.

"I don't expect you to be at my beck and call all my life, but I can't give up all interest in everyone and everything because I'm supposed to be resting. It's not right or practical."

The room was utterly silent on this announcement. Cassandra could have kicked herself for coming at all today. Glancing over at Harriet and finding with a start the older woman's eyes on her, she spoke without thinking.

"I'm sorry, Mrs Thorpe. It's all my fault. I shouldn't have come today."

Tate could feel anger rising inside himself and worked to control it. It didn't take much to understand that Harriet had not believed him and in some silent way was making Cassandra feel at fault. He tried to calm himself before he spoke, but Harriet beat him to it.

"Has something happened, Cassandra?"

"Not exactly. It's all rather complicated."

"And you felt a need to speak to Tate about it."

"Aunt Harriet," Tate jumped in, finally calm enough to do so. "I think you and I need to continue our conversation privately.

"Cassandra, will you please come here?"

Cassandra did as he asked, going to his chair and standing.

"Where is your hand?" he asked, reaching for it. Cassandra offered it, and Tate spoke again when he held it lightly in his.

"My aunt has misunderstood, and I need to explain the situation to her."

"That's fine, but I am sorry."

Tate squeezed her hand a little.

"There's nothing to be sorry about. I asked and you shared. I never wish you to do anything else. What kind of unfeeling fool would I be to expect you to cast your cares at the door and come in pretending all is well?"

Cassandra didn't answer.

"Tell me you'll come tomorrow. Please, Cassandra."

"I'll come, but do send word if you change your mind."

"I will, and you do the same, but understand that I want you to come back."

"All right. I'll go now."

"Thank you."

"Goodbye, Mr Tate. Goodbye, Mrs Thorpe."

The two family members bid her goodbye, but Tate waited only until he'd heard the front door close before addressing his aunt.

"Something went wrong today, Harriet."

"I can see that, Tate. I told Cassandra that you were to have no stress or strain. She told me she understood."

Tate sat for a moment, trying to find the words to put his aunt back on the right path.

"Tell me if this is right: You told Cassandra to come only if she was in a good mood?"

"Not in so many words, but you have enough to think about with your vision. You don't need more problems to dwell on."

"So Cassandra should have sent word that she wasn't up to reading?"

"Yes."

"And how long does she do this? If things aren't settled for her, should she just stay away indefinitely?"

"I don't know." Harriet began to sound uncertain.

"Cassandra has become a part of my daily life. Were you going to find someone else to read to me?"

"I don't know, Tate. I just thought she

was putting too much on you. And I know you tried to explain, but you have been through so much. Maybe you're not thinking clearly."

"Harriet." Tate's voice had remained calm the entire time. "Cassandra Steele is not some servant girl who's being paid for a service. She's a gentleman's daughter and a sister to us in Christ."

"That's very true," Harriet uttered quietly, her voice truly humble. "I think I made her feel bad. I was so surprised that I spoke out of turn."

Tate was quiet.

"What did happen?" his aunt asked.

"I don't know the details, but something was bothering her. I could hear it in her voice and asked her to tell me. Indeed, I insisted."

"Oh, no, and I gave her such an unkind look! What have I done?"

"Harriet, listen to me. Try to believe me when I tell you that I'm not going to overdo. Try not to worry so much."

"I will, Tate, but what's to be done about the way I treated Cassandra?"

"Well, she'll be here tomorrow; you can speak to her then."

"What if she doesn't come?"

"Then you can go to her."

"Yes, yes, that's good," the older woman replied as she used her hankie to mop her suddenly warm face. "I'll do that. I'll talk to her tomorrow as soon as she comes."

Tate smiled in her direction.

"I'm sorry, Tate."

"Thank you, Aunt Harriet," he said, his voice forgiving. "And thank you for caring so much."

Harriet went to hug him, her heart aching over the events of the last few minutes. She debated sending word to Cassandra on the spot, telling her she was sorry to have intruded and that she was welcome whenever she liked, but face-to-face repentance was best. She might not sleep well tonight, but that was a small price to pay for making things right with Cassandra Steele.

Newcomb Park

"I did something today."

It was late. Cassandra had sought Lizzy out in her room. Both women were ready for bed. Lizzy was brushing her hair. Cassandra climbed onto the bed behind her, took the brush, and worked with long methodical strokes.

"Do you want to tell me about it?" Lizzy

prompted when Cassandra didn't immediately speak.

"I went to see Mr Walker. I went to ask him if he and Henry ever talk about spiritual things."

"What did he say?"

"He said they didn't, but that he plans to speak with Henry."

"How do you feel about that?"

"I'm not exactly certain."

Lizzy shifted to see her in the lamplight.

"What exactly did you tell him?"

"I said that Henry confuses me with the way he goes to church but puts things ahead of people. I added that he's self-centered."

"Was Mr Walker surprised?"

"I don't know. He didn't seem to be. Henry is so relaxed with him, ready to speak on many subjects, but Mr Walker can't be missing the fact that Henry is utterly silent when we go to church."

A part of Lizzy wanted to wail and ask Cassandra why she would do such a thing, but in that she saw her own cowardice. She'd known for years that Henry's walk of life was not as it should be. Cassandra was right. He was much too happy with possessions, not people, surrounding him.

Lizzy turned back away, and Cassandra went on with the hairbrush.

"Are you vexed with me, Lizzy?"

"No, I'm vexed with myself and my own timid heart."

"Do you think Henry will learn what I've done and change toward me?"

Lizzy gave a sad little laugh. "He doesn't talk to us now, Cassie. What could really change?"

On this note the women fell silent. Cassandra brushed Lizzy's thick mahogany-colored hair until it was perfectly smooth and then moved to sit beside her. The moment she did, Lizzy took her hand and began to pray.

The days were warming swiftly. Flowers were in riotous bloom on nearly every hillside, a sight Cassandra enjoyed as she trailed Henry on his morning ride. They raced along the ridge, Henry's horse beating hers easily, but Cassandra didn't care. The feel of Iris running hard beneath her was thrill enough.

"I'm going to breakfast with Lizzy," Cassandra said when they arrived back. "Are you joining us, Henry?"

"I'll be along."

Cassandra went ahead of him and found her sister at the table.

"How was your ride?"

"It was lovely. You really must come sometime."

"I'll do that."

"Any mail for me?"

"Yes, and we've heard from Edward."

Cassandra stopped herself from mentioning Morland. She could read the letter herself and not pour salt on the wound by asking. Although when she thought about it, Lizzy seemed rather lighthearted lately. Maybe she was mending some.

"You have mail, Henry," Lizzy said to him the moment he showed up.

He thanked her and took his seat, starting on breakfast even as he read. Cassandra, amid her own meal, read Edward's letter, a small smile appearing on her face.

I certainly miss all of you, but this trip is amazing. The air is hot and dry. I've never felt anything like it. I can actually draw hot air into my lungs, and doing so reminds me most starkly that I am a long way from home.

We moved a few days ago. We've set up housekeeping with friends of Morland's aunt. From here we'll be going into the wilds with a chance to observe the animals at close range. I thought I would feel more afraid at the prospect than I do. My lack of fear is more of a concern than anything else. If I don't write again, you'll know I've been mauled and should have been more frightened.

What do you hear from the new Mrs Barrington? She hasn't written me much at all. You've put her to shame, Lizzy. Did you enjoy the beetle, Henry? I thought him a fine fellow and hope he arrived in good shape. Do ask Cassie if she wants a live one. I might be able to manage that.

Cassandra shuddered at the thought, even as she suppressed a laugh. He was such a pest, but she missed him terribly. She planned to write to him that very day and ask if he was ever coming home.

Upon this thought, Cassandra remembered she was headed back to Pembroke today. She hadn't dwelt on yesterday's incident, but it had come to mind several times. Mrs Thorpe had been very unhappy with her. Would she still be today?

It doesn't matter, Cassie. You still have to go. If after today she doesn't wish you to return, you must do as she asks.

Cassandra refused to let her heart dwell on why the thought of never returning caused her so much pain.

Pembroke

I can feel my temptation to beg You, Father, and I must not do that. You know what is right, Tate prayed before rising, enjoying the quiet of the house at this early hour. *Thank You for this time of darkness, Lord. Thank You for all I've learned. Help me to keep trusting You for the future — my future.*

Help Aunt Harriet to trust You greatly. Help her to see that she can't take care of me as You can. Help her repentance before Cassandra today to be humble and genuine, and help Cassandra to accept it, holding nothing of herself back.

Thank You for the lessons in Jonah, Tate continued, talking out all of his heart to Jesus Christ until Hastings came to check on him. He didn't need him for more than shaving and putting the finishing touches on his appearance, but always the faithful servant, Hastings checked on him often.

"Good morning, sir," Hastings greeted as soon as he knew Tate was awake.

"Good morning, Hastings. What is it like out today? I don't hear rain."

"It's very nice just now. The sun is up and shining. I suspect it might get quite warm."

127

It was their usual exchange on the weather conditions, but never was it just routine. Tate needed Hastings to give him these small details so that his mind could connect to life around him.

"Are you ready for your shave, sir?"

"Please."

Tate sat patiently for this task, again appreciating the regularity of the routine.

"I expect Miss Steele today," Tate mentioned, not noticing that he never addressed her as such. She had come to him as Cassandra, and Cassandra she had remained.

"Will you be in the library as usual?"

"I think we'll start there, but if it's very nice we might move to the veranda."

"Very good, sir. I will see that all is in readiness."

"Are you still looking for those books?"

"I am, sir. I believe I've tracked one of them down."

Tate smiled. "Good. Keep it just between the two of us, and let me know as soon as you have even one of them."

Taking pity on Hastings' shaving efforts, Tate didn't smile, but he wanted to. There would be time for smiling later, especially if the servant could locate the books Tate sought.

Chapter Seven

The Manse

"You look thoughtful," Judith Hurst said to her husband over breakfast.

"I'm sorry." His head came up when he heard her voice. "Did you just ask me something?"

"No, I only commented that you look thoughtful. Want to share?"

"What news have you had on Mr Tate?" he asked.

"Mrs Thorpe's nephew? Nothing recently."

"How often does the doctor check for improvement?"

"I'm not certain. Mrs Thorpe did tell me how much he enjoys your sermon notes, but we didn't speak on his current condition."

"I was just reading about Bartimaeus in Mark 10. When I read about his life, I'm always struck by my own tendency to take my sight for granted. Somewhere in there, Tate came to mind."

"How do you pray for him, Frederick?" his wife asked.

"I ask God to restore his sight, or something better."

Judith stared at her mate. She was so struck by his words that for a moment she was speechless. *How foolish I am, Lord,* she finally prayed, *to assume that the best for Tate is the return of his sight.*

Judith did not continue to question Frederick. Indeed, she was silent for the remainder of the meal, thinking of all the wonderful things that could be better than having one's sight restored.

Pembroke

"I'm so glad you came, Cassandra," Harriet began, not able to keep the warble from her voice. "I'm sorry about yesterday."

"As am I, Mrs Thorpe. Please forgive me."

"No, dear, you misunderstand me. I came into the library and made poor assumptions. I won't interfere with your reading to Tate again."

"You are always welcome, I'm sure."

Harriet hugged her. What a dear woman she was, her heart so ready to give and forgive.

Immensely relieved to have things settled, Cassandra left Tate's aunt and made her way to the library. She half-expected Tate to ask her about the conversation, but he did not mention it. She reached for the newspaper, found an article she had not read to him, and began. It wasn't a long one, but Tate still managed to interrupt.

"Would it be a terrible imposition to move outside?"

"Not at all," Cassandra said honestly, thinking it was a perfect day. "Where would you like to go?"

"To the veranda at the rear of the house. I won't need your arm while inside, but I hope you won't mind helping me when we get out of doors."

Tate came to his feet, as did Cassandra. She hesitated, not certain how to proceed, and then decided to ask.

"Mr Tate?"

"Yes."

"Shall I go ahead of you in the house, or trail after you?"

Tate's head bowed, almost as though he could look down on her.

"Are you sitting down?"

"No."

Tate fought a smile. "You're not very tall, are you?"

"Well, now, that depends," Cassandra stated in good humor.

"On what?"

"On whom you're asking."

Cassandra watched a smile start at the corners of his mouth before he controlled it.

"All right, I'll bite. Name someone who finds you tall."

"I can name several: John Hurst, Lizzy Palmer, Penny Jennings, and Oliver Palmer, to name a few."

"All right, we'll start with John. He would be ten or eleven years old?"

Just holding laughter, Cassandra admitted, "I believe he's six."

Tate stopped trying to suppress his smile. It blossomed fully as he finished questioning her.

"And Lizzy?"

"Six also, I believe."

"Penny?"

"She's older."

"Seven?"

"At least!" Cassandra told him.

"And who was at the end? Oliver?"

"Yes."

"How old is he?"

Cassandra sighed. "I'm not sure. He's still in nappies."

The sound came again. In full volume, Tate's laughter rang out, filling the room and spilling beyond. He did nothing to hide his merriment, and indeed, took some time to control himself.

"Are you still willing to read to me?" he finally calmed enough to ask.

"I shall have to tell you after we arrive on the veranda. If it's as lovely as everything else at Pembroke, I might have to reconsider."

"So it has nothing to do with me?"

"Of course not. You just told me I was short. You won't be forgiven for days."

Tate sighed dramatically. "I need to thank my Aunt Harriet for keeping such a fine home."

"Yes, you should," she continued to tease him. "Now, you never answered my question. Do I go ahead of you or come behind?"

"Just nearby should do the trick. If I'm going to upset something you can give a shout."

Completely unnoticed by either of them, Harriet Thorpe stood outside the library and listened to their conversation. She watched them maneuver their way to the hall and toward the door that would lead them outside, her hand coming to her throat.

If I had chased her away, Lord. If I had done something and she'd never returned . . .

Harriet couldn't go on. The thought was too painful. She simply hadn't seen what was happening. Her eyes had not noticed how greatly Tate had come to need his visitor.

"Oh, my," Cassandra said quietly when they were settled out-of-doors.

"You must be looking at the gardens or the architecture," Tate guessed.

"Both. They're unbelievable."

"How are the flowers this year?"

"Simply lovely. Here," Cassandra plucked a pink bloom from one of the many ornate planters. "Smell this." She placed it into Tate's hand and watched.

Tate raised it to his face and smiled.

"Very nice."

"Do you like flowers and gardening and such?"

"Yes. I have a large garden in London. Why do you ask?"

"The reviews are so mixed in my family. Lizzy doesn't care for flower arranging or for puttering in the garden. Neither does Henry. But Edward and I love it."

"There's one more sister, isn't there? What about her?"

"Charlotte. She loves gardens. When she married Barrington, she told him she would fill the church with flowers, and she did."

"Where have they made their home?"

"They're still traveling, but they'll settle in Bath."

"Have you seen them lately?" Tate asked, having caught a wistful tone.

"No, not since the wedding. They write every so often."

Tate might have been readying to say something more, but Cassandra felt she had talked enough about herself.

"Are you ready for the rest of this article?"

"Yes, please."

The experience took on a whole new meaning in the out-of-doors. The incessant ticking of numerous clocks was replaced by the natural sound of birds and insects. Cassandra's voice even sounded different without the four walls to hold it in.

Tate tried to concentrate, but today it wasn't working. He ended up just sitting back, his legs stretched out, the sun on his head, listening to the husky sound of Cassandra's voice as it floated over him. At that moment in time, he thought he could go forever without his sight and not miss a thing.

★ ★ ★

"Come and see me this week, will you, Steele?" Walker invited just before church on Sunday.

"Certainly. What day?"

"Wednesday. Does that work for you?"

"I'll plan on it."

Sitting in the pew and waiting for the service to start, Cassandra was completely unaware of this exchange. She had prayed for her brother since visiting with Walker and wondered still if she'd done the right thing, but each time she was tempted to worry, she remembered how tragic it would be to have Christ return before Henry could be counted as one of His own.

Even if he's angry with me, I have to do all I can to make sure he knows You, Lord. Help Mr Walker to have just the right words. Help Henry's heart to be open.

The service was starting. Lizzy sat on one side of her, Henry on the other. Cassandra forced her mind to attend, knowing she could learn much about trusting God from the book of Jonah.

The note from Harriet Thorpe had been an invitation. The day it arrived, Cassandra looked at the envelope before opening it, and when she did venture to remove the note, learned that the request was for the next day.

Cassandra,
Will you do Tate and me the honor of joining us for luncheon on Tuesday at noon? No reading on this day, just repast and fellowship to say thank you for your friendship and care. We'll expect you unless we hear otherwise.

Warmly,
Mrs Harriet Thorpe

Cassandra found herself rather excited. She was having one of the loveliest springs of her life getting to know this family. The experience had not been without its bumps, but she had learned a lot along the way. It occurred to her, even as the carriage took her toward Pembroke, that this might be their gentle way of telling her she was no longer needed, but she decided not to worry about that. If the time had come to an end, so be it.

Pembroke

"Are the flowers where she can see them?"
"Yes," Harriet answered patiently, smiling a little. "They're down the table, but they'll

be almost directly to her right."

"And all is in order? Her chair is one with arms?"

"Yes, again."

"You're trying not to laugh."

"This is true." These words were punctuated by a chuckle.

"Why is that?"

"I've just never known you to be so fussy about the table setting."

"This is not just any meal."

"Why is that, Tate?" Harriet asked, her voice telling of her very real desire to know.

"It's not something easily explained. I've become so accustomed to her visits that I fear she thinks I expect them. I want this meal to express how much I appreciate her time."

"That was very nicely put. If you tell her that, she'll understand just what you mean."

"I hope I won't have to say anything of the sort. Such words would probably ruin the party. I hope she'll just understand."

You sound like a man, Harriet thought fondly but saw what he meant.

She glanced at the clock on the dining room wall and hurried to check a few more things. Their visitor would be coming any moment.

★ ★ ★

The carriage arrived, always making better time than Cassandra anticipated, and just moments later Hastings was opening the front door.

"Welcome, Miss Steele. Please come this way."

"Thank you, Hastings."

Cassandra was taken to a room in the opposite direction from the library. The door was closed, and when Hastings opened it, Cassandra was in for a surprise.

"Oh, my," she breathed, taking in the huge windows that looked out to the garden and the walls that appeared to be painted in gold.

"I think she likes it, Harriet," Tate said, bringing Cassandra's gaze to the room's occupants.

"Welcome, Cassandra," Harriet offered.

"Thank you. This room is marvelous."

"We like it," Harriet said simply. "Don't we, Tate?"

"Yes. Have a seat," Tate gestured to the cushioned chair on his right. Harriet went to sit on the other side.

A servant was standing ready to assist, and in moments the three were seated. Food began to appear. Instantly Cassandra could see that she was being treated to a feast, with conversation to match. The three of them talked on all subjects, barely pausing to rest. Cassandra learned of Harriet's travels and how she had met her husband. Some of the things she shared were very romantic, and Cassandra found herself captivated.

On a number of occasions, she was glad Tate could not see her. Throughout the luncheon she looked to him, working to gauge his reactions to stories he must have heard before but also to see if he was enjoying himself. Why that was important to her just now, she wasn't certain.

Not even when the luncheon ended and she was headed for home did she understand exactly why Tate needed to have a good time. Technically he was the host, and it was his job to entertain her, but Cassandra wasn't seeing it that way. All the way home in the carriage she asked herself if he had had as good a time as she had. She fell asleep that night still wondering.

"What does she look like?"

Cassandra was hardly out the door when Tate asked this of his aunt. Harriet stared at the man across from her, weighing her thoughts.

"I just realized something, Tate," she ad-

140

mitted. "That's not an easy question to answer."

"Why isn't it?"

"I don't know exactly. I guess it has to do with the fact that looks are based on so many things."

Tate took a moment to digest this.

"All right. I'll question you."

"Do."

"Is she dark like Elizabeth, or blonde like Charlotte?"

"Neither. Cassandra is a redhead."

Tate's brows went up, but he was smiling.

"And her eyes?"

"Like brown pansies."

"Is her hair dark red or light?"

"Quite dark. Russet."

"Freckles?"

"She's covered with them."

Tate's white teeth flashed as a full-blown smile lit his face.

"She's not very tall." Harriet became expansive. "I think you can tell that. Her eyes light up when she talks or listens, and if she's feeling something, it shows on her face. 'Pretty' or 'beautiful' really doesn't describe her."

"What does?"

" 'Adorable.' Like a child who melts your heart. But then she speaks, and her voice is that of a woman, almost sultry. I could listen to it for hours."

Tate felt his heart turn over, his mind thinking, *I could too.*

"Any more questions?"

"Yes. Does she have any awareness of me, or is she only being kind and polite?"

"She's very aware of you and watches you closely, probably because you can't look back. I suspect that if someday you are able to see her, Tate, she won't be anywhere near so comfortable."

"So you don't think she cares for her looks?"

"She's done nothing to indicate that. I just thought you should be warned." Harriet was swift to add, "I'm not saying she's bold, Tate — nothing could be further from the truth — but her eyes stray to you often. Could you see her, you would probably find it flirtatious, and I know she's not that."

"How do you know?"

"I've watched her with some of the young men in the church family."

"Is she seeing someone?" Tate couldn't hide the note of anxiety in his voice.

"Not that I know of."

With that, Tate was worn out. He'd enjoyed the meal tremendously and hearing about Cassandra had been like finishing a lovely painting, but it had taxed him emotionally. He thanked his aunt and retired to his room, reminding himself that he was supposed to be resting.

Blackburn Manor

"This is spectacular," Walker said, his head bent over the de Witt atlas Cassandra had given Henry for his birthday. "And you say Benwick had this?"

"Yes. Cassandra found it for me."

"She beat me to it, Henry, or it would be in my collection."

Henry smiled and sat back, well satisfied with the comment.

Walker looked at him and laughed a little, but he hadn't forgotten his assignment. He took a seat close by and leaned toward his younger friend.

"I'm glad you brought that so I could see it, Henry, but I have to tell you that I've asked you here today for a different reason."

"All right."

"We're very comfortable talking about maps and such, but it has occurred to me that in all this time we've never spoken of spiritual things."

143

"No, I guess we haven't."

"Why is that, do you suppose?"

"I don't know."

"Well, I for one regret that. I've never asked you about some of the most important things in your life."

"Such as?"

"Such as your parents, and what they believed, and how it's affected you."

Henry stared at him for a moment.

"If you don't mind my asking, Walker, what brought this on?"

"A number of things, the first of which is that I've heard you're very quiet. You're not quiet with me, so it makes me wonder how you live the rest of your life. Are you unusually talkative with me, or unusually silent with others?"

"The latter, I would have to say."

"Why is that?"

"As my sister says, I don't need words to live."

"But how do you share your faith? How do you show people the joy Christ brings?"

Henry began to look uncomfortable, but at the same time he was very humbled by the calm caring he saw in James Walker. Given a choice, he would have avoided this subject like the blight, but the man's voice and manner caused him to listen carefully and to think about his life.

"I try very hard to be an example in my dealings, Walker," Henry offered. "I'm careful to be fair and honest in town and with workers who come to Newcomb Park. And certainly with the staff."

"I'm glad to hear it, Steele," Walker said calmly, but he was done with tact. "But if your own sisters doubt your salvation, something is wrong."

These words shook Henry. He took a moment to ask, "Has Cassie come to you?"

"Yes. Did she tell you?"

"No, but when I noticed that a coach was gone, my man told me she'd come here."

"She cares desperately for you, Henry. I hope there won't be any hard feelings against her."

"Against Cassandra? Never. She's the sweetest woman who ever walked the face of the earth. She seeks my company out, even though I have nothing to say."

The thought — Henry's own words — shook him even more.

Coming to his feet, Henry went to the window. He was not a man of great outward passion. It was true that he didn't need conversation to be content, but that didn't mean he could follow his heart.

"What caused her to come exactly?"

"She's confused by you. She said you value things above people."

Henry turned from the window.

"In truth, I don't, but since I never share my thoughts, how much I love and pray for my sisters and Edward, they never know."

Walker remained quiet. He had decided to speak to Henry, assuming he was a believer, not knowing it would open the floodgates. In the next three hours Walker learned how Henry had come to Christ at his father's knee, Charlotte, just two years younger, right beside him.

He learned of the way he'd met with Pastor Greville in Bath for personal Bible study but now did all of his studying alone. For long stretches Henry talked nonstop, telling Walker of the truths he'd learned from Scripture and the way God had changed his heart in many areas.

"But you never tell any of this to your siblings?"

"No, I guess I don't. I'm a kind person, generous even, and not easily angered. I assumed that they understood the reason I was able to be such a man."

"What would Cassandra say if she was to hear all of that?"

Henry knew in an instant.

"She would ask me why I never inquire about her day or her shopping trips. She would ask how we can go for our morning rides and not say two words to each other."

"So she doesn't speak either?"

"She's only doing that for me."

Walker smiled at Henry Steele.

"Henry, you're one of my favorite people. I feel that way because you're intelligent and we can talk on any subject. I don't know why you haven't been able to do that with your family, but God can change you. I'm sure of it."

Henry sighed. "This might be more than He's ever asked of me before."

Walker was still smiling.

"But if He requires it of you, and I suspect that He does, He'll help you. You know He will."

Henry could not help but agree. He and Walker talked on for the next hour, mapping out a plan and looking at verses that spoke to the man of the family and how much he needed to lead. By the time Henry left for home, he was well and truly spent, but he was also determined to change. He and Walker would meet at the same time next week.

Thinking once again that his sisters had

doubted his salvation made his heart ache.

"I don't know how to talk to them, Father. I don't know how," Henry said softly in the coach as it moved toward Newcomb Park. And from that point on, he prayed until the coach pulled into the drive.

Chapter Eight

Pembroke

The sun was up and warm in a cloudless sky when Cassandra arrived on Friday morning. Hastings told her at the door that Tate was already on the veranda. Cassandra headed that way.

"Hello, Mr Tate."

"Hello, Cassandra. Can you stand to be outside today?"

"Yes. I might have begged for this if I'd found you inside."

Tate waited for her to sit and then handed her the book he'd been holding.

"Here you go."

"What's this?" Cassandra looked down at the new volume.

"Our next book. Have a go at it."

A moment later Cassandra's laughter bubbled out. She didn't know if it was Japanese or Chinese, but she knew one thing: She couldn't read it.

"Where did you unearth this?"

"Hastings is very resourceful," Tate answered with a broad smile, clearly pleased with himself.

"And what if I'd been able to read it?"

"Ah, yes, that would have been fun. The joke would have certainly been on me."

Cassandra laughed a little more.

"Are there other languages you can speak?" Tate suddenly wondered. He was as good with Italian and French as Cassandra was, but until that moment assumed there was nothing else in her repertoire.

"Now that would be telling," Cassandra hedged. In truth, any other language she'd worked on was sketchy, but she didn't want to admit to that just yet.

"You choose to remain a mystery."

"For the moment."

"I might have to keep searching for books."

Cassandra laughed at this and was ready to reach for the nearby paper, but Tate had another question.

"Has anything been rectified in your painful situation?"

"Not that I know of."

"How would you not know?"

"Because at times things happen quietly or slowly. I'm fairly certain that some talking has gone on, but it's rather new, so time might be needed."

"If I were to pray about the situation, for what would I ask?"

Wanting very much to continue to be discreet, Cassandra had to think on that.

"I think we can pray that all hearts involved be open, humble, and patient. Does that make sense?"

"Perfect sense."

"Do you want me to read now?"

"That's fine."

Cassandra reached for the paper but didn't open it.

"Mr Tate, may I ask a question of you?"

"Yes."

"How do you pray for yourself? How do you stay at peace when you don't know what will happen with your eyesight?"

"I pray that I'll keep trusting."

"So the biggest issue for you is trust?"

"Yes. It helps that I was studying Moses at the time of my accident. God asked Moses to trust Him in so many ways. Sometimes he failed, and other times he was obedient. But what stuck out the most to me was God's plan in Moses' life. Clearly God knew what He wanted from Moses and how best to take care of His servant.

"As His child, I believe that God has a plan for me. God knows whether my having my sight restored will bring Him honor and glory. I can't tell you that it wouldn't be an adjustment to remain in darkness, but if I need to stay blind in order to be more pleasing to Him, I can't fight that. If I don't thank Him for whatever He has planned, I'll be miserable and fruitless. I fail in my efforts — every day I fail — but my goal is to be righteous and trust Him."

Cassandra found herself oddly choked up. Had she just met this man, all he'd said might have sounded like a lot of religious platitudes. However, she felt confident that he meant every word. She'd been with him for days, seeing his calmness, his sense of peace, and even his effort to put others ahead of himself.

"Are you still there, Cassandra?"

"Yes." She couldn't disguise the thickness of her voice. Indeed, tears were very close. She forced them back. "I'll read to you now."

Tate didn't comment. He had no idea his thoughts would affect her, but he found it strangely comforting. Coming to need her warmth, sweetness, and sense of caring in his life, he suddenly realized that if she felt nothing for him, it would feel like a rejection.

He listened to her read, no particular emotion showing on his face, but he was pleased right then, very pleased indeed.

Newcomb Park

"How was Mr Tate yesterday?"

For several heartbeats Cassandra didn't answer. She had heard Henry's voice and seen his mouth move but still couldn't quite manage the fact that Henry had initiated a dialog.

"He's doing well. Thank you for asking, Henry."

"I'm glad to hear it."

Henry moved on his way then, Cassandra staring after him. Lizzy chose that moment to walk from the library with a book.

"What is it, Cassie?"

"I don't know. Just something odd."

"Henry?"

"Yes."

Lizzy nodded. "He asked me if I'd visited with Anne Weston lately and how she was doing."

"Did he go and see Mr Walker? Is that where he was on Wednesday?"

"I believe so."

"What do you suppose happened? Should we ask Mr Walker?"

"No." Lizzy immediately shook her head. "Let us take our cue from Henry. Clearly he's trying, and we need to be as open and receptive as we can be."

Cassandra only nodded, still feeling somewhat in shock.

Why do I pray for something and then feel amazed when You bring it to pass? she asked the Lord, a bit miffed with herself and her own lack of faith. *I shall do better,* Cassandra decided. *I shall ask believing and be more willing to trust.*

Having only just decided this, Cassandra realized she'd completely forgotten what she was about to do. She looked toward the library door but nothing jogged her memory. A moment later she gave up and returned to her room.

"How is it going?"

James Walker had slipped into Henry's pew before he could exit.

"I'm exhausted," the younger man admitted, even as Walker studied fatigue around his eyes. "Does God really want me to be someone I'm not?"

Walker chuckled a little, not able to help himself.

"Isn't it like that for all of us, Henry? An emptying. A putting off of the sinful man we were and learning to walk in holiness?"

"Yes, I do see what you mean, but I must admit that I ask myself how talking to my sisters is a step toward holiness."

Walker only stared at him.

"Yes, I know," Henry acknowledged. "I'm showing that I put people ahead of things."

"Did you work on it this week?"

"Yes. I realized I can say what I'm thinking."

"Good."

"I could tell they were quite amazed."

"Your sisters?"

"Yes."

Henry's voice told of his bafflement, but Walker gripped his shoulder and smiled at him.

"You're doing well, Henry. I'm proud of you. I'm expecting you Wednesday, and you can tell me how it's gone, or we can talk about why it isn't working."

"All right. Thank you, Walker."

"By the way, have you told your sisters that you've seen me?"

"No." Henry looked surprised by the very thought, and Walker smiled again, not saying anything this time but communicating clearly with his eyes.

Pembroke

Tate was walking in the garden when Cassandra arrived in the middle of the following week. Aunt Harriet was not far off, but when Hastings took her to the door, she could see that Tate was on his own. The eye patches were still in place, and he was moving slowly, a tall cane in his hand, asking for directions from time to time.

"Hello, Cassandra," Harriet called in greeting. "Come and join us."

"Thank you. I will."

"Welcome, Miss Steele," Tate said, smiling as her footsteps neared. "How are you this fine day?"

"I'm very well, and I don't need to ask how you are doing. Indeed, I can see you won't need anyone to do anything as dull as reading."

"Your reading is never dull," Tate assured her gallantly. "But I will admit to you that this is a very nice change."

"Indeed it is. I think we could stand a full spring and summer of such days."

"I quite agree with you," Tate said, even as he asked himself if he would be able to see her by the end of summer.

"Would you like a basket?" Harriet offered as she approached.

"Thank you," Cassandra said with a smile. "Is there anything I shouldn't pick?"

"No," Harriet said with a laugh. "Take anything that catches your eye."

"I'll need a bigger basket," Cassandra teased, not noticing the way Tate simply stood and listened to her.

"I'll just follow along with you," Tate now said, proud of how calm he managed to keep his voice. "You can tell me what you've picked and allow me to smell one on occasion."

"All right," Cassandra agreed.

Tate, thinking his last line had made him sound like a lovesick school boy, relaxed when he heard her normal tone.

"Do you have a favorite color in flowers?" Cassandra asked after she'd stopped next to a bush full of pale lavender blooms.

"Probably yellow, although I'm also rather partial to red."

Cassandra laughed. "That was an interesting combination."

"It's this fresh air," Tate explained. "It clears the mind and then muddles it again."

"Another interesting combination."

"I can see I'm only going to be teased today."

Cassandra smiled and reached for another stem, having completely forgotten to tell Tate of the flowers she was collecting.

"You're off to a good start, Cassandra," Harriet commented, suddenly back beside them on her way across the yard. "Oh, Tate," she kept on. "She has mostly red and yellow blooms. Just like you enjoy."

Harriet kept moving, or she would have seen the blush that stained Cassandra's cheeks.

"You haven't let me smell anything," Tate said quietly when Cassandra didn't speak.

"Here," she pressed a flower into his hand. "Try this."

"Very nice." Tate fingered the petals. "Shall I name it?"

Rather amused, Cassandra said, "Yes, do."

Cassandra watched as the tall man held the bloom to his nose, his brow creased in concentration. "I believe this should be called fire dragon."

"How did you know that flower by its scent?" Cassandra asked, thoroughly amazed.

Tate laughed. "After my mother died, Aunt Harriet insisted that I develop the love for flowers that Mother had."

"How old were you?"

"It was before my tenth birthday."

"And did it work?"

"Yes. I'm fascinated with horticulture in general."

"Do flowers never make you sad?"

"At first, that's all they did. I cried much of the time. But then Mother's delight of flowers came to me. She was so taken with every blossom and garden. In time they all served as lovely remembrances, not just painful reminders."

For the first time, Cassandra wished she could see his eyes. His voice had been so thoughtful and warm. It hadn't been hard to read, but seeing his eyes would have added to Cassandra's understanding.

"What are you going to pick now?" Tate asked gently, almost as if he could feel her eyes on him.

"I think these small roses," she said, turning swiftly and deciding just as fast.

Tate wasn't certain he should have distracted her, but somehow he thought she might need rescuing. He found himself wishing he could see her eyes. He'd have known then what was on her mind.

His very small sigh went unnoticed. He moved slowly with Cassandra, just content to be near her, and reminding himself yet again that he was supposed to be resting.

Blackburn Manor

"I came across these verses this week, Henry. Can I share them with you?"

"Please."

The men had finished lunch and settled in the study. From his place on the leather sofa, James Walker opened his Bible to Romans 12. Henry leaned close to see the words as Walker read.

" 'Let love be without dissimulation. Abhor that which is evil; cleave to that which is good. Be kindly affectioned one to another with brotherly love, in honor preferring one another.' "

"I have those very verses underlined in my Bible, Walker," Henry told him. "I've read and studied them, but they don't open my mouth any easier."

Walker thought for a moment. There were many things he could say to that, but only one really stuck in his mind at the moment.

"Why don't you write your sisters a letter?"

"They live with me, Walker," Henry clarified, as though the elder of the two had forgotten this point.

"I realize that, but you have all these thoughts in your mind. Why not try to put them on paper? Start the letter by explaining how difficult it is for you to share in person, but that you're trying. I know Lizzy and Cassandra. They will understand."

Henry sat back, his eyes on some distant spot as the idea took seed in his mind.

"That's perfect, isn't it? I mean, they'll at least stop staring at me so oddly when I do try to communicate."

Walker laughed a little.

"Is that still happening?"

Henry even managed to chuckle.

"Cassie nearly filled her lap with hot tea the other morning. I thought I should confine my comments to when she's standing on solid ground with only a book or flower in her hand."

Walker saw great humor in this, and it took some moments before they went on to the other verses he had looked up. Henry determined to memorize a few of them and trust God to remind him when they were needed. All in all, the men spent four hours together. By the time Henry left, he was very tired, but God was changing his heart, he could tell. And he also had the comfort of knowing that Walker was expecting him the very next week.

★ ★ ★

"Does your heart overflow with awe for our Creator God?" Pastor Hurst asked the congregation on Sunday morning. "Look at chapter 1, verse 9. 'And he said unto them, I am an Hebrew; and I fear the Lord, the God of heaven, which hath made the sea and the dry land.'

"Did you catch that? Look at the way Jonah describes his God. 'The Lord, the God of heaven, which made the sea and dry land.' This is not just any old god. And now look at verse 10. 'Then were the men exceedingly afraid, and said unto him, Why hast thou done this? For the men knew that he fled from the presence of the Lord, because he had told them.'

"The moment they hear whom Jonah serves, they are terrified. No matter what they had believed in up to this time, they knew this was not the same. This was not some stone variety god that sits mute on a pedestal somewhere in their home or on the hillside of their village. This God was real and alive, and He'd made the sea that was working to smash their ship to pieces. Why do I know this? Verse 11, 'Then said they unto him, What shall we do unto thee, that the sea may be calm unto us? For the sea wrought and was tempestuous.'

"They weren't just offering lip service here. They asked Jonah what they could do to appease this huge Creator God. And what does he tell them? That's right, throw him overboard. But they don't want this murder on their hands, and they do all they can to avoid that."

Pastor Hurst took a small breath. He was so excited about what he'd been studying that he feared he would rush ahead of himself and miss a point. He made himself calm down before going on.

"The reason I'm so excited about Jonah right now is that I've spent way too many years concentrating on the prophet. Jonah was so flippant in his response to God, but the people he spoke with about his God fell to their knees. I've always read Jonah and thought to myself, 'That's right, Jonah, you can't run from God.' And amid that thought I've missed the example of both the sailors and the people of Nineveh in terms of repentance. No light response there. Their reaction is staggering: terror, fear, belief, repentance.

"I've been struck anew by how lukewarm my own response can be. Am I as awestruck as I need to be? Do I understand the magnificent God in whom I am to delight? I love these sailors. I love their immediate response. I don't want to have a tempest rising up on all sides of me in order for God to get my attention, but if that's what it takes, I'm willing. I'm willing for God to do whatever He must so I can understand and obey Him better."

Henry sat very still through this sermon, knowing he was lacking in this area. He knew that he was too comfortable with life as it was. Such comfort kept him from looking at God as He needed to be viewed.

Beside him, Lizzy sat with thoughts of her own. She had fallen back to thinking about Morland almost constantly and had become discontented. She knew she was wrong. All those times she'd been concentrating on herself — telling herself she was lonely and whatnot — she could have been thinking on the awesome God who loved her.

Cassandra was in bad shape as well. She wasn't yearning for someone far away, but she was so busy with life in Collingbourne that lately she wasn't taking nearly as much time with her Bible and prayer. She too was missing out on the awesome God who had saved her.

The sermon ended in a song and then a long time of quiet prayer. All three members of the Steele family took the prayer time seriously. Cassandra and Lizzy smiled at each other when the service was over and even looked to Henry, who was looking down at both of them.

"I needed that," he thought to say, causing both girls to become emotional. They turned with swift nods so as not to break down in church, and moved to visit with some of the church family.

"Mrs Thorpe?" Lizzy called, just catching that lady before she could climb into the coach to leave the churchyard.

"Hello, Elizabeth. Were you calling to me without my hearing you?"

"No, I called only once because I didn't want my sister to hear."

Harriet's brows rose, but she remained quiet.

"Cassandra's birthday is Friday. We're having a very small party — just the three of us — but I did wonder if you and Mr Tate could join us."

"Oh, Elizabeth, I don't know." That lady's brow furrowed. "You said it would be small?"

"Very. If you join us, there will be five. Nothing lavish, just a few gifts and some conversation."

"I shall check with Tate and let you

165

know. Is that all right?"

"Certainly. And please, Mrs Thorpe, don't pressure yourself or Mr Tate. Cassie doesn't know I've asked you, so there won't be any disappointment on her account."

"And if we are able to come, would you want it kept quiet?"

Lizzy smiled slowly. "I think that might be fun."

"Very well. I will send word tomorrow, and I'll see to it that my reply goes only to you."

"So good of you. Thank you."

Lizzy waited until Mrs Thorpe's coach pulled away, giving her a wave as she went. Her face looked serene as she stood in the churchyard, but in truth she suddenly wanted Mr Tate and his aunt to come to Cassandra's birthday dinner very, very much.

Pembroke

"I would like to go," Tate said. "I think it might do me good."

"Cassandra doesn't know anything about it, Tate. She won't be disappointed if we're not there."

But I will be.

Harriet watched her nephew, not certain if she should say anything else.

"Do you feel I'll be overtaxing myself?" Tate suddenly asked, his voice so humble that Harriet felt humbled herself.

"It occurs to me, Tate," she spoke as the thoughts materialized, "that you are a better judge of such things. I want to cosset you. I want to go overboard with your rest, but you're the one who knows if you're taking it easy or not."

Tate nodded.

"The doctor comes this week," Harriet added, not certain he remembered.

"I did think of that, but thank you for the reminder. I will admit that I'm hoping for good news, but even if I don't hear what I'd like, I need to carry on, don't I?"

"Yes."

"And now what does that have to do with Cassandra's party, you're wondering."

"You read my mind."

"I've done what the doctor has asked," Tate observed, thinking aloud. "And I will continue to do so, trusting his authority on the matter. But progress with my eyes or not, unless the doctor forbids the action, I would like to go to Newcomb Park on Friday evening. I don't see it as not resting, and quite frankly it would be nice to do something for someone else."

"That's a good decision, Tate. I'll get word to Elizabeth Steele. It's a secret, by the way."

"Thank you for your counsel on the matter, Aunt Harriet, and for listening to my roving thoughts. Now, what shall we take for a gift?" With that, Tate was swiftly onto his next line of thought.

The two of them spent the rest of their lunch deciding on the perfect gift.

Chapter Nine

Newcomb Park

"Cassie, are you still awake?" Lizzy asked, opening the door a bit.

"Yes, Lizzy. Come in."

It was rather late on Sunday night. Both Cassandra and Lizzy had been buried in books for the evening, and the time had run away from them. They parted in the hallway, bid each other goodnight, and closed their doors behind them. Lizzy, however, arrived in her room to find a letter on her pillow. The front read, *For Elizabeth and Cassandra.*

"It's from Henry," Lizzy said, now on the edge of her sister's bed and unfolding the pages.

"And it's to both of us?"

"Yes. Shall I read?"

"Please."

"My dear sisters," Lizzy began.

You might think it odd for me to address you in such a manner, especially when we occupy the same home, but because you are well familiar with my communication skills, I hope you will understand and forgive me.

I have been meeting at Blackburn Manor with James Walker for several weeks, and it was he who suggested I write and tell you about it. I know you visited him, Cassie, and you must never think me vexed at anyone save myself. To learn that you fear for my salvation causes me no end of pain, but I can see how easily your mind would stray to such a conclusion.

I have been under the false impression that I could merely act out my belief in Christ. I have lived my life believing I have little need of words. Proverbs 22:1 says, "A good name is rather to be chosen than great riches, and loving favor rather than silver and gold." I think my reputation as a fair man who is honest in my business dealings and as an employer are valid, and I would not wish to trade that, but as Walker brought to my attention, how can I tell anyone about the love Christ has shown me if I never open my heart and share? I now find that I have been so silent in my faith that my own sisters don't even know where I will spend eternity.

This letter is to inform you that I am

working on this area of my life. As you can imagine, it does not come easily to me. Indeed, it is one of the most draining exercises I have ever endeavored. I have such great love for both of you, but telling you this in person is not something that comes naturally for me.

This letter is to beg your forgiveness and patience as I labor in this process, which I hope will lead to further righteousness in my life. I would covet your prayers, and I thank you for your everpresent kindness.

I would also be happy to answer any questions you may have. Please feel free to come to me.

> *With greatest affection,*
> *Henry*

The letter went to Lizzy's lap as she finished. The sisters leaned close to each other as tears streamed unchecked down their cheeks. Amazed that he had so many words bottled up inside, the women struggled to rein in their emotions. Reaching for hankies, they took some time before either was under control.

Cassandra soundlessly rose from the bed. When she moved to the door, Lizzy followed. The shortest of knocks was placed against Henry's bedroom door before Cassandra eased it open. Finding darkness within, she nevertheless spoke from the doorway.

"Henry?"

"Yes?"

"I love you, Henry," Cassandra told him, unable to hold the tears that started again.

"Thank you, Cassie."

"As do I, Henry," Lizzy added, her own voice thick.

"Thank you, Lizzy."

"Goodnight," they both bid him before returning to Cassandra's room.

"Let's pray, Cassie. Let's pray for Henry right now."

The women did just that. For long minutes they sat together and asked God's blessing in Henry's life. They prayed for Charlotte, Barrington, and Edward, confessed their own lack of courage over the years, and then asked God to work a great work in their lives, especially for those still at Newcomb Park, so that they might be a light in Collingbourne as long as God allowed.

Brown Manor

"You're looking well, Mrs Weston," Dr Smith told her after a brief examination. "How are you feeling?"

"Very well, but I do wish I could be up and about."

The doctor asked a few more questions, Weston standing nearby, and then looked at the fine young couple before him.

"You're over five months along now. If you still have no more spotting at the six-month mark, you may be on your feet for two hours a day."

Anne smiled as though he'd handed her the world.

"Any bleeding, dizziness, fatigue, or blurred vision, and you must return to bed. Do I make myself clear?"

"Yes, Dr Smith. Thank you."

"Keep your activity light, and be wise."

Anne lay smiling at the ceiling while Weston saw the good doctor out. Her skin, hips, and back ached from the hours in bed, but a reprieve was on the way.

"You're looking pleased."

Anne beamed at Weston when he returned.

"It's wonderful news, isn't it?"

"Very."

Anne stared at her husband.

"Am I shorter than you are?" she teased. "I believe I've forgotten."

"Well, you were," he teased right back, "but all of this lying down might have given you a chance to grow."

"Only in the middle, I fear."

Weston leaned to kiss her expanding waist. "I'll write to my mother right away."

"Do, Weston. And please ask her to visit again when the baby is due."

"I shall."

Not able to help himself, Weston kissed her again, this time on the lips. He thought she would be in this bed until her pains began. What a wonderful surprise to learn that he was wrong.

Pembroke

The eye patches came away easily, but Dr Tilney commanded Tate to keep his eyes closed. Dr Tilney had also ordered the drapes drawn, so the room was dim. Tate worked at not being anxious, but the temptation to open his eyes was nearly overpowering.

"All right, Mr Tate, you may open your eyes," Dr Tilney said from directly in front of him. "Slowly, I think, would be best."

Tate did so, not able to rush even if he'd wanted. His lids flickered and then carefully opened all the way. He forced his eyes wide for a moment before attempting to look around.

"Remember that the drapes are drawn."

"I see."

"What do you see?"

"Shadows mostly, but things aren't nearly so dark."

"Good. Now I'm going to open the drapes over this one window, so turn your eyes for a moment."

Tate heard the movement to his side and then was told to look back.

"I don't want you to have pain, so turn away if the light hurts."

Tate moved his head slowly, his heart sinking. "What do you see?"

"A lot of light, but things are still out of focus."

"How much light?"

"I think all there is."

Without a word, the doctor moved to the other windows. The room was now fully lit, but as Tate had said, things were blurry around the edges. He watched the doctor come toward him, and found his face a mass of flesh with few distinctive features.

The doctor looked into Tate's eyes and ran a few tests. He questioned him about pain or dizziness as he moved along.

"No, nothing like that," Tate said, discounting the disappointment in his heart.

"I'm very pleased. Two more months

with the patches, and I think we'll know where we stand."

Tate had all he could do not to sigh. Blurry as it was, the light was delightful.

"May I look for just a few more minutes?"

The doctor nodded in understanding. "I'll gather my things and make one more check, but then it's back to darkness."

"Very well."

Ten minutes later the patches were in place, the doctor was gone, and Aunt Harriet was at his door.

"How are you?"

"Disappointed, but dealing with it."

"I'm so sorry, dear. Ring if you need me."

"Thank you."

It has occurred to me — Tate began speaking to God the moment he was alone — *that I thought I knew Your will. I was so certain You would return my sight by now. If I had been questioned, I would have said I was accepting either way, but my present disappointment tells me that I was not ready for this.*

Cassandra lingered in his mind just seconds later. He'd never really considered asking her if she could have feelings for a blind man, so certain was he that his sight would be fully restored.

But that is what I want to know right now, Tate confessed. *Even more than wanting my sight back, I wonder what Cassandra Steele thinks of me. I ache at the thought of her exiting my life. Something akin to grief fills me, even greater than the thought of living life in a haze.*

The more Tate thought on it, the more determined he was to ask Cassandra a few questions, but when he tried to picture himself doing such a thing, something inside him froze.

"This is not good," he said aloud to the empty room. "If I can't get the nerve in my heart, how will I go about it when she's with me?"

With no forthcoming answer, and having to face the fact that he wasn't as thankful as he ought to be, Tate was left alone with his prayers. He determined to agree with God about whatever He planned and to restore the trust he'd worked on from the moment he woke in darkness.

"Which map is your favorite to study, Henry?"

"Probably Africa."

"Why is that?"

"Well, Edward is there, and it's so vast."

Cassandra didn't ask him anything else.

Their morning rides were a great deal more chatty than they'd ever been, but the youngest Steele still tried to be sensitive to Henry's need for silence.

"Will you be going to Pembroke today?" Henry asked just when they were arriving back at the stables.

"Unless I get word."

"Is that what happened yesterday?"

"Yes. The note didn't say why, but I was asked to postpone until today."

Henry had nothing more to say as the two went in to breakfast, but Cassandra didn't notice. She was too busy wondering if she would, in fact, be needed at Pembroke again.

Africa

In his tent, Edward Steele dug around in his bag, sure he'd placed his pad and pencil in there, but he wasn't able to locate them. Pulling out a stack of letters, he noticed that the top one was from his sister, Lizzy. Edward opened it up, remembered reading it the first time. He took it out to the fire where his traveling companion, Thomas Morland, stood attempting to repair a leather strap on his bag.

"Tell me, Morland," Edward didn't beat

about the bush in asking, "have you ever noticed my sister Elizabeth?"

Morland turned to look at Lizzy's brother as though he had taken leave of his senses, but the younger man was staring back, his face serious. "Noticed her?" he questioned.

"Yes. Noticed her."

"How could I not? She's the most beautiful woman I've ever seen."

"Why have you never shown any interest?"

Morland laughed a little.

"You can't be serious. Your sister could have anyone she wished. Why would she pay the least attention to any interest on my part?"

Edward brought the letter back up to his face and read, " 'Out of curiosity, Edward, does Morland ever speak of me or ask after me? I know you won't say anything to him, and he can't see my red face from Africa, but I do wonder about it.' "

Edward brought the letter down in time to see Morland lower himself slowly into a chair.

Morland stared across the fire at the youngest Steele male, his face a bit pale under his tan.

"I thought you knew," Edward said when

he could see how shaken his friend was.

"Not a single hint."

"I'm sorry, old man. I would have asked you a bit differently."

"But she's never given a single clue. Are you certain you understood her?"

"You can read the letter yourself, Morland."

Morland only shook his head, his face a mask of confusion, and asked again, "But how would I know? She's given nothing away!"

Edward smiled a little at the frustration in his voice.

"It was that way with Charlotte. She and Lizzy are both so pretty, and they've never wanted to flirt. Problem is, they've done such a good job that poor blokes like yourself are utterly in the dark. Barrington nearly lost his mind before he knew where he stood with Charlotte."

"What did he do?"

Edward smiled again, the boyish smile that made him so likeable.

"He took the plunge. He told her up front how he felt, with plans to leave the country if she refused him."

Morland didn't laugh or smile, but Edward continued to keep it lighthearted.

"You've already left the country, old

man. All you need to do is write. If she rejects you, you're already out of sight."

"No." Morland surprised him with his seriousness. "This has to be handled in person."

Edward's smile twisted a little.

"It sounds as though our trip is going to be cut short."

"Not at all, Edward. You can stay on and enjoy yourself, but I've got to look into plans to get home to England."

Pembroke

"How are you, Mr Tate?"

"I'm well, Cassandra, thank you. Are you well?"

"Yes, thank you."

Not since the first few days had Cassandra felt so awkward. It was on her mind to ask why she hadn't been needed the day before, but it was as if she'd been forbidden to speak of it.

"The newspaper today?"

"That's fine."

Cassandra began to read without further ado, but something had changed. There was a tenseness in her listener that had not been present before. Her heart felt burdened over what to do. He was supposed

181

to be resting, and to bring the subject up seemed all wrong to her. After all, he was old enough to know what he needed.

Cassandra's next thought chilled her to the bone. If he no longer wanted her and didn't know how to inform her . . .

"Are you all right?" Tate cut in.

"Yes." Cassandra suddenly stopped reading, sounding almost breathless.

"Are you certain?"

"I am, yes." The redhead cleared her throat. "Why do you ask?"

"Your voice sounds strained, as though something is bothering you."

Cassandra saw her chance but couldn't find the words.

"What is it, Cassandra?"

"I just want you to know something. I mean, I'm sure you already do, but I want you to know it again."

"Go on."

Tate's voice had taken on the patient tone that Cassandra found so comforting. When she tried again, her voice was calm.

"I haven't forgotten that you're to be resting, and if ever my coming is too draining for you, I do hope you'll tell me. I would never feel harmed in any way. I only wish you to gain all the rest you need."

"Thank you, Cassandra. I can assure you, I still find your visits very relaxing."

"Shall I continue?"

"That would be fine, but before you do, will you tell me what made you think I wasn't resting?"

"You seem uneasy today."

"Do I?" he asked.

"Yes. I realize there might be days like that, but I don't wish to be the cause."

"How would you be the cause?"

"Well, as I said, if you didn't want me to return and were hesitant to tell me . . ."

"I am hesitating about something today, but it's not about your coming to read for me."

"Is there something I can do?"

"I'm not sure. Shall I let you know if I figure it out?"

"Please do."

Cassandra went on with the reading, relaxing into the article and enjoying it. The next piece was humorous, and it felt good to laugh together. But not until Cassandra had read two more articles did Tate tell her about the day before.

"Dr Tilney checked my eyes yesterday."

"Was it painful?" Cassandra asked, her heart clenching at the thought.

"No, but it wasn't the news I'd hoped

183

for. Two more months of darkness."

"So there was no progress?"

"There was, but I somehow thought there would be more."

"Was it discouraging, or were you able to trust?"

"The trust took a little time. All day, in fact."

"And today is better?"

"Yes. Much. But as you surmised, not complete."

"I prayed for you, hoping you weren't feeling ill."

"Thank you for that."

Silence fell for a moment, Tate's heart telling him to jump, but he couldn't manage it. The questions he had for Cassandra swarmed in his mind, but he couldn't make his mouth move.

"Shall we go on?"

"I think I'm done for today," Tate said, only then realizing she would leave.

"Shall I return tomorrow, do you think, or would you rather send word if you need me."

I need you, Cassandra, please believe that I need you.

"Please come," Tate managed aloud. "Any time that suits you."

"All right."

"Thank you, Cassandra."

"You're very welcome."

A moment later he was on his own, his heart beating hard with emotion and something else he couldn't quite define.

When his Aunt Harriet checked on him a short time later, he still felt spent and hurt with all that was trapped inside of him. Harriet offered to play the piano for him, and Tate gladly moved to that room to enjoy her talent.

Chapter Ten

The Manse

"John, what are you doing?" Judith asked her youngest child rather sharply, causing all of her family to look up from the breakfast table and stare at her. The moment they did this, she heard the tone of her own voice and went to him.

"I didn't mean to sound so cross, dear. I'm sorry."

"Thank you, Mother. Are you unwell today?"

"Just a bit crabby I think, and there's no excuse for that."

"Why are you doing that with your eggs, John?" his father wished to know. The little boy had been lining up the egg pieces on the edge of his plate, and most were spilling onto the table and making a mess.

"Look at me, John," the pastor commanded. "Are you not hungry this morning?"

"Not very."

"Why is that?"

John managed a shrug.

"In the future, when you don't care to eat, you need to say something and not just sit there and play with your food. Understood?"

"Yes, Father."

"Mother?" Jane tried in a quiet voice, but Judith didn't answer. Judith's stomach had acted up earlier, and the smell of breakfast was not a pleasant one. In an effort to keep her distance, she hadn't even sat with the family at the table.

"Why don't you head up to bed," Frederick suggested, his look telling her to go.

Judith exited without a word, and Frederick looked to his children.

"Have we done something?" Jeffery asked, his face concerned.

"No, son, she's feeling unwell this morning; I don't know why she didn't tell you."

"She's tired of using that as an excuse," Margaret explained.

"But she doesn't use it as an excuse," Frederick said in wonder, his brow furrowed in thought. "How do you know that, Margaret?"

"I heard her tell Phoebe. She said she wants to cry all the time, and she's tired of feeling sick to her stomach."

"Was it like this with all of us?" Jane asked.

"A little different each time, I think. A little more emotional with each child."

"She looks tired," Jane commented before everyone went back to breakfast. Frederick made short work of his and was headed up the stairs just minutes later. He found Judith on their bed. She was crying.

"I'm a terrible mother," she sobbed. "John said he didn't feel like eating, and I didn't even make sure he was all right."

Frederick sat beside her, his hand going to her soft, dark hair.

"He's fine, and the girls are right there."

"What's the matter with me, Frederick? I want to cry constantly."

"When did this start?"

"About a week ago. I have a constant headache in my effort to hold tears at bay."

"Well, don't try anymore. Just let yourself cry. I think it was like this with Jane. It will pass."

Judith cried harder.

"What did I say?"

"Nothing!" she wailed in a way that was so unlike her. "I just can't stand it when I'm awful and you're so kind!"

Frederick's shoulders shook with silent laughter, even as his gentle hand moved to stroke her back. They would get through, high emotions and all, and at some point, Judith would join him in the laughter.

Newcomb Park

Let the wicked forsake his way, and the unrighteous man his thoughts, and let him return unto the Lord, and he will have mercy upon him; and to our God; for he will abundantly pardon.

Cassandra began her twenty-fourth birthday with this verse from Isaiah 55. At the end of his sermon on Sunday, Pastor Hurst had read it, and she had been so struck by the words concerning God's pardon that she'd written them down.

Still lying in her bed, Cassandra prayed quietly. She thanked God for His forgiveness, the type that came in abundant amounts, and lay thinking about how undeserving she was of such kindness.

Thank You. Thank You for saving me. Thank You for putting me in this special family and this wonderful home.

For the next hour, Cassandra thanked

God for every blessing in her life, starting with Henry's recent letter to her and Lizzy. By the time she went to breakfast, she wished she hadn't waited for her birthday to take some extra time but started every morning of the year in such a manner.

Blackburn Manor

"How is Henry Steele?" Mrs Walker asked of her husband over the breakfast table.

"He's doing well. He's tired, but that's no surprise since all change takes work."

"I'm so glad the family is back in the area."

"As am I."

"Did he say if Charlotte and Barrington will come anytime soon?"

"He did not. You could check with Lizzy or Cassandra on Sunday."

"I think I will. Why don't we have them to lunch?"

"Good idea."

Mrs Walker made notes on a small pad, deciding to send word immediately and not wait for Sunday. Her husband asked her something a moment later, but at first she didn't hear him. She was too busy mentally working out Sunday's menu.

Pembroke

"I have something to tell you," Cassandra announced to Tate before she picked up the newspaper.

"What's that?" he asked, proud of how unknowledgeable his voice sounded.

"It's my birthday today."

"Congratulations! Will you be having a party?" Again, his voice gave nothing away.

"No, just dinner with Henry and Lizzy. And presents!" she added with a smile.

"I think you like presents."

"I confess I do. My brother Edward sent me a game from Africa."

"Have you already opened your gifts?"

"The one from Edward, yes."

"Before you came this morning?"

"No, it arrived yesterday," she stated matter-of-factly.

"But yesterday wasn't your birthday."

"That's true, but there are different rules for gifts that arrive by post."

"Is that right?" He sounded thoroughly captivated.

"Certainly. You must open those the moment they come."

Tate laughed in a way that Cassandra had not heard for a while. Watching him, she smiled in pleasure, thinking that spending time with him was a lovely start to the day.

"Has anything else come that you had to open immediately?"

"No, but I think Charlotte will send something. She never forgets."

"And your other siblings will have gifts for you tonight?"

"Yes. Henry will have something little and nice, but I think Lizzy might be planning something a bit larger."

"Why do you say that?"

"She's acting a bit odd. She keeps smiling at me."

"She doesn't usually smile at you?"

"Not like this. You'd have to see to know what I mean."

"Ah, yes."

"Statements about your sight don't offend you, do they, Mr Tate?"

"Not usually."

"They fall from my tongue so easily and thoughtlessly."

"I never find you thoughtless."

"I think you are being kind."

"And I think you are overly harsh with yourself."

When Cassandra didn't answer, Tate opted for another rescue. "Are you ready to read?"

"Yes."

The personal conversation was put aside. Cassandra read for almost an hour, and other than wishing her another birthday greeting as she exited, Tate's time with her did not stray to the personal.

"Why must we go to town?" Cassandra asked again, but Lizzy, from her side of the carriage, didn't reply. Lunch had barely been over when Lizzy ordered the coach, and her sister as well.

"You're being very mysterious, Elizabeth."

"It's just something I wish to give myself," she said at last.

"On my birthday?"

Lizzy laughed, completely unrepentant. "Yes. Now sit back and enjoy the day. We'll be there very soon."

Cassandra knew she would get nothing else from her. She was enjoying the day, but a trip into Collingbourne did not figure into her plans.

"Here we are," Lizzy said gaily, the coach coming to a stop in town.

"Where exactly?"

"You shall see soon enough."

Lizzy led them to a small shop, opened the door, and entered. The moment they were inside, a man stood to his feet and came toward them.

"Are you Mr Clay?" Lizzy inquired.

"I am."

Lizzy bowed her head to his bowing acknowledgment.

"I am Elizabeth Steele, and this is my sister. I would like a miniature done of her today."

"Certainly, ma'am. If Miss Steele will just have a seat."

"Lizzy!" Cassandra hissed at her, but the older woman only turned with huge, innocent eyes.

"Sit down, Cassie. You heard the man."

Cassandra had all she could do not to laugh at her sister's triumphant face. Instead she took a quick peek in the mirror that hung on the wall, adjusted two curls at her cheeks, and took the seat offered.

Mr Clay smiled kindly at her and began. Several times Cassandra looked toward Lizzy, but she had moved to look at the frames displayed at the rear of the shop.

In a remarkably short time, the tiny portrait was completed, framed, and paid for. Lizzy led the way to the carriage, only just holding her laughter.

"You dreadful creature!" Cassandra accused, laughter filling every word. "That was terribly embarrassing!"

"I wasn't embarrassed."

Cassandra's mouth opened with surprise over her sister's impertinence.

"I'll take you to a lovely tea at Gray's to make up for it," Lizzy offered, still looking too pleased by half.

"I shouldn't let you. I should be terribly angry."

Lizzy held out the miniature, her face and voice all at once serious.

"It's lovely, Cassie, just as I knew it would be. And we'll always remember that we got it on your birthday."

Cassandra gave in.

"I'll forgive you over tea."

Lizzy's smile went right back in place. She was glad to have the picture — she would treasure it always — but getting Cassandra out of the house for a time would allow Mrs Jasper and Cook to do a few extra things for the party, a party that would allow Lizzy to finally meet Cassandra's Mr Tate.

Newcomb Park

"Lizzy, are you in here?" Cassandra called to her as she opened the bedroom door. She found the room empty. She stood for a moment, trying to think where she hadn't checked. All set for dinner and getting hungry, she was most determined to find her sister.

"Henry," she tried his office. "Have you seen Lizzy?"

"No. Is dinner ready?"

"I think soon."

Lizzy chose that moment to appear.

"We're set for five, Lizzy," Cassandra stopped her, her voice suspicious. "Who did you invite?"

"You'll have to wait and see."

Cassandra had never seen her sister like this. First the trip into town and now two mystery guests.

"Is Anne Weston out of bed?" Cassandra began to guess. "You didn't tell me."

"As a matter of fact, Anne will be up at the end of the month, but they are not coming to dinner."

"Are Charlotte and Barrington coming into town this evening?"

"I wish they were, but no, they are still in the north of England."

Cassandra frowned at her older sister.

"I don't like surprises, Lizzy."

"Don't you?" Lizzy asked with maddening calm.

Cassandra could only stare at her. Lizzy smiled and moved on her way. Cassandra followed, not even aware that Henry was bringing up the rear. She followed her sister directly to the front door, where Jasper was just opening it for their guests.

Harriet Thorpe walked in, Mr Tate holding her arm as she led.

"Mrs Thorpe," Cassandra began in amazement. "Mr Tate."

"Hello, Cassandra." Tate's deep voice sent shivers up her arms and neck.

"Are you all right?" she asked, her voice betraying her uncertainty.

"I am very well, thank you. I am planning on a very restful evening."

"You're certain?"

"Yes."

"You knew it was my birthday all along."

"I confess I did. Your sister invited us over the weekend."

"You even knew what she was planning when I spoke of it this morning," Cassandra accused, all the pieces falling together in her mind.

"Guilty again."

Not until that moment did Cassandra realize that she and Mr Tate had gone to where they always went — a world of their own.

"Please forgive me," Cassandra began when she saw her sister's bemused but smiling face. "Mr Tate, allow me to

197

present you to my brother, Mr Henry Steele, and my sister, Miss Elizabeth Steele."

"It's a pleasure," Tate said, bowing formally.

"The pleasure is all ours," Lizzy offered.

"Please come and make yourself comfortable," Henry invited, liking this tall gentleman very much.

Conversation started the moment the five were at the table. Over beef Wellington they discussed the church family, news from town, Tate's travels in Europe, and Edward's trip to Africa. The time raced by, but Cassandra's siblings were able to observe her with the man she visited each day.

Cassandra was seated closer to Tate than his aunt, so it was the younger woman who, from time to time, directed their guest to things on his plate, or to his utensils or drink. Both Henry and Lizzy caught the ease of this action, as well as Mrs Thorpe's apparent familiarity with the situation.

"Did I just knock my glass over?" he asked Cassandra at one point.

"No, it's standing upright, but some dripped on the side. To your right," Cassandra said quietly, letting Tate know that someone was coming to change his glass. Cassandra waited until he found the new goblet with his hand before going back to her own meal.

"That was marvelous," Harriet said sincerely, the meal coming to an end.

"Thank you, Mrs Thorpe. I think we'll have dessert after Cassandra opens a few gifts."

Harriet smiled at Cassandra's look of excitement. "I love it, Cassandra, that you still enjoy presents."

"I probably should grow up someday, but not today."

Tate's deep chuckle sounded beside her, and Cassandra turned for a moment to look at him. Having him in her home was something she never imagined. All she wanted to do was sit close beside him and watch his every move.

"May I take your arm, Cassandra?" Tate asked when they'd come to their feet.

"Certainly."

With little ceremony, the five moved to the largest sitting room, getting comfortable in the deep chairs, all with a good view of Cassandra and her gifts.

Lizzy gave her a lovely silk shawl, Tate and Harriet had found a book of French poetry, and Henry gave her her own book of maps. Cassandra was delighted with each and every one, but nothing could compare to having Mr Tate at her birthday party. She knew it was a night she would never forget.

"Come in," Cassandra called when there was a knock on her door much later that evening. She should have been ready for bed, but instead she had only taken down her hair and sat before the mirror to study her reflection. She turned to see Lizzy put her head in.

"Too tired to talk?"

"No."

Lizzy went over to the bed. Cassandra was at her dressing table, so Lizzy sat on the end nearest her.

"Thank you for a wonderful day and evening, Lizzy. I shall not forget it for a very long time."

"I'm glad."

Cassandra worked on her hair, able to see her sister in the reflection of the glass.

"What's wrong, Cassie?" Lizzy asked.

Surprised by the question, she turned to look at her sister.

"I don't know that anything is wrong."

"Well, I do. I can read it in your eyes. I saw a change come over you at the end, when Mr Tate and his aunt were leaving."

Cassandra turned back to her mirror. She pulled the brush through her hair a few more times and then set it aside.

"I'm starting to feel things for Mr Tate," she confessed.

"Why is that a problem?"

Cassandra hesitated before saying, "He thinks I'm one of the beautiful Steele sisters."

"You are one of the beautiful Steele sisters."

Cassandra's look was telling.

"You know what I'm speaking of, Lizzy."

"I know how foolish people can be."

Cassandra sighed and turned back to the mirror.

"I'm fine with my red hair, Lizzy; you know I am. My freckles are rather tiresome, but I don't yearn to look like you or Charlotte. He can't see me, Lizzy. I can't have him falling for someone he imagines and then finding me."

Lizzy felt her breath catch in her throat. That someone would not find her sister lovely was so painful to her that she could hardly breathe. Cassandra Steele was beautiful, not just because she was her sister, and not just because her face was utterly lovely — freckles and all — but because her heart was humble and sweet, and her love for Christ was real and deep.

"So you think he might have feelings for you?"

"At times I gain that impression."

"And you do not think he's asked his aunt how you appear?"

"He probably has, but imagining and seeing are not the same." Cassandra met Lizzy's eyes. "I can't stand the idea of seeing disappointment in his gaze. I think it would pull my heart from my chest."

"All right." Lizzy had to get practical or cry. "Let's just imagine that you are quite homely, nothing to look at at all. You don't think him man enough to love your heart, to find you beautiful no matter what your actual appearance?"

"Point well taken, Lizzy, but no less easier to live with. I would ask myself for years if he was disappointed. That's no way to live."

"And it doesn't help that I think you're beautiful?"

"You can see me, Lizzy. There are no surprises for you. In truth, he may find my looks very appealing, but it's that first moment I dread, that first look when I see recognition in his eyes."

"And will you find me utterly cruel if I

suggest that he may never see you, that all of this won't matter in the least?"

"I've thought of that, Lizzy. I've even been so selfish as to think how easy that would be, but something in my heart tells me he will see again, and when that day happens, I will want to do nothing but hide."

Lizzy could see that no number of words were going to bring comfort. She hugged and kissed her sister goodnight, exiting to her own room and telling the Lord that she was going to have to leave this with Him.

I want to fix it. I want to erase the pain in her eyes, but I can't do that. Only You can give her lasting peace, Father. Help me to trust You to that end.

Chapter Eleven

Pembroke

"Do you think she enjoyed her gift?" Tate asked Harriet the moment they met at the breakfast table Saturday morning.

"Without a doubt, dear."

"It sounded as if she did."

"Your ears did not lie. She was delighted."

"And our being there? Was she as pleased as she sounded?"

"Very much so. Did you doubt?"

"No, I just wish I could have experienced it with my eyes, so I'm trying to imagine all I can."

"What did you think of her family?"

"They were very kind. I can tell they love each other very much."

"I think Henry enjoyed you. He's not overly talkative, but he made some efforts on your account."

"Yes, he did. Cassandra has told me that he's close to James Walker. I don't believe I've met him."

Food was served in the midst of their conversation. Harriet fixed Tate's tea the way he liked it and waited for him to pray.

"Did you tell Cassandra about the doctor's visit?" she asked after they began to eat.

"Yes."

Tate's voice had gone rather soft, so Harriet did not press him. That her nephew was falling for Cassandra Steele was only too clear. That his vision was on his mind, and how that might impact his future with her, was clear also.

Much as Harriet wanted to make suggestions about managing a romance, she knew Tate would have to handle this on his own. Just before Tate continued with his questions for her, she had a moment to wonder if he'd ever asked Cassandra whether she could love a man who was nearly blind.

"What did you think of Mr Tate?" Cassandra asked Henry the moment they were on horseback the following morning.

"He seems a fine man."

"So you approve of my knowing him?"

Henry turned to look at her and found her eyes anxious for his approval.

"Yes, Cassie, I do. I would wish you not to rush into anything should a proposal present itself, but from what I know of Mr Tate, I approve of your friendship."

"Thank you."

"Will you be going to read today?"

"No. I'm taking a day off."

Henry didn't question her but nodded, his eyes speaking agreement.

Nothing else was said on the subject, or any subject, for that matter. On this particular morning ride, words were unnecessary.

Blackburn Manor

"I must show you something, Mr Walker," Cassandra announced as soon as they arrived at the house Sunday after church. "Henry has given me a gift."

Cassandra presented the miniature atlas she received on Friday night, and her host's response was all she could have hoped for.

"This is marvelous. A perfect copy. Where did Henry find it?"

"I don't know, but he said I needed one of my own."

"And he's right. Show me your favorite page."

Cassandra turned to Africa.

"Now I wonder why Africa is so interesting to you," he teased.

Cassandra dimpled at him but didn't speak.

"How is Edward?" Mrs Walker asked, ushering them all into the dining room.

"He seems to be doing very well." Henry fielded this question, always so at ease in Walker's presence. "In his last letter to me, he didn't think he'd be away too many more months."

"It's been so long already," Lizzy added.

"And Charlotte? What do you hear from the new Mrs Barrington?"

"I think we'll see them soon. Her last letter said she was ready to settle in at home, and I know they planned to stop for a brief stay before going on to Bath."

"It's a different world when children grow old enough to go out on their own," Mrs Walker told them with a note of wistfulness. "This house rang with noise and laughter for just a few years. Now, unless the grandchildren are visiting, it's as quiet as a tomb."

"Speaking of which," Walker put in, "the grandchildren will be visiting in about a fortnight."

"How fun," the Steele women chimed. "Is everyone coming?"

Mrs Walker told of the family's plans as everyone enjoyed the meal. After that, conversation was never at a loss, and even when the meal ended and they moved to the parlor, the five adults continued to visit.

"I'm going to put Henry on the spot," Walker said once they'd settled in with cake and coffee.

"Oh, my," Henry said, only half joking.

"Forgive me, Henry, but I would like all of us to hear how you came to Christ. Are you willing?"

"If you'd like, Walker," Henry said after clearing his throat. "Certainly, I will."

The women in the room beamed at him with pleasure, causing him to laugh a little and feel even more shy.

"Where to begin?" he started awkwardly, but then remembered to just speak his thoughts. "I was young, but I recall it was at Newcomb Park. Father had been scolding Charlotte and me. I can't remember the incident exactly, but he said that we needed to do a better job of loving and caring for each other. If I recall, we had been doing a good deal of quarreling.

"Anyway, I remember that he suddenly stopped, as though thinking of something. He asked us how true change occurs. I couldn't answer, and Charlotte was quiet as well. He went on to explain that true change happens only on the inside." Henry laughed a little in amazement. "I didn't know what he was speaking of, and for the first time he told us how he'd come to love Christ and accept His forgiveness of his sins. That led to a discussion on sin, and Charlotte and I had to admit that we sinned daily.

"I remember how simple he made it. He used himself as an example. He asked what we would think if a runaway carriage was about to kill us and he jumped in front of us, dying to save our lives. We both cried at the very thought, but he went on to say that God's Son had done that very thing on the cross. I recall that what really struck me was how he said Christ's sacrifice would be trampled if we didn't accept the new life we'd been offered."

Henry paused as the enormousness of it came back to him. "I wanted that life he spoke of. Charlotte did too. Father shared verses from the New Testament about our humble hearts becoming Christ's dwelling place. I wanted Him to come to me and never leave, so I confessed my sins and asked Him to save me.

"And I know it was real, for I didn't want to bicker with Charlotte as much. At times my siblings made me feel cross, but something happened in my heart that day. I was changed from that time forward. I can only attribute it to Christ's love."

Henry had not been looking at anyone in particular, but he now noticed that his sisters and Mrs Walker all had tears in their eyes. It was too much for him. With a quiet word to excuse himself, he went to get some air.

"Did our tears drive him away, Walker?" his wife asked, reaching for her handkerchief.

"They may have, dear, but it's all right. I'll go and see him in a bit."

"Thank you," Lizzy managed.

Cassandra could only nod in agreement, not able to speak for some time.

Pembroke

"Another perfect day," Cassandra said the moment she stepped onto the veranda and found Mr Tate waiting for her.

"I think you must be right. The sun feels very good."

"Do your eye patches allow any light through at all?"

"No, and even if they did, I'm to keep my lids shut at all times."

"Do you wear the patches when sleeping?"

"Yes, even then. Should I sleep rather soundly, I might wake and forget to keep my eyes closed."

"I can see how that might happen."

"Your sister's voice is higher-pitched than yours."

"We've been told that before," Cassandra said with a smile. "Charlotte's is right in the middle."

"I had a good time at your party."

"As did I. I still can't believe the book you and Mrs Thorpe brought. It was lovely."

"What did your other sister end up sending you?"

Before Cassandra could respond, she heard piano music coming from the house. She listened for a moment.

"Is that your aunt playing the piano?"

"Yes."

"Why have I never heard her?"

"She hasn't wanted to disturb your reading."

Cassandra listened for a moment. The melody was beautiful, and the playing accomplished.

"Cassandra, do you play or sing?"

"I play a little, but I don't sing."

"Maybe we should go in so you can play."

"I fear you will prefer your aunt's hand at the keys. My skill is nothing to hers."

211

Tate wasn't certain he believed this but didn't comment. Instead, he suggested, "We could just sit and listen to her for a time."

"I would like that."

Cassandra realized as she settled back that they had never enjoyed music or quiet together. Each time she came, she had to speak almost nonstop. Finding this change so relaxing, she wondered that he had her come at all.

"That was a moving piece," Tate said when the music ended.

He was met with silence.

"Are you there, Cassandra?"

Still no answer.

Tate was almost certain she had not left. He moved to the edge of his chair and reached across to where he thought she might be sitting. He found the arm of her chair and then her hand.

"Cassandra," he said softly, now recognizing she was asleep. He almost called her name again, but stopped, his mind growing distracted with how soft her hand felt in his. He'd held her hand one other time and taken her arm the night of her party. Was her skin always this soft?

Suddenly realizing he was not allowed such liberties, he took his hand away, sat back in his seat, and waited. His aunt began another song some five minutes later, and he heard Cassandra stir.

Cassandra, not certain what had happened, sat up and worked to orient herself. She looked across at her companion. Had he known she was asleep? And why in the world did she suddenly feel so dull and tired?

She swallowed past a thick throat and wished she had a glass of water.

"Do you know the name of this piece?" Tate asked her.

"I think it's Mozart's Concerto in B-flat Major."

"Of course. I can't think how I could have forgotten."

Cassandra wondered if he'd tried to speak to her a moment ago.

"Mr Tate?"

"Yes."

"I think I'll leave a little early today."

"Are you unwell, Cassandra?"

"I don't think so — just a small headache starting."

"Let me ring for Hastings so he can see you to your carriage."

Cassandra allowed this small courtesy, glad for his assistance when her head began to throb in earnest. She barely remembered leaving Pembroke and recalled even less when she arrived home. By afternoon she was in bed, very ill indeed.

"Her skin is so warm," Lizzy told Henry quietly. She had just stepped out of her sister's room and met him in the hall.

"Jasper has sent for Dr Tilney. He'll be here soon."

Lizzy nodded. She had left Cassandra sleeping, and her breathing was normal, but Lizzy was still worried. That worry lifted a slight amount when the doctor came and checked on her, telling Cassandra's family to keep her comfortable and quiet.

"A fever like Cassandra's is not dangerous," the doctor explained. "It just makes her feel dreadful. As long as she can communicate and is lucid while she's awake, I don't think you have anything to worry about."

"So she should sleep as much as she likes?"

"As long as she's coherent when awake, I shouldn't worry."

"Thank you, Dr Tilney."

"I'll check again tomorrow."

The conversation had gone on outside Cassandra's bedroom door, neither participant aware that Cassandra was wrapped inside a cocoon of feverish dreams — almost all of them involving Mr Tate.

"So handsome," Cassandra told the empty room in an illogical mumble. "And kindly. The kindest boy I've ever met."

Lizzy caught part of this remark as she slipped back into the room, but Cassandra did not answer when Lizzy questioned her. More words came forth, some including Tate's name, but Cassandra didn't awaken or speak clearly to her sister for almost an hour.

"Are you there, Cassie?"

"Yes," she answered with her eyes closed. It was too much effort to lift her lids. "I know I must be ill, Lizzy. You sound just like Charlotte."

"It is Charlotte, dear. I've come to see you."

"Oh, Charlotte," Cassandra cried weakly, forcing her eyes open. "You mustn't be here when I'm ill. I so want to enjoy your visit."

"Don't worry, dear. We'll be here after you're back on your feet."

"How is Barrington?" Cassandra asked, barely able to manage the words.

"He's very well," Charlotte said, but she

could see that Cassandra was sleeping again. Tall like Lizzy but blonde with light blue eyes, the oldest Steele sister sat for only a few moments before leaving Kitty on hand to see to Cassandra and heading to find Lizzy.

"Who is Tate?" she wasted no time in asking.

Lizzy smiled. "Did she actually speak of him to you?"

"She mumbled his name just before she woke."

Lizzy smiled.

"Is my baby sister in love?" Charlotte demanded.

"I would say yes."

"When did this happen?" Charlotte's voice was a bit too incredulous.

"Charlotte." Lizzy's voice was calm but direct, and her eyes were a bit stern. "You've been gone for ages."

Charlotte worried her lip. "Everywhere we visited, they pressed us to stay on forever, Lizzy. It was much more difficult for us than it sounds."

"I understand, Charlotte; honestly, I do. And we're all very glad for your long honeymoon, but I've come to see Cassie in a new light. I try not to treat her like a younger sister anymore, and I felt myself coming to her defense when you did."

Charlotte took a minute to comprehend this. Not until that very moment in time did she realize she'd come back expecting all would be as it had ever been. She told herself what a foolish notion that had been and asked, "Do you know this man?"

"Yes, we've met him. We are acquainted with his aunt as well. Harriet Thorpe, his widowed aunt, and Mr Tate came to Cassie's birthday dinner. Did Cassie not write to you that she's daily reading to a man?"

"Yes, she did — a blind man."

Lizzy only stared at her.

"Oh, her *Mr Tate* is blind?" Charlotte said, finally connecting the details.

"At the moment. He fell from his horse some months ago. He's in Collingbourne to recuperate."

"And our Cassie loves him?"

"It looks that way."

"And what are his thoughts of her?"

"It appears as though he cares for her as well."

Barrington and Henry chose that moment to return from their ride. Barrington went immediately to his wife. Henry asked about Cassandra.

"She's sleeping," Charlotte filled in, still

amazed at the change in him.

"I'm going up," Henry said, and exited without waiting for further word.

Charlotte, having come in rather late the night before, now held her sister captive. She wanted any and all news, from Edward in Africa to the change she saw in Henry. With occasional checks on Cassandra, Lizzy brought Charlotte up to date on family and town news over the next several hours. Both women ended up completely drained, and when Lizzy finished, Charlotte determined never to be so out of touch again.

"That was wonderful," Cassandra said weakly, returning the teacup to Barrington. She had managed to drink half of it. "How did you get elected to sit with me?"

"I volunteered."

Cassandra smiled at him. She had liked Barrington from the first moment they'd met. It was an added bonus to know he was very much in love with her sister.

"Tell me the most wonderful thing you did on your trip."

"Besides falling a little more in love with your sister?"

Cassandra smiled. "If I could find a husband half as dear as you, Barrington, I think I would marry on the spot."

"I understand you have someone in your sights right now."

Cassandra smiled, her head back against the pillow.

"There is someone I care for, Barrington, but he can't see me, and I worry about that."

"I can see how you would," he teased. "You've always been so pitied for your horrible looks and disagreeable personality. I don't know how your family stands it."

"Stop, Barrington." Cassandra laughed a little. "You'll have me giggling, and that always makes me weak."

Barrington leaned close and kissed her brow.

"We choose to worry about such foolish things, don't we, Cassie?"

Cassandra looked into his warm, brown eyes and saw caring and wisdom.

"That we do, Barrington," she was forced to agree, even as she felt herself worry a bit more. "That we certainly do."

Pembroke

Tate didn't know a week could be so long. He woke Saturday, as he had all week, his mind immediately going to Cassandra. Was she better? Would she come today? Did she miss him a fraction of the way he missed her?

Lord, I'm not resting, he prayed. He'd been confessing this to God all week and working through his emotions. *Help me not to waste all day thinking about her in an anxious way when I know You are a God who can be trusted. You will take care of her. You will have Your way and be glorified.*

It occurred to Tate, not for the first time, that Cassandra caused him far more anxiety than regaining his eyesight. It would do no good to cut her from his life and go back to his attempt to rest. She was firmly embedded in his heart, and it looked as if she was there to stay.

There was one consolation this morning: Tomorrow was Sunday. If she was feeling better, she would be in church. And then his aunt could see her and bring home a report.

Newcomb Park

"We are missing only Edward," Lizzy told the family just after the prayer. They were gathered around the dining table for lunch after church.

They all smiled at her, agreeing as the

dishes were served and the meal began. Cassandra was a little pale and on the thin side, but she had gone to church and was swiftly regaining her strength.

"Is the house being readied for you in Bath?" Cassandra asked of the Barringtons. "Or will there be work all around you after your arrival?"

"It's supposed to be ready," Barrington answered. "Mother wrote that she was seeing to it herself, so we'll trust it will be prepared in time."

"And will you be home for a while or do you have other plans?" Henry asked. Not overly fond of travel, he couldn't imagine being away from home so long.

"I don't think I shall move from Fairfax Hall for months," Charlotte said. "What do you think, Barrington?"

"I quite agree with you, love. I hope you'll all be willing to visit us, as we are most eager to stay put for a time."

"We shall plan on that," Lizzy volunteered, thinking a trip back to Bath might be fun.

"Who is at Dunham right now, Henry?" Cassandra wished to know, asking about the Steele home in Bath.

"The Harold Browne family of London." Barrington knew the family a little, so he was questioned by the others. It felt a bit odd to have someone living in the home they'd been in for so many years, but no one planned to live there for some time, and leaving it open seemed such a waste.

Cassandra enjoyed the meal immensely but was ready for a nap as soon as it ended. She smiled even as she climbed wearily into bed. Charlotte was home, and she was finally well enough to enjoy her.

Her final thoughts, however, as sleep rushed in to claim her, were of a certain man, a man whom she felt like she hadn't seen all month.

Pembroke

"Was Cassandra at church?"

"Yes," Harriet answered with a smile. Tate was occupying a chair in the foyer, barely allowing his aunt in the front door before he assaulted her with his questions.

"She seemed well?" Tate pressed her, not able to keep some of the tension from his voice.

"She is pale, Tate, but I don't think her sisters would have allowed her out had she not been fit enough."

Tate sat back, not aware of how far forward he'd moved in his chair.

"Did you say sisters?"

"Yes."

"So Barringtons are here?"

"They are," Harriet answered, watching Tate's brow crease.

"Why do you look worried?"

"I'm being selfish."

"How so?"

"If Charlotte and her husband are here, Cassandra probably won't come for a time."

Harriet watched Tate sit very still. She couldn't contradict his thoughts because he was probably right. Little did she know he was praying.

Help me, Lord, to wait on You, but then also help me to find the words. Whenever she comes again, I've got to bolster my courage to ask her some questions. Please bring her back. Please give me a chance to see where I stand.

Chapter Twelve

Thomas Morland stood on the deck of the *Jefferson James*, his eyes wishing for a view of England's shore. The journey away had been exciting, full of adventure, and with no pressure of time. This journey — the return trip — had taken days longer than he figured, his heart and mind eager to be elsewhere.

Making himself turn away from the endless miles of sea, Morland moved toward a chair, seated himself, and reached for the small Bible in his pocket. He turned to the pages he'd been studying in Revelation.

I've always yearned for Your return, Lord, but for the first time I want You to delay. It seems silly to think of anything on earth comparing with heaven, but in truth, I want to see Lizzy so desperately that I hope You tarry.

Morland forced his mind from home and thoughts of Elizabeth Steele. He shifted to get more comfortable and read in chapter 7 for the next hour.

"Are you certain you are up to this?" Henry stopped Cassandra at the carriage to ask.

"Yes, Henry," Cassandra answered him. "Thank you for checking with me."

Henry looked hesitant, so Cassandra waited.

"What is it, Henry? Have you changed your mind about my reading to Mr Tate?"

Henry shook his head no, even as he looked into her still-pale features. What was it like at Pembroke? Was anyone close by to keep track of how she was doing? Could Tate do that with no vision right now? What if she were to become ill again?

"Henry?" Cassandra tried again.

"I just want you to be well, Cassie. That is all."

"I shall be careful, and truly, Henry, I feel much better."

Henry nodded, his eyes still showing concern. He knew he couldn't worry about this, but the closer he became to his family, the harder it was.

As Cassandra went on her way, Henry made a mental note to discuss that fact with James Walker on Wednesday.

Brown Manor

"Well, now," Weston said, smiling at his wife's triumph. "Look at you."

"Don't come any closer," she warned playfully, still standing near the bed.

"Now why is that?"

"Well, from over here, I can still convince myself that I might have grown taller."

Weston laughed as he joined her, his arms going around her in the standing position for the first time in many months.

"This is nice."

"I think so too."

The two shared a kiss before someone knocked. Weston answered the door.

"Mrs Hurst is here to see Mrs Weston."

"Thank you, Mansfield," Weston said, just holding a smile. "Tell Mrs Hurst that Mrs Weston will be down directly."

Weston turned to smile at his wife the minute Mansfield went on his way. Anne grinned back like a mischievous schoolgirl. After making sure Anne was steady on her feet, Weston held his hand out, and Anne claimed it as they started toward the stairs.

Pembroke

Harriet had a great hug for Cassandra the moment she set foot in the house. Cassandra gladly hugged her in return.

"How are you?" the older woman wished to know, now holding her at arm's length so she could inspect her closely.

"Much better, thank you."

"We're so pleased to have you back. Tate missed you."

"I missed both of you," she said. "Shall I go ahead to the library, or is he not expecting me?"

"He's waiting for you."

Harriet didn't add that he'd waited every day. Harriet had waited every day as well. Her emotions almost overflowed as she watched Cassandra move across the foyer.

Cassandra was completely unaware of the other woman's gaze. Pleased to be back, she made a beeline for the library and gave her usual greeting.

"Hello, Mr Tate."

"Cassandra!" Tate exclaimed with pleasure. "I missed you," he added, not wasting time at all. "Come, sit near. Are you certain you're all right?"

"Yes. It was a rather nasty illness, but I am well over it."

227

"I'm glad you are well, for your sake as well as my own," he added wryly.

"How is that?"

"I found the days grew long."

"Did they?"

"Yes." Tate's voice was serious, and Cassandra found herself watching him closely. "My aunt," he continued, "said the Barringtons are here."

"Yes." Cassandra's voice held a smile. "It's been wonderful."

"I hope you didn't feel as though you had to come, Cassandra."

"No, Mr Tate, indeed not," Cassandra said, but she felt tentative. If the days had grown long for him, why did he sound uncertain about having her back?

"Are you positive you wish me to be back, Mr Tate?" Cassandra asked the question in her mind.

"Yes. As a matter of fact, I had large amounts of time to think about things."

When he didn't say what, Cassandra asked, "Anything in particular?"

"Yes, things I wished I'd asked you before you grew ill."

"Oh." This word came out just before Cassandra felt her breath catch. His voice was serious again, and continued to be so.

"Things that I believe I now have the

courage to voice, if you'll allow me."

"These questions," Cassandra began swiftly, afraid he would go on. "You said they have been on your mind?"

"Yes, for some time."

"Have they caused you distress?"

"At times."

Cassandra licked her lips. Was she ready to hear what he had to say? Even as she asked this of herself, she hated the thought of his being in distress for any reason.

"You may ask me whatever you wish, Mr Tate."

"Very well."

"But I must warn you, if I've not given the idea much thought, I will have to return with my answer at another time."

"I believe that to be very fair."

Cassandra waited, her body tense, her eyes on the man across from her.

"You're going to think me foolish, but I actually want to ask you if your skin is soft all the time."

Cassandra laughed a little with relief, even as her cheeks grew pink.

"I don't know. I guess it is."

"And are you always so kind and easy to be with?"

"I'm not perfect, Mr Tate — you must realize that — but I do hope I'm kind."

Tate too licked suddenly dry lips and plunged in, speaking faster than normal.

"Is there any chance, Cassandra, that you could care for a man whose vision was not perfect?"

"Well," Cassandra said thoughtfully, "I don't think a person's looks or situation in life is all that important. Does that answer your question?"

"Somewhat," Tate hesitated, asking himself how far he should push this. He decided not to live in this particular darkness any longer. "Have you ever considered marriage to someone who wasn't as complete in frame as yourself?"

"I don't very often picture myself married, so I'm not certain I can tell you that," Cassandra answered quite honestly, so certain was she that he would never want her.

"If you did picture yourself married, what type of marriage would make you happy?"

"One that was centered on my belief in Christ." Cassandra knew that answer right away. "One that was of love, I think."

"Are there other things of import to you?"

"I don't know. Let me think."

Cassandra's mind raced around a bit, and she even came to her feet and began to pace.

"Are you leaving?"

"No, just trying to think."

"Have I upset you?"

"No, it's a very good question, one that I probably should have considered before now. My parents," she went on, her mind getting settled, "valued one another, yet my father had the final word on things. I can't lead you to believe that my mother was always pleased about it — sometimes they disagreed — but if my father was firmly against something, it would not occur."

"Was he firm about many things?"

"No. That was one of the sweetest things about him. He was only firm when he needed to be. He didn't get into a muddle over things of little consequence, but big things — things involving people and relationships in our family or the church family — were important to him."

Tate listened to her walk around. He would have smiled at the picture it presented in his mind, but he was afraid she would think him laughing at her.

"Respect!" Cassandra said suddenly, turning to Tate. "That's the word I was looking for. My parents had great respect for one another. Even if they became upset about something, they tried to remain calm and talk it out as best they could."

"Belief, love, and respect. Those are very important indeed."

"And honesty," Cassandra added. "I think it's not always easy to be yourself with someone, and that's a form of lying, but as much as we're able, we need to be honest."

"I think you must be very honest," Tate said to Cassandra, believing it with all his heart.

"I hope I am," Cassandra said, even as she worried about her looks, wishing he could see her right now. If his rejection of her was complete, she could move away, maybe to Bath, until she was over him or he moved back to London.

Was it lying not to tell him what she looked like? Cassandra pushed the thought away. With no answer, it only made her miserable. Instead, she asked, "Would you like me to read to you now?"

Tate could hear the need for rescue in her voice. Thinking that in all fairness, he'd found out even more than he asked, he was swift to agree. Still not certain if her own heart was becoming involved with him, he knew that subject might need to wait for another day.

So pleased and thankful just to have her

near again, Tate settled back and listened to the sound of her voice, not letting himself worry about the future.

Newcomb Park

"You're back, Cassie," Charlotte said when she spotted her just before lunch. "How is Mr Tate today?"

"He's doing well."

"Are you reading a book to him?"

"No, just the newspaper."

That Charlotte wanted to ask more was only too clear. Cassandra stood still, waiting for her to continue but not helping out in the least. She even let a small smile peek through, telling Charlotte she was on to her.

Lizzy's right! She has grown up. Why did I never see it before?

"Do you mind if I ask you about Mr Tate, Cassie?" Charlotte tried speaking to Cassandra as she would Lizzy. "Or do you find me intrusive?"

"I don't mind at all, Charlotte."

The women moved to chairs in the small downstairs parlor. They grew comfortable and watched each other, Cassandra waiting again for Charlotte to lead.

"When you read to him, is it uncomfortable with him not being able to see you?"

"Not since the first days. He's very at ease with his present situation, and that makes it easy for everyone else."

"Is there a chance he'll see again?"

"Yes. There's already been some improvement to his sight. He's waiting, allowing his body to continue to heal."

"And he does that patiently — waiting, I mean?"

Cassandra smiled. "I rather admire his trust, Charlotte. He's chosen to wait on God for this. It's wonderful to watch him rest in God's hand."

"Lizzy has led me to believe that you might admire him for more than just that."

Cassandra smiled again. "I will confess to you that I find him very special."

"Do you love him?"

"I think I could love him very easily."

Charlotte saw a bit of herself right now, Lizzy as well.

"You're holding back, Cassie. Can you tell me why?"

"The obvious reason: He can't see me."

It was on Charlotte's tongue to chide her sister, tell her that it didn't matter, but in a flash she asked herself what it would be like if Barrington had never seen her. After a thoughtful moment, she told Cassandra what was on her heart.

"I've only just realized that I've taken for granted that Barrington and I can see each other. I'm sure I'll be guilty of that again. But something else has also just occurred to me: Even though I think Barrington the most handsome man in England and he tells me daily that I'm beautiful, I can tell you that if we didn't treat each other with kindness, if we didn't love and care for each other, not all the physical beauty in the world would make up for that."

Cassandra knew her sister spoke the truth. It made perfect sense. She thanked Charlotte, hugged her, and began to pray. She asked God to settle her heart on this issue and to help her to listen.

I am too often guilty of asking for Your help and then not taking it. Please help me, Lord. I don't know if I can let Tate get close enough to love me, if ever he would. I think I might love him already, but I'm terrified.

Jasper announced at that moment that Pastor Hurst had come to visit. Cassandra was torn between frustration and relief. She knew it was time to talk this out with her heavenly Father but found it was a task she could easily put off.

Heading into the foyer to meet the pastor, Cassandra thought about the fact that her sisters thought her very grown-up of late.

If they knew how much I want to run and hide from Alexander Tate, they would realize that, at least in one sense, I'm still just a child.

Blackburn Manor

"I'm an emotional mess," Henry said with disgust on Wednesday morning. "The closer I get to my family, the more I want to worry and be overly protective. Lizzy headed into the garden last week, and I stood at the window and watched her as though she were going to be captured by a band of marauders."

Walker laughed, and Henry chuckled as well.

"We can laugh at this, Walker," Henry went on, his voice still good-natured, "but in truth, I don't know if I'm any better off than I was before."

"How so?"

"Well, at one time it was the sin of keeping myself away from all others; now it's the sin of worry." Henry sat back, his head shaking in self-derision.

"I won't tell you not to fight that sin, Henry, since God is in control and we have no cause for worry, but I'll still say this:

I'm very proud of you. You're a changed man. It's not every believer who hears of his sin and determines to do something about it. You could have fought me and told me to mind my own business. It felt as though I was asking the impossible of you, but you trusted God and began to change.

"Likewise, that will happen with this temptation to worry. We all have that tendency with our families. I came to Christ late in life, and two of my children have never believed. Their children don't believe — my own dear grandchildren. I ache with that knowledge, but I can't worry. I have to keep praying for them and leaving them in God's hands."

Henry suddenly felt very emotional, another facet added to his life as he learned to show love to others. How God would choose to give him a friend like James Walker he didn't know, but he was eternally grateful.

The men turned to a passage in Hebrews 13, one that reminded them that the God of peace, who raised His own Son from the dead, would help them to do the things that were pleasing in His sight.

After reading the passage over and discussing it, they spent a long time in prayer, Henry giving his family over to God and asking for his trust to be increased, and Walker, for his example before his lost children and grandchildren.

Pembroke

"You've been crying," Tate said after Cassandra had read all of two sentences.

"How did you know that?" she asked, feeling almost betrayed.

"I can hear it in your voice."

Cassandra said nothing for a moment. She thought his not being able to see her red eyes and puffy lids would disguise how she felt.

"Do you want to tell me about it?"

"You weren't supposed to notice," she told him, her voice wobbling again. "And if you're going to be so kind, I'll be in tears all over again."

Tate thought she sounded adorable and couldn't quite stop his smile. He didn't, however, manage to school his face before she noticed.

"You're laughing at me!"

"I'm not, truly, I'm not."

Cassandra sniffed, knowing it was rude but unable to locate her handkerchief. She looked up to see Tate holding his out to her.

"I told you not to be nice to me," she said, tears now coming in earnest.

"Cassandra, what is it?"

"Charlotte and Barrington have left. They've been away from home for a very long time, and they're most eager to get to Bath, but it feels as if they just arrived."

"Would it have helped to remain home?"

"I don't know. I don't think so. At least if we read something interesting I won't have to think about them."

"And I interrupted you."

"It's all right." Cassandra dried her tears, seeing that she'd made him feel bad. It made her want to cry all over again, but she held herself in check.

"Don't worry about my feelings," Tate guessed, frustrating his reader to madness.

"You must stop reading my mind!" Cassandra demanded, meaning it.

Tate laughed, not able to help himself.

"Trust me, Cassandra, there's plenty I can't read."

"What does that mean?" Her tears were now completely forgotten, the handkerchief balled in her hand.

"Only that you're not all that simple to figure out."

"What is it you wish to know?"

Tate mentally stopped in his tracks and

wisely said, "I think those questions might need to wait for another day."

Cassandra fell silent.

"I was rude just now," the redhead confessed. "I'm sorry."

"I didn't find you rude at all."

Again Cassandra was quiet.

"Do you feel like reading?"

"I would be happy to read to you, but not if you would rather I leave."

"Why would I want that?"

"Because I haven't been restful for you. I would never forgive myself if I lost sight of that and hindered your healing."

"That's very good of you, but I find that your presence alone is restful."

"Do you really, Mr Tate?" Cassandra asked in some amazement.

"Yes, and don't you think you know me well enough to drop the Mr from my name?"

"I don't know about that," Cassandra told him. She never thought of him as Mr Tate. She mentally called him Alexander, but she was careful never to say it.

"Well, you let me know when you do."

"All right. I'll finish this article now."

Tate agreed with just a nod, thinking it wise not to say another word. He thought that if he couldn't someday tell this woman that he loved her, he would slowly lose what was left of his mind.

Newcomb Park

Lizzy had no idea what she was doing in the garden, only that it had gotten to be something of a habit.

"When you can't help yourself, and Morland comes to mind," she whispered the horrible routine to herself, "go to the garden. Make yourself pick flowers in an effort to dispel him from your mind."

Lizzy shook her head at the foolishness of it all and determined not to cry. No easy task with Charlotte and Barrington's departure still so fresh in her mind.

With a complete lack of interest, Lizzy chose another bloom, an ugly one in her estimation, and added it to the basket. Not until she shooed a fly away did she look up to see him standing some 20 yards off. The moment they had eye contact, he came forward.

"Morland!" Lizzy said, her breath coming fast. "You're back."

"Hello, Lizzy."

"Hello." She worked to compose herself and think fast. "Is Edward with you?"

"No, he decided to stay on."

"Are you back because someone is ill? Is your aunt well?"

"She's very well. I was ready to come home."

Morland stopped himself from smiling over how flustered she was. Seeing her with more knowledge gave new meaning to everything she did. The calm face she presented to him covered feelings he'd never read in her eyes before. The way she clasped her hands was not a sign of a quiet heart but an effort to stop their shaking.

"Did you enjoy Africa?" she finally asked, nearly smiling in triumph that she came up with a question at all.

"It was marvelous. I'll look forward to telling you about it."

"Is Edward coming anytime soon?"

"In another month to six weeks, I imagine."

"Where did you leave him?"

"He's with the Middletons."

Lizzy nodded. Her brother had written about that. She glanced around, her mind searching for something witty or even intelligent to say.

"Have you seen Henry or Cassie?"

"No, I wished to see you first. Jasper told me you were out here."

Lizzy didn't know what to say to this,

and Morland stopped fighting the smile that wanted to break through.

"If memory serves me, Lizzy, you're not overly fond of picking flowers and arranging them." He paused, their eyes meeting and not looking away. "It causes a man to wonder what a woman might have on her mind."

Lizzy couldn't say a word. Indeed, she could barely breathe.

Morland stepped forward, picked a perfect rose on his way, and held it out to her.

"Add this to the basket. It's almost as lovely as you are."

Lizzy took it without a word and watched as Morland turned and walked toward the house. She waited, expecting to see his carriage exiting the drive, but that didn't happen.

"He's inside!" It occurred to her very suddenly, causing her to almost dump her basket. Forcing herself to move slowly, to hold the basket still and not trip, Lizzy walked to the house, certain that her heart was going to beat through the wall of her chest.

He's back, she said to herself, wondering at this mixture of terror and excitement that filled her.

For an instant she wondered if her

brother might have spoken to him about her feelings but dismissed the idea almost immediately.

Edward wouldn't do that. I know he wouldn't. Don't read something into this, Lizzy, that's simply not there.

Knowing she wouldn't take a word of her own advice, she finished the walk toward the house, willing herself to be as normal as she could be if they again came face-to-face.

Chapter Thirteen

Henry listened with genuine interest as Morland described his trip with Edward, the sights they had seen and the people they'd met, but it didn't leave his mind for a moment that this man was back in England for a specific reason.

"Will you go back, do you think?" Henry asked after some time.

"Someday, I hope, but not anytime soon."

"Why is that?"

Morland smiled. In the past Henry always seemed to be distracted when they talked. Not today. Today he was taking in every word.

"I have some unfinished business here, Henry. It involves your sister. Not until that is settled will I plan to go anywhere or do anything."

"Does Lizzy know that?"

"No. I believed Edward when he told me of her feelings, but I guess I need to see it for myself, not to mention gain your approval."

"You have that, Morland. You always have."

"Thank you."

The men continued to discuss Africa, but now it was Morland's turn to be distracted. Now knowing that Henry approved of his suit, he wanted to do little but see Lizzy. While still traveling it seemed that all he needed to do was return and everything would fall into place. Now he realized that getting close to the lady herself might not prove that easy.

"Jasper just told me Morland is here!" Cassandra whispered furiously the moment she arrived back from Pembroke and found her sister in the library.

"He's in with Henry." Lizzy sounded much calmer than she felt.

"Did Edward come?"

"No, he's here alone."

Cassandra smiled a smug, complacent smile that caused Lizzy to shake her head.

"Stop that this instant."

"Stop what?"

"You know what I'm speaking of. He's come back to England for his own reasons; that's all there is to it."

"You may believe that all you want, Lizzy, but I'm going to remind you on the day you become Mrs Thomas Morland that I knew the real reason."

"Don't you have something to do right now?"

Cassandra took a seat.

"Not at all. I have all day to myself. In fact, I'm going to knock on Henry's door very soon and make sure that Morland knows he's invited to lunch."

"Don't you do that, Cassandra Steele!"

"Henry probably already has."

Lizzy couldn't take her sister's satisfied eyes. She positioned her book in front of her face to hide her anxiety. She lowered the book just a heartbeat later, knowing she needed more of a distraction.

"How did it go with Mr Tate today?"

Cassandra rolled her eyes.

"He could tell I'd been crying. I was so embarrassed. I think he reads my mind."

"Well, he's had to. I think you must give off many unseen signals that Mr Tate has learned to read."

Cassandra gawked at her. "When did you come up with this?"

"A long time ago. Picturing the two of you married has been an interesting pastime. If Tate doesn't regain his eyesight, I don't think you'll miss it in the least."

"Why do you say that?" Cassandra

asked, forgetting to be outraged that her sister had already figured them as a husband and wife.

"Because your relationship has never included that. He's always had to go beyond his sight to get to know you, and he'll go on doing that."

Cassandra had to think on this. Her sister had a very good point, but she didn't want to talk about Tate right now. She wanted to see Morland. Cassandra stood.

"Where are you going?"

"To see Morland."

"Sit down," Lizzy told her, but Cassandra only shook her head, looking like the older of the two.

"Dear Lizzy. You wanted him here, but now you're afraid to see him."

Not until the words were out of her mouth did Cassandra realize how closely they paralleled her own feelings for Tate. She left the library without another word and went to her brother's study.

Morland greeted her with a hug, and she learned in the first minute that she had been right. Henry had asked him to stay for lunch.

Henry and Cassandra exited the carriage ahead of Lizzy. For this reason, she had no idea that Morland had come forward to give her a hand. Not until her hand was in his did she realize who it was.

"Good morning, Lizzy," he greeted her quietly in the church courtyard.

"Good morning, Morland."

"Did you find any more flowers?" he asked, his eyes giving away a slight gleam of teasing.

Lizzy smiled a little.

"I believe Cassie chose a few more. I left it to her."

"Maybe the item that was on your mind is now settled?"

Lizzy looked into his eyes but couldn't answer. Her heart was too full of questions and a certain measure of panic.

Morland did not torment her. He walked beside the family as they went into church, greeting those who welcomed him back and then taking a seat next to Henry. Lizzy, very aware of how close he'd sat, forced her attention on the service. Her thoughts strayed on occasion, but for the most part she listened.

She would have been struck dumb to learn that Morland was in the very same state. Having Lizzy one person away from him in a church pew was not unusual. He'd sat with the Steele family on countless occasions, but this was not just any Lizzy. This was the woman he knew would be open to his attention. This was the woman whom he'd never allowed himself to imagine as his wife but now had the freedom to do so.

It was nothing short of God's intervention that he heard any part of the service.

Pembroke

"We were in Jonah again," Harriet told Tate over lunch. "I've certainly learned a lot from that small book."

"I enjoy the notes Pastor sends."

"He apologized to me several times about not getting those done this week, but he said several unexpected events popped up, making it impossible."

"No matter. Maybe you can tell me what you remember."

"I would love to," Harriet said with great enthusiasm, having taken in every word, but thinking on one point in particular. "I was especially struck by Pastor's explanation of verse 10 of chapter 3. That's the one that says God repented of the evil that He said He would do. I've struggled with that verse for years because it's so hard for me to picture God ever needing to repent, but Pastor said this word is used in every sense except the sense that God was doing something wrong.

"It still means a complete change of mind, a change in the way He would treat these people. God was delighted with the way the citizens of Nineveh turned from their evil ways and had a complete change of mind."

Harriet suddenly laughed. "And then, even when I was asking myself if it's possible for an almighty, all-knowing God to change His mind, Pastor cautioned us to remember that God does respond to us. He responds to our prayers. He said we should not detract from God's eternality in any way, but that Scripture is written in a way that helps us understand God and who He is.

"Terms like 'delight,' 'approve,' 'joy,' and 'grieved' are used all through the Old Testament. That's not because God is surprised by anything but because He does respond to us. Pastor said the word 're-pent' in that verse is better described as 'respond.' He explained the repentance of the people caused God to delight in them and respond by not destroying them."

Tate laughed with her. He'd had some of those very thoughts.

Harriet went on, sharing what came to mind and making the meal pass swiftly. In fact, she did such a fine job of keeping Tate's interest that that man actually forgot to ask about a certain woman, one who was usually on his mind.

Newcomb Park

"It was nice that Morland could join us for lunch," Henry remarked from his place on the drive. He and his sisters had walked out to see him off.

"Yes, it was."

"He seems to be around quite a bit," Henry commented, his eyes on Lizzy. Cassandra scooted into the house, leaving them alone.

"Well, it's only normal that he should be, Henry," Lizzy replied, using some logic. "He's been a friend of the family for years."

When Henry didn't reply, Lizzy looked up at him. His look was calm — she would expect nothing else — but she suddenly felt like a child caught in trouble.

"Why are you looking at me like that?"

"Why won't you look at Morland as we dine?"

Lizzy worried her lip. "You noticed that, did you?"

"Yes, Lizzy. Do you think the man returned to England to see how our garden was doing?"

A small laugh escaped Lizzy. It was so unlike Henry to be sarcastic. Nevertheless, he was still watching her, clearly waiting for some type of answer.

"What do you suggest I do?"

"Give the man some encouragement. As you've said, he's been a friend of the family for years. Unless you know something I don't, you have no cause to fear him."

"No, of course not."

Henry sighed, still not sure he was getting through.

"Have you forgotten so soon, Lizzy, how miserable Barrington was before he learned to read Charlotte?"

Understanding dawned for the mahogany-haired beauty. She nodded, thanked her brother, and turned to go inside. She now knew of what he spoke, but following through on his suggestion might be a harder task than understanding his reason for doing so.

She spent a good part of the afternoon picturing herself flirting with Morland or giving him special looks. Each time she visualized it, she blushed to the roots of her hair or burst out laughing.

"I did something on my own," Cassandra said the moment she arrived on the sun-filled veranda Monday morning.

"And what might that be?"

"I brought a book to read, but if you don't care for it," she added swiftly, "we can go on in the newspaper."

"I'd like to hear it," Tate said without hesitation. Hearing what Cassandra thought enjoyable was very interesting to him.

"Shall I begin?"

Tate just covered a smile. She had sounded so uncertain.

"Or we can visit for a time," Tate suggested.

"I'll read!"

This was said so quickly that Tate had to cover his mouth with his hand. She was panicked about something — there was no mistake about that — but he would probably have to bide his time to find out what.

Cassandra began to read *Rip van Winkle*. She was halfway through the first chapter when something occurred to her.

"Mr Tate?"

"Yes?"

"Have you read this book before?"

"Yes."

Cassandra sighed. "Why did you not tell me?"

"Because I would enjoy hearing it again."

She sighed again. "Why do I feel as though you have me come because you can't find it in your heart to tell me not to return?"

"That's a very good question, especially since I don't feel that way. One would be tempted to ask why *you* think I feel that way?"

"I don't know," Cassandra admitted, wishing she hadn't even asked if he'd read the book. "Suddenly I doubt everything I do."

Tate couldn't help but wonder if her doubts would disappear if only he would declare himself. But he couldn't do that without a better measure of her feelings, and to date, that hadn't happened.

"May I tell you something?" Tate asked, deciding to try for the next best thing.

"Of course."

"There is one thing you don't need to doubt. You need never doubt my enjoying your visits. I'm sorry I've done such a poor job of expressing how much I want you to come. On days when you don't, I find myself quite lonely."

"I miss you too," Cassandra admitted before she thought about it. Her face full of extra color, she asked, "Shall I go ahead and read?"

"Please."

Keeping strictly to business, Cassandra did just that. She'd read the story before and only half attended. Tate didn't listen at all, except to the sound of her husky voice, the way she pronounced words, and the proximity of her voice, telling him she was close by. He prayed for patience and for Cassandra as well. Somewhere in his heart he was certain he would be healed.

Help her, Father. Help her to be ready. If the time comes when I can see again, she'll need to be prepared, because nothing short of Your hand will hold me back.

Collingbourne

"Hello, Morland." Cassandra greeted him with a huge smile. They had happened down the same aisle at Benwick's. She hadn't been expecting it, but Cassandra was always glad to see him. Lizzy was behind her, and Cassandra was very impressed that Morland finished his greeting to her before shifting his gaze to her sister.

"Hello, Lizzy."

"Hello, Morland. How are you?"

"I'm very well. Would you and Cassandra be available to join me for tea? I'm going to Gray's."

For a moment, Lizzy was caught by his eyes. She had a full list to shop for yet, but right now all she could see was this man.

"What time?"

"In an hour. Does that work for you?"

"Yes."

Morland smiled at her, his eyes warm as he studied her. "I'll see you there."

Lizzy only nodded, her face having taken on a dreamy expression. She wasn't even aware of the way Morland had gone on his way. When she came back to earth, it was to find Cassandra staring at her.

"Are you all right?" Cassie asked softly.

"Yes. How long has it been? How much longer do I have to wait?"

"Only about 59 minutes."

Lizzy's hand went to her mouth to smother laughter. Cassandra's did the same. With unspoken agreement, they split up. If they stayed together they would only laugh and carry on, and that wouldn't do at all.

When Henry came looking for them close to 40 minutes later, they had calmed down

257

long enough to tell him of their plans for tea. Even he managed a smile at the older of his two sisters. Lizzy thought that by the time she left town, everyone would know of her feelings for Morland, but then she decided it was all right. As long as the man himself knew, nothing else mattered.

Pembroke

Tate woke early on the second day of June, earlier than usual. He could tell the day was already warm, but something more was happening. His head felt amazingly clear, his eyes utterly normal. He hadn't experienced headaches or throbbing for some time, but today was different. Today was better.

Dr Tilney was not scheduled to check his eyes for another month, but Tate needed him today. Something had happened in the night; he was certain of it. He didn't hurry to rouse Hastings or the household but lay quiet, praying.

I've been foolish and worried about a lot of things recently, Lord, and I'm sorry. Help me to keep leaving things in Your hand and not run ahead of You. And if I'm wrong, Father, and my sight is not there, please help me to keep trusting You.

Cassandra traveled home in a state of shock. Of all places to learn about Tate's returned eyesight, she never dreamed it would be at the manse. It wasn't that she wasn't pleased for him; she was. But how did word travel so swiftly that Pastor and Judith would hear ahead of her?

"And to think I was headed there to read," she said to the empty coach, so glad that she had learned in time and could tell the driver to take her home.

Newcomb Park

"Is there nothing I can say, Cassie?" Lizzy begged, tears in her eyes.

"Please don't cry, Lizzy. It's not forever. I just need to get away to think."

"Just wait for Henry to return. Just wait for that."

Cassandra looked at her sternly.

"You're hoping he'll talk me out of it, Elizabeth, or tell me I'm not to leave at all!" Cassandra stopped and tried to calm down, pushing Tate's ever-present face from her mind. "Send word to me as soon as he's gone to London. He'll return to his life, Lizzy, and I'll come home. Everything will be as it was."

Lizzy held on for dear life when they hugged, and Cassandra allowed her. The look on the younger girl's face was so crushed and hurt when she let go that Lizzy almost snatched her back.

Lizzy waited only until the coach was out of sight before returning to the house, her tears coming in a torrent. Her pain would have been double had she known that Cassandra was doing the same thing in the coach headed for Bath and Fairfax Hall.

Pembroke

Tate looked down at the note he'd just penned to Cassandra, amazed at how clearly he could see the words. He explained everything to her concerning the doctor's wishes and his own desire to do as much as he could.

Much as it pained him to do it, he sent the letter and did not deliver it himself. For all the time he'd waited, a few more days shouldn't seem like much, but Tate had a feeling they would be the longest two days of his life.

Newcomb Park

"Oh, Henry, you're home!"

"What is it, Lizzy?" He gripped her arm. "Are you hurt?"

"No, it's Cassie. She's left."

Henry had seen Morland on his ride and brought him home. That man stood by while Lizzy told Cassandra's story. She worked not to cry but wasn't able to manage it.

"I'll go," Morland said at one point, and both Steeles turned to dissuade him. "No," he clarified. "I'll go after Cassandra."

"She won't listen to you," Lizzy said.

"I won't try to bring her home. I'll just make sure she arrives safely at your sister's. As soon as she's settled, I'll return."

"Thank you, Morland," Henry said. "I wish to send a letter with you. I'll put it together right now."

Henry strode from the room, leaving Morland and Lizzy alone. Lizzy tried to conceal her blotchy face, but Morland would have none of it. He approached without hesitation and took her hands in his.

"I thought if I came back to England, it would all be so easy."

"Did you?" Lizzy asked, a little sniff escaping.

"Yes, and now I find that the lady herself is terrified of me, and never once did I imagine our sweet, stable Cassandra capable of running from any problem."

Tears filled Lizzy's eyes.

"She doesn't think she's beautiful. She doesn't believe Tate would ever want her."

"Well, at least I know that it runs in the family."

"What does?"

"The beautiful Steele sisters are all quite bad at letting a man know when he can get close."

Lizzy could only nod, forced to agree.

"I know your heart is hurting right now, Lizzy, but I'm headed to check on Cassandra. I won't come back unless I know she's all right." Morland stopped talking and bent very close before going on. "But hear me well, Elizabeth Steele. When I return I'll be getting close — very close indeed."

Lizzy could only stare up at him. She was completely motionless when he bent a little further and brushed her lips with his own. A moment later he let go of her hands. Henry was returning with the letter for Cassandra. Morland bid them both goodbye and went on his way. Lizzy didn't remember taking a breath for the rest of the day.

Chapter Fourteen

The coach's speed began to decline, but at first Cassandra didn't notice. She had been dozing, not wanting to think about what she was doing, but when it began to bounce to a stop, she sat up and put her head out.

"Is there trouble?"

"No, Miss Steele," their faithful coachman, Bernard, said. "You have a visitor."

Only then did Cassandra see a horseman dismounting and coming toward her.

"Morland!" she exclaimed in shock and surprise. "Is everything all right?"

"At home? Yes," Morland answered as he pulled himself inside and put his fist to the roof to send them on their way. "In this coach, I'm not so sure."

Cassandra's personal maid had gone up on top when Morland climbed in, but Cassandra almost wished for her presence. She had started this and would finish it, but Morland's appearance made her doubt.

"Did Lizzy and Henry send you?"

"No. I offered to catch up with you and

make sure you arrived safely at your sister's."

"You didn't have to do that."

"I did, Cassie. Lizzy is very distressed, and you must know I can't stand to see that."

Cassandra nodded. She felt so selfish, but she didn't know what else to do. She closed her eyes against the image of Tate's face looking at her with disappointment and surprise. Her stomach rolled at the thought.

"Did he ever tell you he loves you?" Morland came right out and asked, breaking into her tortured thoughts.

"No."

"Did you tell him you love him?"

"No."

"So your fear of rejection is great."

"Very great. I never thought myself so weak, but I am." Cassandra took a breath. "He'll return to London, and when he does, Lizzy will send for me and I'll go on as before."

"I'm going to marry Lizzy someday, Cassie. She won't be at Newcomb forever."

"But I'm happy there with Henry," Cassandra reasoned. "He and I will do well together. I won't pine for someone of my own."

His look was so skeptical that Cassandra lost all patience.

"What am I to do, Morland? He's never seen me! I think he might very well be in love, but it's not with me. It's with the woman he imagines me to be!"

Morland easily read the pain and frustration in her face and eyes, and his heart turned over. Hadn't he known that very pain when he returned and Lizzy was as she'd always been, distant and uncertain around him? Even knowing how she felt didn't instantly change everything.

"Are you angry with me?" Cassandra asked when he remained silent.

"I'm not, Cassie, and I didn't catch up with your coach so I could dissuade you. I've come to see that you arrive safely at Charlotte's. That is all. Oh!" Morland remembered the letter. "Henry sent you this."

Cassandra took the missive from his outstretched hand but knew she couldn't read it right then. Her satchel was nearby, and she tucked it in there.

Morland watched her and was again reminded of how close this action was to desperation. He thought to change the subject by asking her about the book in her hand, but tears came to her eyes when she answered, and he settled back to ride in silence.

Pembroke

"I had forgotten the beauty of this stained glass," Tate told Harriet as he walked slowly through Pembroke, seeing it for the first time in years. "It's magnificent."

"Thorpe's favorite window," Harriet remembered fondly as they stood before the huge stained-glass window at the end of the upstairs hallway. It was an unusual spot for the art, and all the more eye-catching because of it. "I never did show Cassandra around Pembroke, but I know she would love to see it."

"Thursday," Tate said with a smile. "I'll show her Thursday."

"Is that what day she's coming to see you?"

"No, I told her in my note that I would come to Newcomb Park, but I'll bring her back here for lunch. Does that work for your schedule?"

Harriet agreed, looking into eyes that she'd waited so long to see — smiling eyes, eyes that loved her, eyes that looked at everything with a boyish new interest.

Eyes that couldn't wait to see the woman he loved.

Fairfax Hall

"Oh, Morland," Charlotte said, the morning he prepared to climb back into the Steele coach for the ride home. "I can't thank you enough."

"It was my pleasure, Charlotte. Tell Cassie to take care of herself and that I shall see her when she arrives home."

"Indeed, I shall."

Giving his own word of thanks, Barrington shook Morland's hand and then stood with his wife to wave the coach on its way.

"Are you angry?" Charlotte asked of her spouse the moment they were alone.

"Why would I be angry?"

"We've only just arrived home, and we were looking forward to being alone."

"Wanting to be alone or not, how could I take one look at Cassie's heartbroken face and be angry?"

Charlotte's eyes filled with tears. "How could anyone not love her?"

"We have only her word that he doesn't, and I for one tend to believe that he loves her very much."

"You've never met the man. How could you possibly know that?"

"I'm in love with one of the Steele sisters," he said simply. "I know how irresistible they can be."

Barrington kissed her surprised lips and caressed her waist before slipping a possessive arm around her to lead her inside. And only just in time, for Cassandra was awake, dressed, and looking for her sister. That she had already been crying was only too obvious.

The newlyweds made no comment, however, but set about showing Cassandra around their home, feeding her a fine breakfast, and making her feel as welcome as she was.

Cassandra enjoyed the time immensely. She was quite willing for any distraction that would take her mind from Collingbourne and a man whose eyes she'd never seen.

Pembroke

"I can't tell you how much the sermon notes meant, Pastor Hurst. It is indeed a pleasure to meet you."

"I'm very glad to hear it, Mr Tate, and news of your recovery has brought joy to many."

"I know the church family was praying for me. I plan to be in church this Sunday. I'm looking forward to meeting everyone."

"Will you be returning to London soon?"

"My plans are not confirmed at this point. I'm in no hurry."

"We hope you'll be with us for a time. August can be rather warm, but most summers here are very nice."

Pastor Hurst did not stay overly long, and it gave Tate great pleasure to walk him to the drive and wave as his small buggy took him away.

The pastor gone, Tate did not hurry back inside. He hadn't seen the view from the front door of Pembroke in many years. He spotted a flower bush of unusual color, one he'd never seen before. Going over to study it, he made mental plans to show it to Cassandra on the morrow.

Newcomb Park

"She is well?" Henry questioned.

"Yes," Morland answered, thanking Lizzy for the glass of water. "I didn't see her the morning I left, but I know she's in good hands. Charlotte was very glad to have her, as was Barrington."

Both Steele siblings exchanged a look.

They had not wanted to worry but had given in to that temptation. They wanted Cassandra home with them immediately, but knowing that Morland had seen her safely to Charlotte's was the next best thing.

"I will confess to you that I am rather weary." Morland had finished his water and set the glass aside. "I think I will head to my aunt's now."

"Thank you, Morland," Henry said again. "Can you join us this evening for dinner?"

"I would enjoy that."

Lizzy watched him leave, thinking she had never seen him so tired. The moment he was out the door, she went in search of Cook. Whatever they had for supper needed to be special.

Fairfax Hall

Dear Cassie, Henry's letter began. It had taken until the next day for her to open it.

I am a very observant man, if not a vocal one. I had only one evening in the company of Mr Tate, but one evening was enough. He loves you, Cassie. He thinks you're wonderful.

I know all about fears. They're not logical, and because we have a God who is in control, they are sin. I'm not saying this to be harsh. I have no wish to scold you. But I would urge you to think wisely on this subject and listen to those around you.

Cassandra had to stop reading. If she listened to those around her, she would never have left Collingbourne. But then she would be forced to face Alexander Tate.

Folding the letter without looking at another word, Cassandra slipped it into the pages of her Bible. She had only just stopped crying. If she finished the letter, she would most certainly be in tears again, and right now she wasn't willing to risk it.

Newcomb Park

Tate arrived midmorning. He asked to see Cassandra Steele, not noticing the servant's moment of hesitation. The young gentleman was shown to the small parlor, where he stayed on his feet, eager for his first glimpse of Cassandra. When the door opened just minutes later, the woman who entered was not a redhead.

"Hello, Mr Tate. It's nice to see you."

"You must be Miss Elizabeth."

271

The two bowed formally to each other before Tate smiled.

"Do you know whether Cassandra got my note? Has she forgiven me for not coming sooner?" he asked, not waiting for an answer. "The doctor wanted me to rest at home another week, but I was only willing to do that for two more days. I didn't try to explain all of that in the letter, but I hope Cassandra understood."

"She's not here, Mr Tate," Lizzy answered with regret. "And she never received your note. She left before it arrived."

To Lizzy's amazement, Tate smiled.

"She's run, hasn't she?"

"Yes. How did you know?"

Tate laughed. He was finding that regaining one's sight had an amazing effect on one's outlook.

"My aunt commented on your dark hair and beauty the first time she met you," Tate now explained. "I had met your blonde sister, Charlotte, in London and thought her beautiful. When Aunt Harriet told me that Cassandra had red hair and freckles, it wasn't hard to imagine her not feeling as though she measured up.

"But it was more than that," Tate went on, Lizzy listening in surprise. "I could hear the hesitancy in her voice. One day we spoke of honesty, and I could tell she was trying to be herself with me but wasn't quite able to manage the job. I know now that she was upset about how I would view her."

"And how will you view her?"

"I'll view her for exactly what she is: the most beautiful woman I've ever known."

Lizzy's tears would not be stopped. Even with this near stranger in her midst, she began to cry and could not stop.

Henry happened by, heard his sister's cries, and went in. Not bothering with formalities, Henry nodded to Tate and went to his sister.

"It's all right, Lizzy. Don't cry anymore."

"He loves Cassie," she managed.

"Of course he does. Did you ever doubt?"

It had all been too much. For a time Lizzy was inconsolable. Only when she began to calm a bit did Tate try to speak.

"It's most rude of me to stay on when you are so upset, but if I leave, I don't know when I'll learn where Cassandra has gone. I have to go after her, you see."

Both Henry and Lizzy looked at him.

"I suppose you've been sworn to secrecy," he guessed.

"We have not," they said in unison, and

both laughed, laughs of relief and genuine pleasure. Lizzy took a moment to mop her face, and Henry spoke.

"She's in Bath, at Charlotte's. I can give you the exact directions."

"I would be only too happy to have them."

"She's so certain . . ." Lizzy, now able to speak, began. "I don't know if you'll convince her as easily as you have me."

Tate nodded.

"I think she'll believe me. I have something I've never had before."

Lizzy's heart sank over her disregard of his situation. But all she could think about was Cassandra.

"How awful of me not to say anything, Mr Tate. I'm so pleased you've regained your vision. I remembered you in my prayers daily."

"Thank you. Now, at the risk of being rude, I must head home and pack. I have a trip to make."

Lizzy went to him.

"Please tell her how much we want her to come home."

"I shall do that." Tate smiled down at her and was smiled at in return. "As soon as you're my sister-in-law, Miss Elizabeth, I shall give you a hug."

Tate went with Henry for directions to Fairfax Hall. The men shook hands, and Henry repeated Lizzy's request. As soon as Tate was able, he was on his way.

"Will you walk with me in the garden?" Morland asked Lizzy when supper was over.

"Yes."

It was a quiet couple who made their way outside, the sun setting fast. Lizzy wondered what Morland was thinking, and Morland wanted to hold Lizzy's hand.

"That was a fine meal," Morland said instead, keeping his hands at his sides.

"I'm glad you enjoyed it."

"Did you know that pork is one of my favorites?"

"Is it?" Lizzy asked, but Morland only smiled. There was no artifice in this woman.

"Yes, it is, and I know you don't care for apples and that you prefer chicken to beef or pork."

"How did you know that?"

"One pays attention over time."

"Not if one isn't interested."

"Who said I wasn't interested?"

"You did."

"When did I say this?"

"You didn't have to say it, Morland. I just knew."

Morland stopped their slow progress over the grounds with a hand to her arm. He didn't keep touching her but waited until she faced him to speak.

"What should I have done, Lizzy?"

"It's not your fault, Morland. I'm sorry I made it sound that way." Lizzy met his eyes. "I take it you came back because Edward told you of my feelings?"

"He read a letter to me. I must confess, until that moment, I had no clue."

Lizzy turned away in shame. "He wasn't supposed to do that."

"No?"

"No!" she said firmly now. "No woman wants to know that a man has come to her in this way."

"You're not so different from Cassie, are you?"

Lizzy looked at him. "What do you mean?"

"I mean, you haven't run away, but you're no easier to convince."

Lizzy bit her lip.

"Don't you get it, Lizzy? You had no idea that Edward spoke with me about your letter. He could have shown it to me; I would have asked if you knew he planned to say something; he would have said no; and I would have gone on with my trip."

"But instead you came home."

Morland gave a short laugh. "I began making plans on the spot. Believing we had a chance, I couldn't get here fast enough."

"What are you saying, Morland?"

Morland shook his head, his hands going out in frustration. This only lasted a moment, however. Seconds later he pulled Lizzy close.

"I'm saying," he began, "that I love you. I've loved you for a very long time."

Lizzy sighed as Morland held her.

"I thought I would die when you went away. I tried not to love you, but it never worked."

"I had no idea, or I should never have left."

Morland kissed her now, ever so gently, before moving back a little and reaching for her hand. He linked her smaller fingers in his own and continued their walk. He had been enjoying the flowers and the sunset, but now he saw none of it. Turning to look at each other constantly, the two talked and walked for the next two hours. Not until Henry came looking for them did they go back inside where the three of them continued to talk until well after midnight.

When Lizzy finally climbed the stairs for bed, she realized she hadn't thought of Cassandra in hours. Praying that her sister would listen to Tate and be wise in the Lord, Lizzy fell into a dreamless sleep, never once forgetting that Thomas Morland loved her.

Fairfax Hall

Charlotte heard someone at the door. She was on her way to check on lunch preparation, but she stopped and waited as Ward answered the wide portal at the front of their home.

A tall, dark-haired man was given entrance. Ward saw the mistress of the house standing by and went on his way.

"You must be Mrs Barrington," Tate said with a bow. "I'm sorry to intrude on your home, but I'm hoping to speak with Miss Cassandra Steele."

"Cassandra is here. May I tell her who's calling?"

Tate smiled in a way that both of Cassandra's sisters found utterly charming.

"Please just tell her she has a visitor."

Charlotte went on her way, tracking Cassandra down in the garden room at the rear of the house where she was working

278

on an arrangement of flowers.

"Cassie, someone is here to see you."

"Oh," she looked up, her face pleased, thinking Morland might have returned. "Who is it?"

"A visitor."

Cassandra needed no time in understanding. Her eyes grew large, and panic filled her face.

"Send him away."

"I can't do that, Cassie. Won't you just see him?"

"No!" She began to wave her hands, her eyes casting about. "I see I need more flowers. No visitors today, Charlotte. I'm simply too busy."

With those words, she went out the nearby door and into the garden. Charlotte stood still, wondering where that "grown-up" sister had gone. Seeing no help for it, she turned back to the foyer.

Tate took one look at Mrs Barrington's face and smiled again.

"Did she run?"

"I'm afraid so."

"How far did she go this time?"

"Just to the garden."

"Do you mind?"

Charlotte now smiled. "Not at all. I'll show you the way."

Taking him to the exact door her sister had used as an exit, Charlotte stepped out.

"I don't see her right now," she said, keeping her voice low, "but I would go toward the arbor. There's a seat on the other side, and she enjoys the view from there."

"Thank you, Mrs Barrington."

"I'm making the assumption that you'll be staying for lunch and dinner, Mr Tate."

"Thank you for the invitation. May I let you know in a short time?"

To Charlotte's answering smile, he moved on his way. He heard a voice, Cassandra's voice, talking to herself as he approached, so he stopped on the other side of the arbor, out of sight.

"Did your sister not tell you that you had a visitor?" he called.

"She did," Cassandra returned, speaking right up. "But I'm very busy right now. I can't see anyone."

"That's too bad," Tate said gently, keeping himself well hidden. "I can see everything."

"Tate?" Cassandra said softly after a moment.

"Yes?"

"I'm very glad for you."

"Thank you."

The two fell silent. Tate was desperate to see her but more desperate to be the man she needed. Wanting that more than anything aided his patience.

"I just learned that your family calls you Cassie. It fits you."

"When did you learn that?"

"When I stopped to see you in Collingbourne and found you'd left."

"Tate, you do understand that I am pleased for you; truly I am."

"I know you are, but are you not happy for yourself as well?"

"I don't know what I am."

"What is it you want me to know about you? What is it that you think I won't love?"

"My looks."

"And you think those are a mystery to me?"

"Yes."

"Cassie, I asked my aunt ages ago what you looked like."

"But that doesn't mean you really know."

Cassandra held her breath when she heard him move. She didn't look in his direction but sat very still when he came around the arbor and joined her on the bench.

Watching from the house, Charlotte began to cry. That he would speak to her from around the arbor was one of the sweetest, most romantic things she'd ever seen.

With Tate around the corner there was nothing more to see, so she went in search of Barrington. Suddenly she needed him to kiss her and hold her very tight.

Chapter Fifteen

Cassandra could not look at Tate. She could feel his study of her profile and wanted so much to see his eyes, but the disappointment she'd imagined a thousand times kept her gaze forward, her eyes on the lovely garden beyond.

"What are you afraid of, Cassie? I know it's not me."

"No, it's not you. You're the dearest man I've ever known, but every woman wants her husband to find her lovely, and I don't think you will."

"Do I get to have a say, or has this all been decided?"

"You decided it, Tate." Cassandra's voice was sad.

"When did I do that?"

"One of our first days together. You said you were being read to by one of the beautiful Steele sisters."

"And you don't think I was?"

Cassandra looked at him, too perplexed not to.

"You know what I mean. You've now seen Lizzy and Charlotte, and I can assure you that when people refer to the beautiful Steele sisters, they are thinking only of those two."

Cassandra would have looked away, but her eyes finally found his.

"Oh, my," she whispered. "Your eyes are blue. I never dreamed they'd be blue."

Tate only smiled at her.

"Can you really see?"

"Very clearly."

"What happened?"

"Just full healing, I think. I woke on Tuesday morning and knew something had changed in the night. We sent for Dr Tilney, even though it was a month early. He removed the patches, and I could see."

Cassandra smiled at him; she couldn't help herself.

"I'm so pleased for you, Tate. I know how much praise you'll give to God for this, but I also admire you and the way you handled all of it. It was a huge example to me."

"But now you're done with me?"

Cassandra looked back over the garden, her heart feeling helpless and exposed. She loved this man. She would love him if he never owned his sight, but now that he did, she couldn't help but wonder if he was terribly disappointed.

"I have red hair," she said, stating the obvious.

"I can see that."

"It's curly and unruly most of the time."

"Um hm."

His tone, blatantly flirtatious, almost made her smile.

"What about my freckles?" she asked at last, turning to him in frustration.

Tate leaned close, his eyes caressing her face.

"I guess I'll have to spend a lifetime kissing every one."

Cassandra's heart stopped and then thundered on.

"Did you just ask me to marry you?"

Tate moved until his forehead touched her.

"No, I did not. I would love nothing more, but I will restrain myself."

Cassandra continued to watch him.

"From this point, we will return to Collingbourne and have a proper courtship. I will come to your parlor and gaze across at you. I will get to know your family. I will work to show you what is in my heart."

Cassandra looked as pleased and surprised as she felt.

"You don't find me repulsive?"

Tate laughed before saying, "It might be easier if I did."

"Why is that?"

Tate asked himself if she could be that innocent.

"Why, Tate?" she tried again.

"It would help me with my thoughts about you," Tate said carefully.

Cassandra continued to pay attention, but no comprehension dawned on her face.

"Private thoughts, Cassie."

Nothing. She still didn't know. Tate saw no help for it.

"Thoughts that need to be reserved for marriage."

Color swept to her hairline, and Tate smiled at the sight. Irresistibly drawn, two of Tate's fingers moved up to stroke her cheek.

"Well, that certainly answers that question," Tate commented.

"What question?"

"Your skin *is* amazingly soft."

Cassandra could only smile up at him.

When Tate stood and held out his hand, she took it. He led her to the house, to the very door from which she'd fled.

"Come inside, Cassie," he said gently. "I must tell your sister that I accept her offer for lunch and dinner."

Collingbourne
The Church

"Are you alone, Mrs Thorpe?" Pastor Hurst asked, thinking to see Tate with her.

"I'm afraid I am, Pastor. Tate had to visit someone on short notice. I'm sure he'll be back this week."

"He's still feeling well?"

Harriet smiled, thinking about the last time she'd seen him. It had given her such pleasure to watch his zeal and excitement as he followed after Cassandra.

"Yes, he's very well. Thank you for asking."

Harriet moved on her way then, still finding pleasure in the memory of Tate's face but not able to stop herself from wondering if things were all right.

Please believe him, Cassandra. Please believe Tate when he tells you how much he loves you.

Newcomb Park

Henry was just headed out on his ride when a messenger arrived with word. Jasper tipped the man as Henry opened the letter and read. It was from Barrington.

*I'm bringing Cassie home. Should be with
you late Monday. Tate coming in his own
carriage. Cassie is well and will explain all
when she arrives.*

Barrington

Henry went on his ride, but not before
he found Lizzy and gave her the letter. He
tried to stay and comfort her when she
grew weepy again, but when she urged him
to go, he gladly fled.

Brown Manor

"I hope you know I'm using you as a diversion," Lizzy admitted to Anne. She'd explained the whole story and was now spent.

"Nonsense, Lizzy. Of course you must
come and tell me about Cassie. You know
I would wish to hear."

Lizzy came to her feet and moved
around a bit.

"I thank you, Anne. If I had been forced
to sit at home all day and wait for her to
arrive, I think I would have gone mad."

"Is there not more to tell me, Lizzy?"
Anne gently urged. She was out of bed but
still taking things slowly.

"About Cassie?"

"No, about yourself. Word has it that

Thomas Morland has come home and is spending a good deal of time at Newcomb."

Lizzy smiled and took her seat again.

"Ah, Lizzy," Anne went on, "you don't need to explain a thing. I can see it's all true."

"I never dreamed he would come," she said with a sigh. "I had given up hoping he would ever notice me, and all along he knew I was here."

Anne wanted to know every detail. Lizzy was only too glad to tell her. Her heart felt lighter for just talking about it. When she was finished, Anne's maid came and told her the time.

"I've been up for more than two hours, Lizzy. I really must lie down."

"Of course, Anne. Shall I see you upstairs?"

"Jenny will do that."

The two friends hugged and smiled at each other like schoolgirls.

"I have a selfish request," Anne whispered, just before she let her friend go. "Don't get married until after the baby comes. I want to be there."

Lizzy laughed. That particular topic had yet to be spoken of, but it got her to thinking. Indeed, it remained on her mind all the way home.

Thornton Hall

Marianne Jennings needed to be alone. She loved her family very much, but suddenly she felt a need to separate herself. Whenever this happened, she went to the maze that stood outside her home.

If she were to look up at the house, she would be looking at Penny's window, a window which gave a perfect view of the maze and that entire corner of the yard. There was a time when she needed someone directing her from that window to get through the maze, but no more. It was as familiar to her as the open fields, and now in an effort to gain solitude, she wandered the gravel path, hedges above her head on all sides, and just let her thoughts roam.

I have no reason to be down, Father, but I am. My heart is so sad. My siblings were just here with all their beautiful children. We had a marvelous visit. But lately I just want to cry over nothing and everything.

Marianne asked God to examine her heart. She worked to be thankful, and when she did she felt tears coming on. Weary of her own emotion, she squelched them and continued to wander through the maze.

"Mrs Jennings?"

Marianne smiled at the sound of her husband's voice.

"Where are you, Mrs Jennings?" he called, his voice a tad singsongy.

"I'll never tell."

Marianne moved into an alcove that led nowhere, sure he would never find her without direction.

"Marianne?"

Marianne smothered laughter and moved a little deeper, wishing the day wasn't so bright. If she could have hid in the shadows, he would never . . .

"Well, now," Jennings said suddenly, having spotted her. "I do believe you might be hiding from me."

Marianne laughed and put her arms around him when he came to her. Jennings pulled her close.

"How come you're out here?"

"I just needed to be alone, I think."

"I would offer to leave, but you'll still have someone with you."

Marianne nodded, sure he was talking about God, but Jennings went on.

"I have it figured out."

"What's that?"

"It was the same way with Catherine. You didn't feel ill in the morning, but for some weeks you were rather blue."

Marianne's mouth opened, and Jennings smiled at her.

"It's been weeks," he continued, pressing his point home.

"How could you know this without my having once thought of it?"

Jennings shrugged.

"Just naturally brilliant, I guess."

"Oh, Jennings! I think you may be right. I've been too busy to really take notice."

Jennings smiled tenderly down at her and kissed her. When she looked into his eyes again, she found that flames had replaced the tenderness.

"Now, Jennings," she protested when he pulled her even closer.

"Hush," he said, already breathless.

Marianne did just that, her arms going around his neck. She only hoped the children were not watching from Penny's window.

Newcomb Park

Lizzy wrapped her arms around Cassandra in a way that said she would never let go. She held her small, younger sister and cried tears of relief.

"Did Tate see you?" Lizzy finally managed.

"Yes, and Lizzy, I'm so sorry I didn't listen. I was so foolish and blind."

"We won't let you go away again," Lizzy told her. "Our hearts can't take it."

Barrington kissed his sister-in-law and then went to Henry, who was waiting to thank him. The hour was late, and all were tired, but Henry still asked Cassandra to see him in his study. Cassandra never thought to deny him and went there as soon as she thanked Barrington and told him she'd see him before he left in the morning.

"Sit down, Cassie," Henry suggested as soon as she'd entered and shut the door. "I need to tell you something."

Cassandra thought she should start by apologizing, but Henry didn't give her a chance.

"I'm still working to get this right, Cassie, so I've asked you in here so I can express my regrets and ask you to forgive me."

"For what, Henry?" The youngest Steele couldn't imagine.

"For not going after you. Morland volunteered, and I let him go, thinking the letter would be enough. Tate came along just after, and I let him go. It was my place as your brother, the oldest in this family, to go after you, make sure you were safe, and try to reason with you."

Henry shook his head a little. "I found it easier to remain here, and that is what I did. I regret it very much."

"But, Henry, don't you see? None of this would have been necessary if I had remained and let Tate speak with me."

"You should have stayed, Cassie. I realize that. But no matter what you chose to do, I have responses of my own to answer for. Walker has been talking to me for weeks about my responsibility to lead and serve as the head of this family. I should have gone to Bath. I should have checked on you myself and brought you home."

Cassandra felt as though she could weep. She had put Henry in a terrible position, but how to describe to him the utter panic that filled her? She never dreamed that Tate would come after her. She never believed he could love her. She thought that her leaving would rescue them all. There would be no need to be ashamed in front of Harriet Thorpe or Tate before he returned to London.

"Late as it is, Cassie, I do wish to know what happened. I take it Tate arrived at Fairfax Hall and proposed to you."

"On the contrary, he said we're going to have a proper courtship. He said he'll come to visit, sit in our parlor, gaze at me, and get to know my family."

Henry couldn't stop that small shake of his head.

"And you ran from this special man."

"Foolish, wasn't I?"

"As we all are at times, Cassie. Do you forgive me?"

"I don't think there's anything to forgive. Do you forgive me?"

"Always."

Henry stood and came to her chair. Cassandra rose to hug him, thinking that the change in him was still something of a miracle.

Weary as she was, she retired but couldn't sleep. It was very late before sleep came to claim her, but she was up in time to see Barrington off, thanking him for all his special care.

Pembroke

"Cassandra is home safely?" Harriet asked over breakfast. She had been asleep before Tate arrived the night before.

"Yes. Barrington brought her back."

"You weren't with them?"

"No, my coach was 30 minutes ahead of theirs, and I came directly here."

"Tate." Her hand reached for his. "I

must know. Did you ask Cassandra to marry you?"

Tate smiled.

"No. We're not going to rush this."

"But you do care for her, and she cares for you, does she not?"

Tate's mind went to the way she looked in the garden at Fairfax, her surprised and trusting eyes when she realized he was not repulsed by her. And he thought about the remainder of the day: the way she looked at lunch and dinner, and the sweet way she smiled at him as they sat and talked with Mr and Mrs Barrington.

"I would say our feelings are quite mutual."

Harriet sat back with a sigh.

"I can't tell you how pleased and relieved I am. I tried not to worry, but I was so fearful when she went away."

"Why was that?"

"Well, Tate," his aunt said logically, "I knew she'd taken your heart. I knew you would follow her anywhere."

"That's true," Tate said. "I would."

"Why did she go?" Harriet suddenly asked, tired of trying to guess.

"She thought I would find her looks abhorrent."

Harriet's mouth swung open in surprise.

"You can't be serious."

"*She* was very serious."

"But she's adorable, absolutely lovely!"

"She didn't think I would find her thus."

Harriet sat up and sternly shook her head. "She must have been confused about how completely you now see. There is positively no way you could look at that girl and find anything wanting."

Tate had to laugh. "Aunt Harriet, I'm not the one who needed convincing."

"Of course not." Harriet calmed and even managed to butter her toast. "I was just being defensive."

"Well, don't be too harsh on her. She truly believed that I would compare her to her sisters and be disappointed once I'd seen her."

Harriet's own heart pained her as she thought about Cassandra's turmoil. She had been slightly put out when she'd heard of it. But Tate was right, Cassandra didn't need anyone to criticize her. It looked as though she'd been harsh on herself. Nevertheless, the older woman prayed that Cassandra would understand that true beauty lies within.

Newcomb Park

Cassandra spotted him a moment too late. She was headed to the library and didn't have to go through the parlor — and wouldn't have if only she'd realized that her sister had a visitor. He'd spotted her as well.

"Hello, Morland." Seeing no hope for it, Cassandra greeted him. Even as her face turned pink, she wished she'd gone the other way.

"Hello, Cassie. How are you?"

"Fine." She knew she couldn't leave now without being rude. "How are you?"

"I'm well. Cassie?"

"Yes?"

"Why are you embarrassed in front of me?"

Cassandra's shoulders slumped.

"Oh, Morland, I caused everyone so much trouble. I feel ashamed."

Morland was silent for a moment.

"Did you know your sister cared for me?"

Cassandra blinked at the change in subject but still said, "Yes."

"Did Henry?"

"Yes."

"And Charlotte? Edward?"

Cassandra nodded.

"Now, who should feel ashamed, Cassie? I went to Africa, having completely missed everything I now see in her eyes."

Cassandra smiled at him.

"Thank you, Morland."

"For what?"

"For being here — for coming as soon as you knew."

Cassandra didn't stay, but Morland didn't need her to. After all, what else could he have done? He hadn't known, but Cassandra was correct: As soon as he found out, he'd returned to England.

Chapter Sixteen

Blackburn Manor

"Hello, Mother." Marianne greeted Mrs Walker warmly, receiving a kiss and an embrace.

"Don't tell me," her mother teased. "Have you actually come alone? Have you actually dared to visit without bringing any of my beautiful grandchildren?"

Marianne laughed as her mother looped an arm in hers and led her to the parlor.

It was a constant source of pleasure to Marianne that her parents never expressed second thoughts over their adopted grandchildren. Marianne had married a man who was a guardian to three of the sweetest children in England. Marianne had loved them from day one, and her parents had been no different.

"I wanted to come alone this time," Marianne began when they were seated. "I have news for you and Father."

"You don't have to tell me," Mrs Walker

answered, her smile kind. "I already know."

"How could you? I found out only yesterday."

Mrs Walker chuckled a little, even as she shook her head with the memory.

"Your sisters and brothers were all just here, dear. You grew weepy every time someone hugged you or one of the children wanted into your lap for a story. You even cried when you watched all the nieces and nephews grapple to hold Catherine."

Remembering that it had been exactly that way, Marianne laughed at herself.

"Why is it like that, Mother? I have so much to be thankful for. I work hard to remember that, but then I end up crying all the time."

"Tears don't necessarily mean you're not being thankful, Mari. People are emotional for all sorts of reasons. If you know your heart to be in line with God's, then you must not worry. You're also married to a godly man, who I know would be happy to help you in this. If you suspect you have things to work on, maybe sins you are unaware of, Jennings will help you."

As might be expected, tears came to Marianne's eyes. Her mother moved close to hug her. When Mr Walker joined them, she was just composing herself.

"Did you come to tell us your news?" her father teased, having listened to his wife's wise words on the subject.

Marianne laughed, but the tears started again as well. Her parents laughed with her and at her, thinking her a most special daughter. Marianne thought they were special as well, but if she dwelt on that, she would be in tears all over again.

Richmond

"Good morning, Aunt Penelope." Morland greeted the elderly aunt he lived with when in Collingbourne, kissing her cheek as he joined her at the breakfast table.

"Good morning, Morland. I'm surprised you're still here."

Morland smiled at her teasing tone.

"Lizzy must have had plans this morning."

Morland's smile widened. "Indeed, she did."

"When are you going to ask that girl to marry you and be done with it?"

Morland shook his head. "I find I don't care to rush this. I never dreamed that Elizabeth Steele would want me for a husband. I want to enjoy this time, if you take my meaning."

"Even if I didn't, Lizzy needs to know

that she's getting the most wonderful man in the country."

"You don't speak with bias, do you, Auntie?"

"Of course not!" she blustered. "I've never heard of such a thing. I am never biased."

Morland smiled at her.

"Don't you dare give me that sassy look, Thomas Morland. I know enough about you to send Lizzy Steele running for her life."

"Such as?"

"You never mind that!" She dismissed the subject with a wave of her thin, well-spotted hand. "Now, what day are you bringing Lizzy to lunch?"

"I don't know. Why don't you select the day, and I'll extend the invitation."

"Very well. Tuesday! Tell Henry and Cassandra they are to come as well. And Edward."

"I don't believe Edward has returned yet."

"Well, he must come soon."

"Why is that?"

"He can't miss the wedding," Aunt Penelope explained as though Morland was a simpleton.

She continued on about what she would

wear and how pretty Lizzy would look in her dress. Morland let her talk. It wasn't at all hard to hear conversation about Lizzy, and as for picturing her in her wedding dress, Morland was all ears.

Newcomb Park

Cassandra was in the garden when Tate arrived Wednesday. They had both been home since Monday night, but Tate had not called on Tuesday. He'd shared with Cassandra how much he needed to be in touch with his business manager, so she wasn't overly surprised not to hear from him.

In truth, Cassandra was rather eager to see Harriet Thorpe. The two women had shared something special all those weeks, and now it was over, at least in part. Cassandra didn't want their relationship to be broken in any way, but she knew better than to call on her and possibly disturb Tate. Now this morning, not many hours after her ride with Henry, the man in question sought her out in the garden.

"Good morning, Miss Steele." Tate bowed, his eyes smiling even before his mouth could join.

"Good morning, Mr Tate." Cassandra

did a small curtsy, flower basket hanging from her arm.

"You are busy this morning."

"Not overly. Just gathering a few flowers for the dining room." Cassandra suddenly felt shy and snipped another blossom so she could lower her eyes.

"Was your family pleased to see you?"

"Yes, very. Did your business correspondence go well?"

"Yes. I shall probably hear back from Pierrepont any day now."

"He is the gentleman handling business affairs in your absence?"

"Yes."

"You must have a great trust of him."

"I do. We've known each other many years."

"And do you have much property to manage?"

"A fair amount."

Cassandra wondered if he was being modest but didn't know how to ask.

"I think you have something on your mind." Tate had been watching her very carefully.

Cassandra looked at him, understanding that his seeing her was going to add a new dimension to their relationship. She was still trying to decide how to reply

when Tate pointed to a flower.

"Pick this one."

"Why that one?"

"It's the same color as your dress."

Cassandra smiled and did as she was told, adding it to her basket, all the while asking herself why she was suddenly so shy. It felt as if the days of easy talk and camaraderie at Fairfax Hall were months in the past.

Tate could see that something was on her mind, but he didn't press her to talk, at least not right then. He followed along and watched as she selected flowers, carefully collecting them for the basket.

"Where will these flowers go?" he asked, choosing a safe subject.

"To the dining room," she answered with a smile, having already told him that.

"You said that, didn't you?"

"Yes."

"Why are we nervous with each other?" Tate asked quietly.

"There are probably several reasons," Cassandra answered with her eyes on the garden, "but the one that comes to mind right now is how little we really know of each other."

"I feel I know a lot about you."

Cassandra looked at him.

"Why don't you feel as though you know me?" he asked.

"Because of the way I came into your life. Your past was not my business. I didn't visit Pembroke to question you. I came to read and give you rest."

"And I felt free to ask more questions of you," Tate guessed.

"Exactly."

"Ask me something."

"All right." Cassandra was not about to let that pass. "Just now when we spoke of your holdings, you described them as a fair amount. Were you being modest?"

"Yes," Tate answered without hesitation, going on to explain about his property. He was not as rich as a king, but his properties were substantial.

"Thank you for telling me."

"Does it matter so very much?"

"I think everything matters. When we were at Fairfax Hall, we spent all of our time telling Charlotte and Barrington how we'd met and gotten to know each other. Then you took time to relate your accident, and I realized it was the first time I'd heard all the details.

"Had you asked me in the garden that day to marry you, I would have said yes. I see now that God was protecting me. My heart would have rushed ahead when it was clearly wise that we go slowly and make sure of each other."

"And that's why you're shy with me today?" Tate had to ask, as it was his idea to have a proper courtship in the first place.

"I think it must be. I feel as though you have the advantage on me. I feel ignorant and off guard."

"I'm glad you told me," Tate said and then admitted something shocking. "I was coming over today to propose to you."

Cassandra gawked at him. "But you said . . ."

"I know, and I would have been foolish to ignore my own advice in Bath, but sometimes my heart runs ahead of me."

Cassandra smiled at him.

"What is that smile for?"

"Some days I wonder if you're human."

Tate laughed in the way she loved.

"I fear I'm all too human, Cassie. Have no concern on that end."

"Can you stay for lunch?"

"Thank you. I will."

With the gentlest of movements, Tate took the small cutting tool from her hand. For the next hour they walked and talked, and Cassandra had only to point to the blooms she wanted.

Her heart taking its turn in running ahead of her, Cassandra nearly shook her head at her most recent doubts. At the moment she wanted to throw her arms around this man and never let go.

Morland found Lizzy alone in the large parlor, gazing out the window. Jasper had let him in, and while the door into that room had not been silent, she did not turn from her place on the window seat. He approached quietly, uncertain whether she'd even heard the door and not wishing to startle her. She heard him when he was halfway across the room and turned in surprise.

"I'm sorry, Lizzy."

"It's all right."

Morland could tell she was upset.

"Is this a bad time?"

Lizzy shook her head, even as tears threatened. Morland went to sit beside her. She didn't speak, so he took her hand and held it.

"I've had word from Anne Weston," Lizzy said when she could speak. "The doctor has sent her back to bed for the remainder of her term."

"How much longer?"

"The end of August. More than two

months." Lizzy looked at him. "I so want her to have this baby, Morland. I want it so much."

"It would be a very nice thing."

"And Weston. I haven't known him very long, but his care of her is so tender."

"All they can do is obey the doctor's orders and trust God for this small life."

The words were too much for Lizzy. At the mention of the tiny person inside Anne, she broke down. Morland sat patiently, hating to see Lizzy like this but knowing it was probably for the best. He had never feared tears as many men did, and had no issue with Lizzy's need to cry.

"I'm sorry."

"Not at all."

"I think I've cried more since you returned than I have all year."

"Should I go back?" he teased.

"I would send Henry after you."

Morland's thumb stroked the back of Lizzy's hand and reminded her where her thoughts had roamed the night before.

"I was thinking about you last night," she admitted, feeling a change in subject was needed.

"Good thoughts?"

"After a time."

Morland smiled. "Was I in trouble?"

"Not exactly, but for a time I convinced myself that your feelings were only confused."

Morland's brows rose, and Lizzy hurried on.

"It's logical, Morland. After all, you could view me as a sister. We have known each other for years."

Morland laughed and sat back to regard her from a distance.

"Why is that funny?" Lizzy demanded.

"It's funny because of all the hard work I do to be a gentleman."

"You are a gentleman, Morland."

"I don't always feel like acting as one."

The way he watched Lizzy was warm and tender, and she smiled at her own stupidity.

"Feeling better?"

"Yes. About both things. I need to visit Anne. I think I would feel better if I saw her. And of course," she added quietly, "I always feel better when I see you."

With no need for words, the two regarded one another for long minutes. Lizzy was still working to believe that he'd come back, and Morland was still working on the wonder that she cared for him.

"Stay for dinner?" she invited.

Morland sighed. "I thought you would never ask."

★ ★ ★

Tate was back at Newcomb. He'd lunched with the Steeles, gone home, and returned after supper. Now the four of them, Lizzy, Cassandra, Tate, and Morland, sat around the card table, talking over a game of ruff.

"She's loaded," Morland said, watching Cassandra arrange her cards.

"How do you know?" Tate asked.

"She always bites her lip when she has so many good cards she doesn't know what to play first."

"Not fair, Morland!" Cassandra scolded him, still studying her hand. "You're giving away old family secrets."

"Well, if I didn't, you just did."

Cassandra ignored him and played trump.

"What did I tell you?" Morland said as he and Tate both surrendered cards.

"We shouldn't have let them talk us into these teams," Tate observed, surprised by how much Cassandra wanted to be Lizzy's partner.

Lizzy smiled, just short of laughter.

"You are looking way too pleased with yourself, Miss Elizabeth," Morland scolded, but all she did was smile a little more and take the next hand.

"That settles it," Tate put in. "We're

going to mix things up next time."

More competitive than Tate would have imagined, the women shared a smile. In the next hour they outscored the men three out of four times, and the men were crying for revenge.

"But you can't really get revenge unless you remain a team and beat us," Cassandra said, her voice a little too sweet.

"That's not going to work," Tate said, not falling for it. "And to make things more interesting, I think Lizzy should be my partner, and you should be Morland's."

Both women laughed at his nerve but agreed. Morland quietly went along, but he knew he got the better end of the deal. For all her unworldly ways, Cassandra was a dab hand at cards. The team of Cassandra and Morland thrashed Lizzy and Tate in less time than it had taken the women on their own.

"I should have warned you," Lizzy said to Tate, not sorry in the least. "Cassie always carries me. She's so unassuming, we get away with it every time."

Cassandra did her best to look innocent, but Tate was not fooled.

"I shall have my revenge," he promised.

"In what game?" Cassandra boldly asked him.

"I don't know, but hear me well, Cassie, when I tell you that this is not over yet."

The occupants of the table laughed at him before Lizzy rang for tea. They put the cards away, and Henry joined the four of them as they visited over hot cups of tea and biscuits.

The evening ended all too soon, both women taking the stairs at a slow pace.

"I do believe I'm in love, Cassie," Lizzy said quietly.

"I would never have guessed."

"And you?"

"I'm still mulling it over."

Lizzy laughed. "The only thing you're mulling over is what type of dress you want."

The women hugged goodnight and went their separate ways, but it was a good long time before either of them slept.

"We are happy to welcome a certain gentleman into our midst this morning," Pastor Hurst began. "Many of you have been praying for Mr Tate, and for the first time he has been able to join us.

"I've asked him to take the dais and say a few words to us about his recovery and some of the things he's learned. Mr Tate, if you'll come now, we are most eager to hear from you."

Cassandra hadn't known about this and suddenly felt her heart pounding as he rose from the pew he shared with his aunt, so tall and handsome, and went to the front.

"First of all," he said in the deep voice Cassandra loved, "I wish to thank you for all your prayers. I know God used those prayers in my life. I am most grateful to have my eyesight restored to me, but I'm also grateful for the things I was able to learn in that time.

"I think my life had gotten very busy before the accident, but I was doing some studying on the life of Moses. When I think on his life, I can't help but notice how often God demanded Moses' trust. God never let him make excuses for not obeying — not when he had to leave Egypt, and not when he was asked to go back.

"When my world went black, I tried to remember that. God asked hard things of Moses, and He has the right to ask hard things of me. It does no good to be angry with God. He has a plan, and no plan of His can be thwarted. I worked to agree with His plan about my vision. I didn't want to be blind. I wanted to see again, but I knew if God's plan was different, I had better learn to accept it.

"At times I was fearful. At times I didn't think I could wait, but God often reminded me of His provision and care. I'm sure He was able to work in my heart because of your prayers. Thank you."

Cassandra had a hard time not staring over at Tate as he took his seat. Pastor Hurst was speaking again, and she did her best to attend but would have been forced to admit that she was distracted.

He's so special, Father. Thank You for bringing Tate into my life. Help us to follow You. Help us to get to know each other and to know the right time to proceed. You've seen our hearts. You know how anxious we can be. Please help us to trust in Your timing.

The hymnals had been put away. Cassandra missed one entire song. Lizzy checked with her to see if she was all right. She gave a swift nod and bent her mind to paying attention to the sermon.

"My aunt has plans and left as soon as the service ended," Tate told Lizzy after church, "but I have none."

"I'm glad to hear it. We'll plan on your joining us, Tate," she invited, knowing that Cassandra was still inside.

"Thank you." Tate bowed a little and

watched as Morland took Lizzy to her carriage. He watched them for a moment, wishing that he felt more free to be with Cassandra in public. He wasn't put out by always having to visit her at Newcomb, but seeing Morland and Lizzy together made him want more.

I've just been invited to lunch with the Steeles, and I'm complaining, Tate caught himself. *What foolishness. I'm sorry, Father. Help me to see these things for what they are: just moments in a long life — nothing to be concerned about at all.*

Tate walked toward his carriage, knowing he would see Cassandra in a matter of minutes. As Cassandra emerged from the church, her heart knew a moment of indecision when she spotted him and wondered if Lizzy had had a chance to ask him to lunch. Nevertheless, she went to their carriage without stopping.

"Yes," Lizzy said the moment her eyes met Cassandra's. Cassandra laughed about it all the way home.

Newcomb Park

Dear Edward, Henry's letter opened to his brother. Lunch was over, and the others had gone outside.

I'm not sure you should stay away much longer. Morland has become a permanent fixture, and a certain gentleman, whose sight has been restored, is seeing an awful lot of our Cassie. I don't claim that a double wedding will take place, but I shouldn't be surprised to see one long before Christmas. I can't think this is something you would want to miss.

The four of them are playing pall-mall in the yard just now. They wanted me to join, but my aim is dreadful.

I certainly miss you. I do wish you'd come home, but for the first time in many years, I have a yearning to travel. If you plan to return to Africa, I might like to go along. You, of course, can tell me if this interrupts your plans. I will count on your honesty.

Henry heard laughter just then and went to the window. Lizzy had just hit the ball between the wickets and against the stake. Cassandra and Tate were applauding from the side as she held her mallet up in triumph, and Morland was bowing over her hand in homage.

Henry smiled at the sight, and thought, *Come home soon, Edward. We miss you. We need you to celebrate with us for this short time we are here.*

Chapter Seventeen

Tipton

"Why, Marianne," her sister-in-law said as she approached her outside, surprised to see that Marianne hadn't joined the men in archery.

"Hello, Liddy. Come and sit by me." Marianne touched the seat beside her, reiterating her invitation.

"Where are all the children?"

"Catherine is asleep; Sophie is sitting with her; and the rest have gone to visit the horses."

"Do they never get tired of them?" Lydia asked, taking a seat and thinking how good it felt to get off her feet.

"I think not."

"Why don't you have a bow in your hand?"

"Jennings prefers that I not participate."

"Are you getting too good for him?" Lydia teased.

"I'm sure that's it."

Marianne's mild tone caused Lydia to look at her longtime friend. "What's going on?"

Marianne looked right back. "What do you think?"

A moment later Lydia was hugging Marianne, who tried not to laugh loudly.

"We haven't told the children. We want to wait for a time."

"But how are you?"

"I'm very well. Just teary at all moments of the day."

"That's how it was with Catherine. Do you remember?"

"I did as soon as Jennings and my mother reminded me," she said dryly.

"I'm so happy for you. That's three of you now, isn't it? You, Anne, and Judith."

"As far as we know." Marianne's eyes suddenly twinkled. "Unless Palmer knows of others."

Lydia laughed before asking, "Did you hear that Anne has been confined to bedrest again?"

"Yes. Do you know how she's doing?"

"Lizzy Steele visited her and told Judith that her spirits are a bit low, but she's talking about it and working it through."

"Is Weston doing all right? I should think it would be almost as hard on him."

"That's a very good point. I wonder if Palmer or Jennings has called on him recently."

At the moment Palmer, Jennings, and their oldest sons, Frank and Thomas, were all battling on the archery field. But the women would ask the men about Weston. They planned on doing that very thing as soon as they were finished with their game, but the children came back, full of ideas about the pony and trap.

The men were pressed into service, giving rides and entertaining for a time. Before they knew it, the afternoon had sped by, and the Jennings family made ready to leave. With a swiftly shared word, the women decided to speak to their husbands individually and then leave it in their hands.

Henry and Cassandra stared across the carriage at Lizzy, who was fidgeting with her dress, acting as if she were headed to her first ball. She didn't notice their scrutiny for some time, but froze when she did.

"What?" she asked.

"That's what we are wondering: What?"

Lizzy went back to smoothing the folds of fabric in her lap. Her posture tried to say nothing was wrong, but it didn't work.

"Why are you nervous, Lizzy?" Cassandra came out and asked.

"I don't know," she admitted, not even attempting to sit still, "except that I've only met Morland's aunt twice, and I can't recall what she thought of me."

"Has Morland given you no clue?" Henry asked.

"I didn't ask him."

"Well, Mrs Long can't object overly much if we've all been invited to lunch."

Lizzy nodded, but her heart was having a hard time agreeing. They arrived at Richmond long before she was ready, and the moment Morland saw her, he read what her siblings had seen in the carriage.

"No one is going to bite you," he said softly, smiling a little when he wanted to laugh.

Still in the foyer, Lizzy frowned at him crossly.

"For a man who very recently didn't appear to know I existed, you have certainly learned to read me well."

Morland only smiled a little more, which drew another frown.

"Welcome," Penelope Long greeted them, coming to her feet just long enough for them to join her in the main salon.

"Please sit down. Lunch will be served shortly, but we'll wait in here. My, Henry, you are looking very well. How old are you these days?"

"I am 20 and 9, Mrs Long."

"No wife?"

"No, mum."

"Well, you have time," she told him, thinking it a comfort. "And you, Cassandra. I had forgotten your red hair. I rather like it."

Cassandra smiled at her.

"Morland tells me that a gentleman has been calling on you."

Cassandra nodded even as she blushed.

"Ah, yes. A little color to your face gives you away. Now, Lizzy," she switched without warning, "you haven't been to see me in a while, and I want this to be the first of many times. Do you think you can manage that?"

"Yes, Mrs Long. I should enjoy visiting you."

"Even if Morland is not in attendance?" she teased, and Lizzy smiled at her. "Come and help me, Morland. We shall feed these friends before they grow weak and faint on my carpet."

Lizzy learned in a hurry that she had panicked over nothing. Mrs Long was delighted to have them, and although strongly opinionated on many subjects, very willing to offer her hospitality and friendship. Lizzy could see why Morland adored her. She was swiftly on her way to loving Aunt Penelope as well.

Pembroke

Cassandra's Tuesday was full with lunch at Richmond and dinner at Pembroke. The evening started with a tour of that grand home. Both Harriet and Tate walked her through and stood back in pleasure when she spotted the stained glass upstairs.

"Oh, my," she said softly. "I had no idea."

"My Uncle Thorpe's favorite window, wasn't it, Aunt Harriet?"

"Yes. He loved it."

"I can see why."

From the upstairs hallway, they went to Harriet's bedroom. She had a balcony that overlooked the gardens at the rear of the house, and for a long time Cassandra stood frozen in place.

"I don't know if I would ever leave this spot," she decided. "I would have all my meals served here, receive all my guests in this place, and simply sit here all day."

Harriet laughed with pleasure and turned to show her something else, but Tate bent and whispered in her ear, "I think I can arrange that."

Cassandra blushed at his warm tone as well as his words and hurried after Harriet as she began to point out the finer details of a painting back out in the hallway. If Harriet noticed Cassandra's crimson face, she ignored it and continued the tour.

When Cassandra had seen everything, she was so overwhelmed that at the start of the meal she was rather quiet. In truth she lived in a lovely home and had done so her entire life, but Pembroke was special. Not as large and grand as Brown Manor, one of the grandest homes in the area, Pembroke was nevertheless so architecturally lovely and perfectly placed that she thought she'd never seen the like.

She was still thinking on it at the end of the meal when they retired to the music room, and Harriet began to play. Tate and Cassandra had claimed opposite ends of the long sofa as they watched Harriet at the piano. She played for the better part of an hour before taking a break, and as soon as she did, Tate invited Cassandra to play.

"I was serious when I told you that I can't compare to your aunt."

"But it would still be nice to hear you," Tate argued.

Cassandra's look was long-suffering. Harriet caught it.

"Do you enjoy playing, Cassandra?"

"Not overly."

The other two occupants of the room were so surprised by this honest admission that it took a moment for them to respond. When they did, it was with laughter.

Cassandra felt herself blushing again and wishing she didn't have such fair skin.

"We won't press you any longer, Cassandra," Harriet vowed. "Will we, Tate?"

But that gentleman didn't agree.

"How can I go along with that when it causes her to blush so nicely?"

"Oh, Tate, leave the poor girl alone," Harriet admonished him good-naturedly as she went to ring for tea.

"You were quiet during dinner," Tate said, his eyes watchful.

"A little overwhelmed, I think."

"With me or the house?"

"Maybe a little of both." Cassandra looked at him. "I wonder how long it will take for me to become accustomed to your being able to see."

"I'm still in wonder," Tate admitted, casting his eyes around the room. "I couldn't wait to see my Bible, the out-doors, the sun, and the stars again." Tate looked back at his guest. "And that was all before I wanted to see you."

"That was a nice thing to say."

"I have nice thoughts about you."

"That's funny," Cassandra teased. "I find I have rather lovely thoughts about you."

"Until I want you to play the piano."

"Why is that so important?" she demanded, her face displaying chagrin all over again.

"Anything you do is special. I thought you were just being modest."

Cassandra's look was skeptical. "I think you will find," she admitted, "that I am very much who I appear to be. There's nothing terribly hidden about me."

"That's reassuring, but what you've just told me is that I can plan to see you blush every day, that you're going to run if something scares you, and that large, beautiful homes and tall, sighted men overwhelm you a bit."

Cassandra just kept from laughing.

"I think that sums me up quite well."

"In that case, I'll tell you about me. I love to see you blush; I'll come after you every time; and I hope someday that you'll very much love large, lovely homes, and tall, sighted men. Or at least one tall, sighted man."

Cassandra looked into his blue eyes, such a lucid color that she wanted to stare for hours. Tate looked right back, knowing he would never in his life meet another woman who would so thoroughly capture his heart. She was beyond lovely to him and so sweet that she melted his heart with nearly every glance.

There was so much he wanted to say, but Harriet was coming back. It didn't occur to him until just then that she could have requested tea from the music room. Tate knew he would have to thank her for giving them a few minutes alone.

The Manse

"Frederick, why are you here?"

"Because Jane ran and fetched me. Are you all right?"

Judith took a moment to think and then realized she was lying on the living room floor.

"I bent over too swiftly," she said rather dazedly. It was coming back now. "I don't think I actually fainted. I just felt dizzy and then lay down."

"But your eyes were shut," Jane said, her

white face peeking over her father's shoulder.

Judith smiled at her. "It was the first time I'd stopped moving all day, Jane. I think my body thought it was time to sleep."

Frederick helped his wife to her feet and then into a chair. Her color was good, and she was very steady, something he told his heart to emulate.

"You look shaken, Frederick."

"I am. I had the most horrible thoughts, all flashing through my mind in a matter of seconds."

Judith put a hand to his cheek, and he spoke again. "You're worried about me, and I thought you might be dead."

"No, I'm made of sterner stuff than that, Frederick."

"Nevertheless, you shall retire to bed, and I will find help until Phoebe has returned."

Judith had no argument. A rest in bed sounded lovely, and with someone coming, she knew the children would be well looked after.

Her husband close behind her, Judith took the stairs slowly. When she was settled under a light coverlet, Frederick sat beside her.

"Dizzy?"

"No."

"Not even with love for me?"

Judith laughed, and he bent to kiss her.

"Is it selfish to want it all, Judith?"

"What's that?"

"You and the baby?"

"I was asking the same thing. I was asking God to let me be here for you and the children and still meet this little one."

Frederick took her hand in his and held it tightly.

"We'll choose to trust, Judith. Even if we feel as though we're in the belly of the fish, we'll choose to trust."

Not willing to be parted from her, Frederick stayed close, holding her hand as they talked. He sat on the edge of the bed until she fell asleep. From there he stood next to the bed, looked down on the wife he loved, and asked God for the desire of his heart.

Newcomb Park

Cassandra was in the garden again. The mid-June flowers were a riot of color, and she was as tempted as a child in a confectioner's shop. She was working along, not expecting to see Tate for another hours, when she noticed he was rounding the house and coming her way at a fierce pace. She smiled until he neared, giving her a clear view of his face.

"Tate, what is it?"

"I must away to London. I don't have time to give you details, but Pierrepont has cheated me." Tate's face grew red as he burst forth, "My man Banks in London has just alerted me! I must be off."

"Tate," Cassandra called to him as he was turning away. "Is there nothing I can do?"

"No." He nearly ground his teeth, his agitation clearly evident. "How could this happen?" he asked under his breath. "I trusted him, and now behind my back —" Tate cut off, barely glancing at Cassandra. "I must go," he growled.

"Tate." Cassandra's voice stopped him. "I'm so sorry. I hope everything is all right with us."

Tate's face darkened a bit more. "Nothing is all right," he said curtly, this time moving on his way, his long legs covering the distance in little time.

Cassandra did not call to him again, nor did he look her way. She had never seen him in such a state. Even after his vision returned, she had known only his kindness and attentiveness. Cassandra was stunned. Unable to move from the spot where he had left her, she was still standing with her basket 20 minutes later when Henry found her.

"Cassie, did I see Tate?" he asked, looking about.

"Yes, but he's gone."

"I thought he was staying for dinner."

"He's gone to the city."

Henry finally looked at his sister's face.

"I wish to speak to you, Cassandra. Let us go into my study."

It wasn't the most inviting room in the house, but only wanting privacy, that never occurred to Henry. Cassandra might have preferred the parlor or a sitting room, but right now she didn't notice. She looked across the desk at her brother, having taken a wooden chair, and spoke softly.

"Tate's business manager has cheated him. He's only just received the news."

"And he's left for London?"

"Yes."

Cassandra gave a full rundown of what had occurred in the yard, and ended with, "I'm so confused, Henry," she admitted, looking a little lost. "Just last night he intimated again that he wished to make me his wife. He followed me all the way to Bath."

Cassandra paused. "It might have been selfish of me, Henry. He so surprised me; maybe I shouldn't have mentioned us, but today he was a man I've never seen before."

As Henry's mind raced, one thought came rushing to the fore. *Tate was so trusting of God concerning his eyesight, but now that money is the issue, he's forgotten God is still in charge.* Before he could give voice to his thought, Cassandra went on.

"He was so trusting about his eyes, but now he's fallen apart over the loss of some money. I can understand his concern, but he was so distraught that it seemed as though we could no longer have a future."

Henry was on the verge of asking whether she had voiced this to Tate but stopped. He had left others in charge in the past and did not plan to repeat that action.

"Cassandra," Henry began, taking charge. "I want you to give me Mr Tate's address. I wish to write him a letter."

Cassandra bit her lip. The old Henry would never have done this. Suddenly this new Henry was a little scary to her.

"Go on now," he said gently. "Get word to Mrs Thorpe or whatever you need to do, and get that address."

Still not certain how she felt about that matter, Cassandra did as she was told. Harriet had given her a note one time that had been on Tate's stationery, his London address printed at the top. The note was in her room. She found it for her brother and then at his request waited in the study while he wrote.

"Read this," he said after some time, coming out of his chair and inviting Cassandra to be seated. She sat in the overly large leather chair and read the following:

Mr Tate,
Cassandra has told me of your dilemma. I am sorry. I'm equally sorry that I am forced to write this letter to you. It has not passed my notice that though you trusted God for your eyesight, you have had an entirely different view concerning your finances.

Cassandra Steele does not live in this world unloved and unprotected. I can't allow you to see my sister or have any contact with her without first applying to me. It is unacceptable that such a situation would cause you to act in such disregard for her feelings. She was very shaken by having your attentions on Tuesday evening in your aunt's home and then receiving your harsh disregard of her feelings some 24 hours later.

It gives me great pain to communicate

this to you, and I hope that by the time you receive this you will have come to your senses and repented. Does not the God who planned your blindness also have say over your business dealings? Even if you are left penniless, is He not always in charge?

I am praying for you. I hope you will find things not as grim as they first appeared, but most of all I hope that you will regain the trust you once had. My sister's feelings are not based on a life of luxury she hopes to have with you. She has, however, been under the impression that you have a strong regard for her. Now we are both left to wondering.

I am sending this letter on to you, but as of this writing I am planning on coming to London myself. If we should miss each other, I will warn you again. Although I have not forgotten that you are my brother in Christ, you are not to have contact with Cassandra, either by letter or in person, until you have my permission to do so.

Sincerely,
Henry J. Steele

Tears filled Cassandra's eyes as she finished. Henry saw them and came to her. "I'm sorry, Cassie," he said with a hand to her shoulder. "I would have had it very different."

"I know, Henry. Will you really go to see him?"

"Yes. It's late today, but I shall leave in the morning."

Cassandra felt a tear slip down her cheek. "What if he doesn't wish to see me again?"

"Then we will have all been fooled by his nature, and it will be some time before the pain abates — yours most of all."

Cassandra thanked him, her heart feeling bruised all over. She left the study and went in search of Lizzy, only to remember that she had gone to see Anne Weston.

Making an effort to remember that God was at work in her life as well, she tried not to feel so utterly desolate. Thinking that a good hard cry might be in order, she retired to her room to read her Bible and then indulge herself. God, however, had other ideas. She read in David's psalms for a time, read of his pain, and then fell asleep. By the time she woke up, Lizzy was there to comfort her.

"Talk to me, Lizzy. Tell me something interesting."

"All right," Lizzy agreed, trying to think fast.

Henry had been gone for several hours, and the women suddenly found themselves at loose ends.

"Mr Palmer was visiting Weston when I arrived at Anne's yesterday."

"How nice for him. Is he doing well?"

"He seems to be very well, glad for the company."

"I never did ask how Anne was doing."

"Much better. Her spirits are greatly lifted. She's so excited to meet this baby and doesn't want to do anything to jeopardize that."

"It sounds as though she's being wise."

"That she is."

Silence fell long before Cassandra was ready. Lizzy's heart ached with this new turn of events, but she wanted to be strong for her sister. She almost hoped that Morland wouldn't come. He would be a comfort to Lizzy, but his presence would also magnify Cassandra's loss.

"Let's go to Collingbourne," Lizzy suggested. "I don't have a shopping list, but we could go to Gray's for tea and then window-shop a bit."

Cassandra didn't reply.

"Don't like the idea?"

"I'm afraid I'll think of Tate and not be the best company."

"We won't worry about that. We'll have such fun looking around that we won't cry until we're on the way home."

Cassandra laughed a little, thinking it just like Lizzy to have a plan. Gathering their things in the next few minutes, they ordered the carriage for town. They'd only just left when they had a visitor, one they wouldn't see until they arrived home.

Chapter Eighteen

Well, this is just fine! Edward Steele thought good-naturedly after Jasper had greeted him, given him the news of the family's whereabouts, and left him in the empty foyer. *I'm home after how many months away, and there's no one here to greet me.*

The second youngest Steele sibling smiled and shook his head, knowing that his lack of communication had caused this. Morland had no more left Africa when Edward realized he missed his family. He wasn't long in following, so with just a few stops along the way, he was now standing in Collingbourne and no one knew of it.

With another smile, this one a little more mischievous, he headed to the stairs to see his room. From there he planned to station himself in the sitting room with a book. When his family returned, he would be lounging in complete comfort, looking as though he'd been there all month.

Collingbourne

"Now I know you're upset, Cassie," Lizzy said, peeking over her shoulder at the hat she was holding. "What a horrid hat. You're not really thinking of buying it."

"No, but the ribbon caught my eye."

"It's a dreadful color, Cassie. What are you thinking?"

Lizzy's tone was Cassandra's undoing. She giggled a little before she could stop herself.

"Hello, Miss Elizabeth. Hello, Miss Cassandra. Is there anything I can show you?"

"We're browsing today, Mrs North. Thank you."

Lizzy turned Cassandra away before she could speak.

"I don't care how sad your heart is, buying a hat that you shouldn't wear to your grave is not going to help."

"I was thinking of Mrs North." Cassandra's voice was melancholy, her brow puckered in a small frown. "I'm sure she would like to make a sale."

"It's time for tea," Lizzy declared, wanting to laugh. "Before you go into total depression, I must get you out of here."

Planning to leave on the spot, Lizzy was

340

surprised to find something that did catch her eye. Cassandra spotted it at the same moment. A bolt of dress material, not quite ready for display, sat off to one side of the doorway. The color, a rich green, would have been lovely on both women.

Before they thought of tea again, they had purchased enough for two items. Cassandra planned on a dress, and Lizzy would have hers lined for a spencer jacket. Not until they were relaxing in Gray's, tea and cakes before them, did Lizzy mention Cassandra's behavior.

"Pathetic," she teased her, eyes rolling.

"Well, Mrs North did have a sale, so that makes it all right."

That this would be Cassandra's logic only made Lizzy want to laugh again. She tucked into her teacup and worked to squelch the urge. She had thought they might browse all day but changed her mind. As soon as they finished, they headed for Newcomb Park.

Newcomb Park

"Edward!" Morland said with surprise before clasping his friend in a great hug. "When did you arrive?"

"Just an hour ago." Edward hugged

Morland in return. "Only to learn that my family has fled the nest."

"Is no one home?"

"No. And I desperately need someone to tell me why Henry would go to London."

"All right, but you'd better sit down. It's rather complicated."

Morland explained the situation to Edward, whose heart was very affected for his younger sister. That Cassandra had finally found love was wonderful to him, but not like this.

"I suspect that Lizzy got her out of the house for a diversion."

Edward nodded in agreement. "Jasper said they went to Collingbourne."

"But tell me, why are you home?"

"You'd no more left Africa when I realized I missed the family. I was close on your heels, but I made several stops en route. So tell me, when do you and Lizzy wed?"

"I don't know. I haven't asked the lady yet."

Edward's face was comical. "Don't tell me she's not interested!"

"Oh, she's interested, but we're enjoying this time."

Edward grinned in his engaging way. "You're one in a million, Morland. I hope Lizzy knows that."

"Well, you can tell her if you think she doubts."

A noise at the door brought both men to their feet.

"Hide!" Morland commanded, even as Edward was taking flight, concealing himself behind a long drapery.

"Hello, Morland," Cassandra greeted just seconds later, still removing her silk bonnet. "Have you waited long?"

"No. Where's Lizzy?"

"Just behind me."

"Did you shop?" Morland asked, hoping he didn't sound as full of laughter as he felt.

"A little. Lizzy," Cassandra had called, turning to the door. "Morland is here."

"Oh, this is a nice surprise."

"I'm glad you think so, but I have another."

"This sounds interesting."

"Should I leave?" Cassandra asked.

"Not at all. I think you'll both enjoy it."

The women looked at each other. That Morland was enjoying himself was very evident.

"Come right over here and sit down," Morland directed. "That's it. Good, good. Eyes closed."

"Morland, what in the world . . ."

"Eyes closed, Lizzy. Very good. Okay," he said, elongating the word, "you can open them."

A moment later Morland watched with pleasure as Edward reunited with his sisters. There was no halting the laughter that followed; Edward was always so fun. They hugged him, cried a little, and hugged him again.

"How could we be in town when you arrived? How could we have missed your coach?"

"I don't know, but I was dreadfully put out. I pouted until Morland arrived. Good thing you've had sense enough to keep him around, Lizzy."

"You haven't changed a bit," she accused him. "Although you are tan. Was it dreadfully hot?"

"Yes. I did so enjoy the coolness of England's clime as we drew near."

"Henry's away," Cassandra informed him.

"Morland explained."

Cassandra nodded, her smile becoming a bit more tentative.

"So, what plans do we have for the evening?" Edward asked. "Do tell me that we're going to have a leisurely meal and play cards in quiet repose — Cassandra the

Great as my partner, hmm?"

Both of his sisters laughed. He was always such a charming card. Lizzy was happy to tell him that they would do that very thing, and even happier to invite Morland to join them.

"At the end of the day," Cassandra said from the corner of Lizzy's bed, "diversions or not, I still ache to see Alexander Tate."

"I'm sure you do." Lizzy's voice was filled with compassion. "It wasn't my plan to distract you to forgetfulness, Cassie, but to make the day go by more swiftly."

"And I'm thankful for your efforts, Lizzy. I had a lovely time. Edward's arrival was the icing on top."

Lizzy didn't comment, even though she agreed. Her mind was still on Tate.

"What is it that troubles you the most, Cassie? Are you angry with Tate?"

"No, not at all. I've never seen Henry like he was. I almost pity Tate having to face him. He was fierce, Lizzy. But above all else, I don't want Tate hurt again. He's not been horseback riding or even ridden in a carriage much since the accident. I think how difficult it would be to lose his vision again after such a short time. I want him to be safe."

"And that's why you're not angry with him," Lizzy concluded.

"Yes. I will admit that I am hurt by the things he said, but even that is tempered by my compassion."

"And what of your own heart? Have you care for that?"

Cassandra smiled a little and shook her head in wonder.

"What a funny creature I am, Lizzy. First I run to Bath out of fear for my heart, and then I forgive a man when he's offered no apology out of regard for his heart."

"What do you pray for him?" Lizzy wished to know.

"I pray for the things Henry wrote in his letter — mostly that Tate would remember that God is still in control and he can trust Him."

"And for yourself?"

"The very same prayer."

Cassandra leaned now and kissed Lizzy goodnight. She slipped out the door and to her own bedroom, ready for sleep.

Pembroke

"I was not aware that you were still in Collingbourne, Mrs Thorpe. Your note

346

was a great surprise," Cassandra told her after the older woman had given her a hug.

"Did you think I'd gone to London?"

"Yes."

"Tate was not at his best," Harriet stated simply. "I felt it wise to let him go alone."

Cassandra nodded, realizing that this lady would have no idea how her last conversation with Tate had gone.

"Shall we go to the veranda? It's such a nice day out."

"That would be fine."

Cassandra felt herself relaxing. She had arrived at Pembroke, dread filling her, until she understood that Harriet Thorpe was only continuing the friendship they had begun. She didn't even ask if Tate had stopped to see her. In turn, Cassandra did not mention it.

"My brother Edward has arrived home."

"He was in Africa?"

"Yes. It's wonderful to see him."

"Has he told you all about it?"

"Bits and pieces. He's something of a character, so we have to do a little puzzling together. It sounds as though he had a marvelous time."

"Does Morland know he's home?"

"Yes. He was actually at the house ahead of Lizzy and me."

"And have Lizzy and Morland made any plans?"

"No," Cassandra told her, knowing she would be discreet.

"I would ask the same question of you and Tate, but I think I'll know that even before either of you tell me."

Cassandra only smiled and took a sip of water. That her heart felt like a strong hand was wrapped around it squeezing tightly did not show on her face. Cassandra was relieved to have Harriet change the subject.

They visited for a time, and Cassandra even ended up staying for lunch. She was attentive to all of Harriet's comments on Tate, and Harriet took her lack of words on the man as shyness. When she left, her heart breathed another sigh of relief. She hadn't broken down or been questioned by her hostess.

Harriet saw her off, thinking that shy girls were her favorites. *She didn't even ask me about him,* Harriet thought, truly impressed. *Cassandra: a sweet wife who is at times a little shy. She is just what Tate needs.*

London

Henry had not been to London in some time, but many of the sights and sounds were familiar. It was quite warm, and therefore not a popular time to be in the city, but the streets were still busy. Henry spent a good deal of time looking out the window at neighborhoods previously unknown to him. The instructions they had been given to Tate's home, however, seemed to be leading them in the right direction.

As he'd been asking himself for many miles, Henry wondered again if he'd been too harsh on the man. He had only heard Cassandra's side of the story — not that he didn't trust her — but not until after he'd sent the letter did he put himself in Tate's shoes.

It was Henry's hope that he would never grow so agitated and overreact, but in truth the Steele family had never been dealt such a financial blow, and he could only surmise as to his response.

The coach lurched and moved on its way. Henry felt as though he'd been traveling for weeks. But at least they'd made it to town. The wait to see how Tate was doing would soon be over.

Preston Manor

Tate laid his head back against his desk chair and prayed for wisdom. With every inquiry he learned of more deception in Pierrepont's dealings. It was starting to look as though he'd been planning things for a long time. The business manager could not have known that his employer was going to experience a fall and be confined to the country, but he had certainly wasted no time taking advantage when it happened.

And always in the back of his mind — no matter what he was facing at the moment — was Cassandra. Tate took a few minutes of luxury to fully think of her and pray for her, but Hastings interrupted him when he knocked softly on the door and entered. Tate sat up, his face showing the concern and fatigue that filled him.

"What is it, Hastings?" Even his voice sounded tired.

"Mr Steele is here, sir."

"Bring him right in. Thank you."

Tate was on his feet when Henry entered but had no energy to move around the desk. Henry, on the other hand, came right to him and shook his hand.

"How are things, Tate?" the older of the two asked.

"In my heart, things are all right — much better — but the situation is not good. Pierrepont has commandeered many of my holdings, selling them and secreting the money away. But I don't wish to discuss that, Henry, until you read my letter." Tate reached for an envelope that lay on his desk. "I was getting ready to send this to you when I received your missive." This said, Tate handed him the letter. "Please read it now."

A fine leather chair sat opposite Tate's desk. Henry made himself comfortable and began to read.

My foolishness in leaving Collingbourne in such a state pains me deeply. Not for myself, but for Cassandra and my Aunt Harriet. I calmed down enough to realize what I'd done by the time I reached London, but you were so right; my actions have been reprehensible.

Please do not cut me off from your family, and most especially Cassandra. Please give the enclosed letter to her. I would even prefer that you read it before doing so. I love your sister. I lost sight of that for a few hours, but it's true. If you and Cassandra are willing to give me another chance, I will not disappoint you again. My financial losses are great, but what are they compared to the loss of your friendship and Cassandra's love?

I await your word on this matter. I await it prayerfully, in hope that you can forgive me.

> Most sincerely,
> A. Tate

The moment Henry finished his letter, he opened his sister's. He started to read, but stopped and folded it again.

"Thank you for your letter, Tate. I am very willing to continue our friendship, but I feel that your words to Cassie are private. Why don't you give me the gist of the letter rather than my reading it."

"Thank you," Tate said, actually feeling emotionally spent. "I say some of the very things I speak of in your letter, and then I tell her I love her and ask her if she can forgive me. If she can, I ask that we continue our time of courtship and make plans for the future.

"Just so you know," Tate went on in case Henry was tempted to speak, "my income *has* been affected by all of this, but I can still support your sister and see to her every need."

"I didn't doubt that, Tate, but you must know by now that Cassie doesn't yearn for jewels and a life of luxury. If she's surrounded by believing family members who love her, she is most content."

Tate nodded, more tired than he'd ever been in his life but also experiencing great relief.

"She is a treasure, Henry. I have known that for some time."

"That she is. So!" All at once, Henry got down to business. "I probably don't have as many connections in London as you do, but is there anything I can do to help?"

Tate took the next hour to outline some of what had gone on. He'd been blinded the previous November but had not moved to Collingbourne until January. In the months he was there convalescing, property had been sold, and the money was unaccounted for. Capital stock in several companies had also been sold. Pierrepont had tampered with account books and business ledgers.

It wasn't hopeless. Tate still had income. But the shock of it all still had Tate reeling a bit. Henry heard him out and then introduced his plan.

"I need to send word to Newcomb Park that I have arrived in London and will be here for a time. I have an old friend whom I haven't seen in years. I think he might be able to help."

"Thank you, Henry. I hope you will stay

here. I have plenty of room, and I think we can make you very comfortable."

"I accept. I'll write that letter and then pay a visit to Edmond Ellenborough."

"You know Ellenborough?" Tate referred to a detective in London, one whose reputation for finding people was well known.

"Yes," Henry smiled. "If he can't track down Pierrepont, I don't know who can."

Some of Tate's fatigue drained away. A plan of any kind was a step in the right direction. It might turn out that Ellenborough would not be able to help him at all, but at least he could say they had tried.

Tate supplied stationery, a pen, and ink. The moment Henry finished his letter for home, the men were on their way.

Chapter Nineteen

Newcomb Park

Both Steele sisters were on hand when Henry's letter arrived. As they stood in the foyer reading it, Edward joined them.

"From Henry?" he guessed.

Lizzy passed it to him, and both women watched as he read.

Dear Lizzy and Cassie,
I will be in London for a time. I am staying at Preston Manor with Tate. His findings were grim, but we are attempting to locate his business manager and put a halt to his deceptions. If you find you have need of me, contact me here.

Cassie, enclosed is a letter for you from Tate. He has my permission to contact you. I shall see you all soon.

With warmest regards,
Henry

"Did you read the letter, Cassie?" Edward asked.

"It wasn't in the envelope. I don't know what happened to it."

"Let me see it."

Hoping his sisters had missed something, Edward looked but found nothing. He looked into Cassandra's eyes, wishing with all his heart that he could somehow cause this letter to materialize.

"It does say Tate has permission to contact you," Lizzy pointed out. "Is that not a good sign, Cassie?"

"I think it might be."

"But you're not sure?"

"Well, it's a bit complicated. I was just asking myself what I should do if a letter arrived from Tate before I knew if Henry had spoken to him, because he'd told Tate not to contact me without permission. I want to hear from him, of course, but not against Henry's wishes.

"We know that Henry has spoken with him, but maybe Tate only gained permission to write and tell me he won't be back."

"If he felt that way, why would Henry stay and help him?"

Cassandra's face was thoughtful.

"That's a good question. It would seem

that Henry's staying to help him is a good sign."

"We will just assume that it is, Cassie," Edward declared. "In the meantime, write Henry at Tate's address and tell him there was no letter."

Cassandra looked uncertain about this, and Edward made it an order.

"Do it now."

"Why?" she argued with him.

"Because it will give you something to do besides wonder and speculate."

Cassandra nodded slowly, thinking it couldn't hurt — or could it?

"Does that make me seem a bit anxious?"

"Cassie, you are anxious," Edward pointed out.

"But I shouldn't be."

This stopped her older brother in his tracks. That Henry was not the only one to change in his absence was swiftly coming to light for him. He had never been in the habit of babying Cassandra the way Charlotte and Lizzy had, but he had coddled her nonetheless.

"I'm sorry, Edward." Cassandra was contrite. "You're trying to help, and I'm making it tough on you."

"No need to apologize, Cassie. You're

certainly correct about not being anxious, but I don't think it's wrong to distract yourself either."

Cassandra suddenly saw the point he'd been attempting to make and excused herself. Both Lizzy and Edward watched her head to the stairway.

"Do you truly think it's a good sign, Edward?" his older sister asked.

"I haven't seen Henry in many months, and yet I know my brother. He traveled, something he is not fond of, all the way to London to confront a man on Cassie's behalf, and now he's staying to help him out. I may not know *this* Henry very well, but I'm still taking all of that as not just a good sign but as a miracle."

Lizzy smiled. "He certainly has changed."

"I can hardly wait to find out for myself."

Cassandra's siblings suddenly found themselves in need of their own distractions. They went their separate ways, prayerful for Henry and Tate in London but trying not to dwell on the situation overly much.

London

Ellenborough had not been in on Saturday, which is why Henry's coach could

358

be seen taking him toward Ellenborough's office on Monday morning. This was a more familiar part of London for the man from Collingbourne. For this reason and several others, his mind didn't dwell on his surroundings but was once again on the service at Tate's church the morning before. Henry had been very pleased by the whole experience.

Pastor Annesley had the congregation studying in the book of 1 Peter. He'd not covered many verses, but what he'd shared had been insightful and helpful to Henry. Henry knew Tate loved his sister; he'd known it long before the younger man had voiced such thoughts. Had Henry any doubts about the man's character, his love for Cassandra wouldn't have meant a thing. Also now knowing the type of church he chose to worship and fellowship in gave him even more hope of his sister's future happiness.

"I never did ask you, Henry — how do you know Ellenborough?"

Henry brought his attention to the inside of the carriage, to Tate, the coach's other occupant.

"I was in school with his younger brother."

"How old is this man?"

"I'm not exactly certain. He's at least ten years ahead of me, if not fifteen. He was long out of school by the time William and I went through."

"And do you still have contact with his brother?"

"No, I'm afraid that's a rather tragic story. William is dead. In fact, it was his brother's mysterious death that sent Ellenborough into detective work."

"Did he ever solve the case?"

"Not to my knowledge."

Tate fell silent then, working to take it in. Henry Steele was turning out to be vastly different than he had imagined. He wasn't without his peculiarities, such as the way he would fall silent for long stretches of time, but Tate was coming to genuinely admire him.

"Here we are," Henry said when the coach pulled up. The two men stepped onto the street, and Henry led the way to the door of a dark, small-looking office. A man looked up from his position behind a desk the moment they stepped in, his brows rising in question.

"Is Ellenborough in?"

"He is. Do you have an appointment?"

"I do not. I would like you to tell him that Henry Steele is here."

It was not said unkindly or with any force, but the man rose without question.

He knocked softly on an interior door and slipped inside. Almost no time passed before the man was back and inviting Henry and Tate to enter.

"Henry Steele." Ellenborough met him in the middle of the room. "How many years has it been?"

"Too many, Ellenborough. How are you?"

"I am very well. In fact, I was thinking about you not six months ago. Do you know, I've never solved William's murder."

"I'm sorry to hear that; truly I am."

"Well, come in," the detective invited, even as Henry did the honors. The moment the two men met, Ellenborough took his seat behind a large, messy desk and sat back as if he had all the time in the world.

"What can I do for you, Steele?"

Henry gave an abbreviated version of Tate's situation and then waited to hear that the man was too busy or didn't take those types of cases. The secretary and the cluttered atmosphere of the entire office reminded Henry that this man was no longer just the older brother of an old friend.

"Did you say Pierrepont?"

"Yes."

"First name?"

"Charles."

"And he was your business manager, Mr Tate?"

"For many years."

"You seem surprised, Ellenborough," Henry commented.

"I am. I've only just heard from another man — Plunkett of Chelsea. Plunkett claims that his business consultant has disappeared with some assets. His name is also Charles Pierrepont."

Tate had all he could do not to put his hand to his head. Had all of this been staring him in the face and had he missed it? Had his vision been of so little use to him even before the accident? Could Pierrepont have been that good at deceiving all of them?

"I take it you want me to find the man?"

"Yes, very much."

Ellenborough pulled a sheet of paper toward him and began to write. He asked Tate for names — correctly spelled — addresses, a bit of personal history, and details that included dates of employment and Tate's accident. But when he asked for the whole story from Tate, he sat back and listened without interruption.

When Tate finished, Ellenborough was quiet, thoughtful. Tate took his cue from Henry and said nothing, but he felt his body tensing, moisture beading his upper lip.

"I'll look into it," Ellenborough finally answered.

"Thank you," Tate said, feeling he could breathe again.

The men didn't stay any longer. Ellenborough told Henry to visit again soon, Tate thanked the man, and they made their exit.

"I can't thank you enough," Tate said once they were both back in the carriage.

"Well, let us hope he can find some leads."

That Henry didn't want to be given any credit was obvious. Tate let him have his silence, wondering if there was anything else he should be doing. Even without voicing it, Tate thought he knew the answer: Trust God first and then trust Mr Ellenborough to do his job. It was no coincidence that Henry knew him. God would use whomever He chose to accomplish His purposes.

Newcomb Park

I won't tell You, Lord, that I must have this man, but I will confess that I think he's wonderful. I know he had those moments when he

363

was angry and upset, but I would want him to forgive me in such a situation. Can I offer any less?

Thank You for Your plan. Help me to wait on it. I could rush ahead easily. I could pace and be vexed with You, but that's foolish, and I've been foolish enough in the relationship with Tate to last a lifetime.

For a moment Cassandra was quiet. She had written to Henry as Edward had suggested, but now she just wanted to be alone with her thoughts. She stayed in her room, the door shut, and tried to remember some of the verses from Sunday. She ended up opening her Bible but had more to pray about.

When I think of the way You are able to work, I feel amazed. I know Tate did not enjoy his fall or the long days in darkness, but had You never brought him to this place, I might never have met him. Thank You. Thank You for seeing every need so clearly.

Please be with Morland and Lizzy, Father, Cassandra suddenly remembered to pray. *I want my sister's happiness, and I don't wish her to hold back on account of Tate and me. Help her to proceed in You, believing I will be fine.*

And in that moment Cassandra knew she would be. She wasn't overjoyed at the thought of never seeing Tate again, but she knew that God would comfort her heart and give her all she needed.

She cried then, tears of mourning and tears of letting go of her pride and wanting her own way, but also tears of thankfulness that no matter what the outcome, she didn't have to go through it alone.

The Manse

"And you haven't heard from Henry since Monday?"

"No."

"That must be a bit hard." Judith's voice was filled with compassion.

Cassandra smiled. "As you can see, Judith, it is really you who's doing the rescuing today, not the other way around."

The pastor's wife shook her head with a rueful smile. "We'll see how weary you are after a day of reading to the children and going on outings. You may change your mind about that rescue."

Cassandra only laughed. She was looking forward to the experience, even when the two youngest children joined them and John looked uncertain about his mother's departure up the stairs.

"Shall we read a book, John and Margaret, or would you rather play outside for a time?"

"A book."

"Outside."

Cassandra surprised them both into smiling when she burst out laughing and suggested, "Why don't we read outside?"

They were all for this, and not many minutes later the three trooped out of doors, coverlet and book in hand.

With little pomp or ceremony, Cassandra settled the counterpane under a large, shady tree, sat down, and opened the book. John sat beside her, ready to listen, but Margaret kept to her feet.

"I thought we were going to play."

"You can, Margaret. When John and I have read awhile, we'll probably join you. Or you can sit with us for a time, and we'll all play later."

Cassandra could read the indecision in Margaret's eyes but didn't wait for an answer. She began to read to the little boy beside her and didn't even look in Margaret's direction when she joined them. Wanting to be compassionate, however, she kept the reading time short and soon suggested they play a game.

"Can we play blind man's bluff?" John wished to know.

"That's not as fun with only three people," Margaret told him.

The children began to discuss this, Margaret even suggesting another game, but Cassandra heard little of it. The words "blind man" were still stuck firmly in her mind. They conjured up images of a man no longer blind but still as dear, and many questions about where he was and whether his mind was as preoccupied with her as hers was with him.

Newcomb Park

Henry was so tired of speaking, he thought his head would burst with pain and pressure. Lizzy and Edward had been full of questions, seemingly dozens of them, and in all of this, he still hadn't seen Cassandra. When they paused for breath, he ventured a question of his own.

"Where is Cassie?"

"She's at the Hursts for the day, giving Judith some rest."

Henry stood. "I'm going to lie down before she comes home."

That he needed some time alone was clear. Brother and sister were quiet as he walked from the room and for several minutes after he left. Cassie would be home in a few hours. Did they tell her all that Henry had to say or leave that to the brother who was exhausted in his efforts toward communication?

The Manse

"How were they?" Judith asked Cassandra at the end of the day. The children were in the dining room with a small meal, and Judith was walking Cassandra to the door.

"Very well. We had a marvelous time. Judith?"

"Yes."

"We don't know each other extremely well, but may I tell you something?"

"Certainly."

"I think Margaret fears you're going to die."

"Did she say as much?"

"No, but she questioned me about my mother, and when I told her she was dead, she asked more questions and was very relieved that she hadn't died in childbirth. I could see the rest all over her face. And as soon as she knew that, she didn't want to know anything else about my mother. She changed the questioning to life at Newcomb."

Judith put a hand on the younger woman's arm, her eyes closing for several seconds, her chest sighing deeply.

"I can't thank you enough for sharing with me. Frederick and I have been suspicious of something for a while now, but nothing specific has come to the fore. This will help us with the right words and verses, Cassie. Thank you. A thousand times, thank you."

Cassandra told her not to hesitate to ask again and went on her way. It had been a marvelous day, and she still got to go home. In that, there was always the possibility that there would be word from Henry or Tate.

Newcomb Park

"Your brother is in his study," Jasper told Cassandra the moment she set foot in the front door.

Cassandra's heart leaped, but she only thanked him quietly and walked that way. Her knock was a little loud, but Henry didn't comment.

"How are you, Henry?" Cassandra asked right away. "Was the trip very tiring?"

"A bit, but I'm doing well," he answered, reminded of her sweetness as she asked about him first.

"Must you return right away, or are you home to stay?"

"I'm home to stay."

"I'm glad. We missed you. How is Tate?" she asked at last, and her questions, without the anxiety that Lizzy and Edward showed, caused him to believe that their siblings had spoken to her.

"He's well. I'm sure you'll hear from him again."

"Did you get my letter, Henry?"

"No." He looked surprised. "I must have missed it."

"It explained to you that I didn't get a letter from Tate. Your letter arrived on its own."

"So you don't know . . ." Henry said with wonder, his voice trailing off.

Cassandra stood silently, her face looking young and vulnerable.

"He still loves you, Cassie," Henry took pleasure in telling her, "and deeply regrets the way he treated you."

Cassandra's entire body sagged with relief.

"All this time you waited," Henry said softly, his voice filled with compassion.

"Thank you for going, Henry," she said quietly. "Thank you so much."

Henry took the next few minutes to explain the situation to his sister. He ended by saying, "Do not doubt that he cares for you, Cassie, but he must stay in London and sort things out."

"Of course. Thank you for telling me. Maybe he'll write to me again."

"Or you could write him."

"I would wish to see his letter first, I think. Do you understand what I mean?"

"Yes. I will search for it, Cassie. Maybe it's in my correspondence or traveling bag."

"Well, I'll be here all evening should you find it."

Henry smiled at her attempt not to pressure him. He was still smiling when she let herself out the door. Once on his own, he prayed for her and for the man in London whose heart must surely be in two places.

Richmond

"Are you certain we should leave her?" Lizzy asked Morland as he led her outside to the garden.

"Yes. She might not even be asleep. It's her way of having a time of quiet."

Lizzy smiled, not at all surprised that Penelope Long would use such a tactic.

Lizzy had been invited to lunch with Morland and his aunt. She had been glad to accept. The meal was sumptuous and the conversation lively, but when they'd retired to the parlor for coffee, Aunt Penelope lasted only a matter of minutes. Morland had been talking when Lizzy noticed that the old woman's head had fallen back and she appeared to be sound asleep. After Morland saw it, he signaled to Lizzy, and in minutes they were stepping out into the sun-filled yard and garden.

Morland started a slow walk among the flowers and hedges. At first there was silence, but then Morland spoke his thoughts.

"There's something we haven't talked about, Lizzy."

"Probably many things, but what is on your mind?"

"Children."

"Our children?" Lizzy asked, using wording that caused hope to burgeon in Morland's heart.

"Yes. I've always pictured myself with many — like your family, not mine. What have you pictured?"

"Many, I think, especially knowing what good friends they can be during all the growing-up years and even into adulthood."

"Do you know how many times I envied Edward?"

"Did you?"

"Yes."

For a few minutes they walked in silence. The day was warm, the sun beating on their heads, and the smells from the garden were glorious.

"I also want a large garden," Morland said, half teasing.

"As do I."

Morland stopped. "You do?"

"I love flowers, Morland."

"No, you don't."

"Yes, I do. I just don't enjoy picking and arranging them. I'm happy to leave that to Cassie."

"You won't always live with Cassie," Morland pointed out.

"And a house must be full of flowers?"

"Yes." Morland just held his smile.

"Well, then," Lizzy retorted, thinking fast and also fighting a smile, "I shall live close to Cassie, and she can come weekly and fill the house."

Morland shook his head lovingly and took her hand in his. He continued their walk thinking, *If you're going to be with me, Lizzy, I think I can agree to just about anything.*

Chapter Twenty

"Please don't miss the example of these people, the significance of the swift repentance of the men of Nineveh," Pastor Hurst urged on Sunday. "Turn to the book of Matthew, chapter 12, where we'll see in verse 39 that Jonah is mentioned. I think it's easy for us to be hard on this man, but he is one of God's prophets, and God used him in a mighty and powerful way."

The church building sounded with the rustle of turning pages. When things grew quiet, Frederick Hurst continued.

"What I really want you to center on just now is verse 41. Follow along with me while I read part of this verse. 'The men of Nineveh shall rise in judgment with this generation, and shall condemn it; because they repented at the preaching of Jonah.'

"Jesus is telling His followers that they are not getting it. We're so certain that if we could walk and talk with Jesus, it would be easier to believe, but these men had His presence, and it still wasn't enough. The folks of Nineveh didn't ask for a sign. They didn't say, 'Just show us something special and our hearts will turn.' No, they knew the end was near and they'd better take this seriously.

"In the book of Jonah, only a man is speaking. God's prophet, yes, but still a man. In the book of Matthew, it's God Himself, standing and talking to these dear men, but they still wanted a sign.

"My friends, how seriously do we take God's Word? The words Jonah spoke were from God. The words we read in Matthew are from God. Do we repent when we know we should, or are we waiting for something special from God?"

Pastor Hurst held up his Bible. "It's all right here. It's here for our reading, re-proof, instruction, and teaching. It's here to comfort and command us. It's here to wonder and wound us. Everything God expects from us, His children, is spelled out here, if we'll only look and learn."

Listening to him, Cassandra was only too happy to close her eyes on the final prayer. She had been so flippant that morning when she read her Bible. Her mind had wandered back and forth to Tate a dozen times.

I have a copy of Your precious Word, and I

don't even stop with the wonder of that. I just page through it, knowing I can come back another day. I'm sorry, Father. I'm sorry I haven't seen it for what it is. Please instruct me and teach me.

The first bars of the last song were being played when Cassandra came to her feet with the rest of the congregation.

"Are you all right?" Edward whispered.

"Yes, thank you."

He held the book for both of them, and Cassandra castigated herself again. She had so much to be thankful for, and yet she fell into discontentment so easily. Edward was home! Yes, she missed Tate, but Edward was home, and that was reason to rejoice.

Blackburn Manor

"So tell us, Edward," Mr Walker urged over lunch. "What will you miss the most about Africa?"

"The wildlife. It was spectacular."

"Were you not afraid, Edward?" Harriet Thorpe asked; they'd only just met.

"Yes, when we camped outside, especially at night with only a tent to separate us from the nocturnal creatures. But most of the time we were at a distance."

"Tell them about the heat," Lizzy suggested.

"Ah, yes," Edward said with a smile, his teeth looking brilliantly white in his tan face. "It was very warm. Our July has nothing on African heat."

"And what did you do for relief?"

"Find some shade and wait for night to fall."

"When you could be afraid of being eaten again," Cassandra commented and everyone laughed.

Edward laughed as well but went on to regale them with his tales and experiences. By the time he was finished, most of the table's occupants were ready to pack their bags.

"Henry might go with me sometime," Edward said casually, shocking the room into complete silence.

It stayed that way so long that Edward and Henry exchanged a smile.

"They're teasing us," Lizzy said when she saw them.

"No," Henry said simply, "we're not."

The second silence was more comical than the first, but both men knew if they laughed they would never be believed.

"That's one of the things I most appreciate about you, Henry," Mr Walker commented with a smile. "Just when I think I know you, I come around another corner and find I don't."

Color crept into Henry's face, but he smiled a little and nodded in Walker's direction. Taking pity on him, the host diverted the conversation in an effortless manner, and it wasn't long until the men were headed into the study and the women wandered into the parlor.

They'd only just arrived in that room when Mrs Walker remembered that she had wanted to show to Lizzy a tapestry she was working on. Telling them they would return soon, the two women left Harriet and Cassandra on their own.

"Something about you is different," Harriet charged Cassandra the moment the other women exited the room. "What is it?"

"Different?" Cassandra hedged a bit, not entirely certain what she was referring to.

"Yes, and I want to know what it is. Not until just now did I realize that you were not yourself that day you came to lunch."

Cassandra played for a moment with the folds of her dress. Harriet didn't speak, but the younger woman knew she was waiting.

"Tate didn't leave in a very good humor,"

Cassandra said carefully. "He left me in doubt of his intentions."

"What did he do?"

"He was very angry and said that everything had changed. I didn't know what to think. I wasn't very certain that I would ever see him again."

"Oh, Cassandra, I'm sorry you had to go through that. Tate was just as upset when he left Pembroke, but I of course have known him years longer. It's very unusual for him to respond in such a way, and when he does, his repentance is swift and genuine."

"He did communicate through my brother that he still cares."

"He didn't write you directly?"

"He did, but the letter was lost."

"And you were left here wondering and waiting," Harriet guessed.

"At times it was awful. I fear I sinned repeatedly with my questioning of God and His motives."

Harriet took her hand.

"I can't count how many times I've failed God, Cassandra. He's so good and faithful, but I don't choose to trust."

"That explains it very well."

"But now you know, so you're doing better."

"As a matter of fact, I had begun to do better before Henry arrived home, but yes, it's lovely to know that Tate still cares."

Harriet smiled. "I could have set your mind at ease."

Cassandra shook her head. "Edward and Lizzy tried. I didn't believe them."

"Why did you believe Henry?"

"He'd seen the letter that was lost. He knew how Tate felt."

"And Tate loves you."

Cassandra smiled, her face growing pink. "Yes, it would seem so."

Harriet's smile was tender as she observed the sweet curves of Cassie's profile. Cassandra Steele had the most adorable round button nose and softly rounded chin. It gave her a guileless, childlike demeanor.

"I think you might be staring, Mrs Thorpe," Cassandra teased her.

"I'm just so pleased that Tate can see how lovely you are."

"He does like the way I look. I worried about that. It's more important to me than it should be, but I'm mostly pleased that he loved the inside of me first."

"That's a wonderful gift. We all assume we're going to be young and good-looking forever. If that's all we marry, it will never last. How nice to know that although you enjoy each other's features, the real love is built on something much more important."

"That was nicely put."

"I manage to find the right words every once in a while."

Cassandra laughed at her choice of words before noticing the way the shade had moved to the veranda outside.

Cassandra suggested they go out through the double glass doors and sit outside. It was a bit warm, but Harriet liked the idea. When Mrs Walker and Lizzy returned, they joined them. The men were not long in following, and the lively conversation from lunch simply continued out-of-doors.

"When will this weariness go away?"

"What type of weariness?"

It was the following Wednesday, and Henry was meeting again with his friend back at Blackburn Manor.

"Forcing myself to converse is so tiring. Will it ever get easier?"

"I think it's safe to say that it will, but it might take some time."

Henry looked exhausted just thinking about it.

"Do you know Galatians 6:9?" Walker asked.

"I'm not sure."

" 'And let us not be weary in well doing; for in due season we shall reap, if we faint not.' "

"Now it's familiar."

"Well, most folks forget to memorize the verse ahead of it. Verse 8 says, 'For he that soweth to his flesh shall of the flesh reap corruption; but he that soweth to the Spirit shall of the Spirit reap life everlasting.'

"Don't forget what you're working toward, Henry. We have to keep fighting the flesh — in your case, fighting the urge to keep quiet when there are important words to be said — so that we reap of the Spirit. And by the way, one time I looked up the word 'reap.' I thought I knew it to mean glean or harvest, but it also means to obtain or win."

"That's excellent. Thank you for telling me."

"We certainly enjoyed visiting with your family on Sunday."

"We enjoyed it as well."

"When do you leave for Africa?" Walker asked with a smile, more in jest than anything else.

"Between you and me?" Henry asked.

"Yes."

"Right after my sisters get married."

Walker's head went back when he laughed. It was the last response he'd expected, but as he'd admitted on Sunday, Henry Steele could be something of a surprise.

Newcomb Park

"Oh, look at this bouquet, Mrs Jasper." Cassandra frowned at the dead flowers on the corner table of the dining room. "It must be the heat."

"I think you must be right, Miss Cassandra. I'll get this out straightaway."

"All right. I'm going to go to the garden to pick some blooms."

"It's warm out, Miss Cassandra."

"I'll be all right."

"Very well. I'll take care of this vase while you're out."

Cassandra put a bonnet on her head, found her basket, and left by the front door. There were very few flowers in the front yard, but it was worth a peek. Seeing nothing of interest, she headed around the house to the gardens. Not really in the mood to pick flowers, she felt a bit restless this day. She was hoping the activity would calm her.

It was not a short walk. She was almost to the garden when she realized that while tying her bonnet, she'd left her clippers inside the front door on a table. Still wondering if it was worth the effort, she started back.

Her mind very much on her task, she rounded the corner and ran smack into someone. Head coming up, she looked into Alexander Tate's face for the first time in many days.

"Tate!" Cassandra felt as if she'd been running. "How are you?"

Tate took her hand.

"I am the most contrite of men."

Cassandra began to shake her head to deny him, but he stopped her.

"Do not be easy on me, Cassie. I do not deserve it. I am so dreadfully sorry. I acted without regard for you or the future we might have."

"Please don't pain yourself any longer, Tate, I'm fine. Truly I am. But tell me, you must have found Pierrepont, or you wouldn't be here."

"On the contrary, he has not been located, but I told Ellenborough he could contact me in Collingbourne and returned." Tate stopped and looked into her lovely eyes. "I told him this was a matter of some importance."

Cassandra was out of breath all over again.

Tate reached up, his hands gentle, and untied her bonnet. He smiled once he slipped it from her head.

"I wanted to see your hair."

"I only wore the bonnet so I wouldn't freckle more."

"You may freckle all you wish, but I don't want you to burn. Shall we find some shade?"

Cassandra managed only a nod.

Barely able to keep their eyes from each other, they walked to the back of the house, to the shade-covered seats to the east. They sat down and for a little time just watched each other.

"You received my letter?"

Cassandra laughed a little.

"As a matter of fact, I did not. I wrote Henry to tell him that it hadn't come, but he missed that letter."

Tate reached into his breast pocket and handed her the letter she'd written to Henry.

"I'll let you deliver this if there's still a need."

"Thank you."

"So I need to tell you what the letter said, don't I?"

"Henry told me," she said, blushing for a reason she couldn't name. "Was the city very warm?" she asked to change the subject.

"Yes. Warm as it is here, it's significantly cooler than London."

"Are you in Collingbourne for a time?"

"Well, until my business is complete."

Cassandra felt her heart sink, thinking his reason might be more personal.

"Business of a rather personal nature."

Cassandra's eyes came to his. What she saw there nearly barricaded her breath completely, but she managed to squeak a few words out.

"Business with me?"

"No one else, Cassie."

Cassandra couldn't look at him for a moment. It was too wonderful to be true.

"I had lunch with your Aunt Harriet on Sunday. We were at Blackburn."

"That's very nice," Tate said, just fighting laughter over how often she'd changed the subject. "What did you eat?"

As her mind searched for the information, Cassandra's face was almost too much for him. Her brow lowered and her eyes scanned the sky as though looking for the menu up there. Tate had all he could do not to kiss her.

"I can't recall."

Cassandra saw it then, the twinkle in his eyes, and knew she was being teased.

"Fair enough," she replied. "What did you have for lunch last Sunday?"

"Beef."

Cassandra frowned at him. "You weren't supposed to remember."

"My chef in London always fixes beef for Sunday."

"Not fair! Tell me at least two side dishes."

Tate couldn't do it, and Cassandra began to relax.

"Why were you outside?" Tate asked next.

"I was going to pick a few flowers."

"It's rather warm for that, isn't it?"

Cassandra shrugged. "I find myself needing things to do."

"I can understand that. If I hadn't been centered on finding a certain business manager, I would have paced the floor for thoughts of you."

"I thought of you too," Cassandra admitted, and this time she did not look away or change the subject. "I was hurt, Tate — you need to know that — but not angry. I so wished I could speak to you; a thousand times I wished it."

"And I so desired to change my reaction to the news. You would have thought that I had been in charge all along."

"It's so easy to delude ourselves in that way," Cassandra agreed. "But, Tate, I would make one request of you. If you must leave again, can you take more time to speak with me about it? I wouldn't detain you, and I understand when urgency is needed, but I felt as if you were upset with me to the point that it was over between us. It was very hard to be left in such question."

"I have no plans to ever repeat my actions from that day, Cassie. I'm glad you told me how awful it was for you. It helps my resolve never to fail you in that manner again."

"Thank you, Tate."

"Now, why don't you invite me to dinner, and I'll head to Pembroke and tell my aunt I'm back."

"You haven't see her?"

"No." Tate brushed at his sleeve. "Can you not see the dust?"

"I didn't notice."

The idea of going to his aunt's was lost to him for the better part of a minute. Cassandra was watching him, her eyes not seeing anything but his, and the last thing he wanted to do was leave.

"I must go," he said at last, his voice

quiet. "I think for now it would be the best thing."

Cassandra, whose heart had begun to pound, swiftly nodded. She walked him to his carriage and stood while he climbed in.

It was a quiet couple that said their goodbyes, their eyes still watchful, but neither one was discontented. Tate would return in a few hours, and Cassandra considered sitting around and thinking about him until he arrived.

That evening, Lizzy watched Morland, whose eyes had barely left her since he arrived. Tate was not with them yet, and although she'd asked Morland if something was amiss, he'd only shaken his head no, not answering further.

At present Edward had his attention, but the moment the two men stopped speaking, his eyes went back on her. Morland kept his seat, but Edward wandered over to where Lizzy was looking for a book she'd been telling Henry about.

"You do know that Morland loves you, do you not, Lizzy?"

Lizzy gawked at him and whispered. "Edward, what a question! Was there really some doubt in your mind? Do you think I wish the man to hang about so I can dash his hopes to bits?"

Her outrage amused him. He smiled, not sure why he asked, but also not sure why Morland hadn't asked the question. He somehow thought Lizzy was holding him off.

"What are you smiling at?"

"Nothing," Edward answered, trying to look innocent.

Lizzy rolled her eyes and went over to where Morland was sitting.

"I can't locate that book."

"Which book was it, Lizzy?"

She told him.

"You loaned it to me. I still have it."

"Oh, I'd forgotten. Would you be so kind as to give it to Henry when you're finished?"

"Certainly. You look lovely tonight, by the way."

"Is that why you're staring?"

"That, among other things."

"Such as?"

"I don't think I can wait any longer, Lizzy. I miss you when we're not together. I ache to talk to you after only one day apart."

Lizzy looked into his eyes, feeling the very love he described. She would have gone on looking all night, but Jasper announced that Mr Tate had arrived. The group in the library stood to receive and welcome him. Cassandra and Henry joined them moments later, and all went in to dinner.

Cassandra was not thrilled to be asked to play after dinner, but she did so without complaint. The only person who had not heard her perform was Tate, but for this activity he was the only person who mattered.

Hoping desperately that he couldn't see her warm cheeks, she sat down and started a familiar piece. It was more interest than skill level that hindered Cassandra, as she did in fact play well. She did not, however, fool herself. Charlotte, whose dynamics and phrasing were more accomplished, was the better pianist.

Lizzy had even less interest in performing; her tastes ran to tapestries and books, but she enjoyed listening to music.

"Very nice," Edward said when Cassandra was done, the occupants of the room giving her applause.

"How about some Bach," Lizzy asked.

Cassandra gave a slight nod and began. She had yet to look at Tate but knew he was watching her. He'd done little else all evening. She remembered that they had ended their afternoon together with eyes only for each other. With that in mind, Cassandra found the piano a distraction.

That Tate wanted to keep looking at her was only too clear. What he might not know is that she wanted to look back.

"Are you going to play for us, Lizzy?" Edward had the cheek to ask when Cassandra finished and moved away from the instrument before anyone could suggest another piece.

"No," she said sweetly, her eyes sending a message before she turned to Morland. "Don't you start," she warned him when she saw the gleam in his eyes.

He only smiled.

"Your sister doesn't care to play?" Tate asked quietly when Cassandra came back to sit near him.

"No more than I do."

Well remembering her view on the matter, Tate only smiled.

"It looks as though we're stuck with cards," Edward commented, going for the deck.

The women, thinking they might be asked again to play, were on their feet in a moment. Both of the men in their lives noticed this but only smiled without comment. Morland and Tate liked music, but pushing the women they loved to perform — even women they believed played beautifully — was the last thing they wished to do.

Chapter Twenty-One

Henry had not stayed to breakfast with the family. He and Cassandra had ridden early and she had gone to the table, but as soon as Henry received the morning post, he retired to his study. He surprised the family by joining them again not five minutes later.

Cassandra, Edward, and Lizzy watched him take his regular place at the breakfast table, their food forgotten.

"Have Morland and Tate been exchanging plans?" Henry asked of his sisters.

"Why would you ask that?" Lizzy ventured.

"Because I have received a request for your hand in marriage, Lizzy, and one for yours as well, Cassie. They have come in the same post."

As though they'd practiced the move, both girls' hands came to their mouths before they exchanged looks. They grinned at each other like children and then looked back to Henry.

"I can see by this melancholy reaction that I must say no," Henry said dryly, pushing from his seat amid his sisters' laughter. They were chattering before he could exit the room.

"I think it would be so wonderful to have a double wedding, Cassie."

Cassandra sat very upright, as though she'd been affronted.

"How could you think anything else? I've wished for us to have a double wedding for some time now."

"With baskets of flowers!" Lizzy went on. "That's a must."

"Yes, but now, should our dresses match or be different?"

"I think different, Cassie. We have separate tastes, and I'm a few inches taller. One style might not work for both of us."

"That's true. I think we should go into town today and start shopping."

"I have to see Anne Weston this morning, but we can go directly after."

It wasn't until that moment that they noticed Edward. His head turned back and forth between them as they talked, as if he were watching a ball fly to and fro over a net.

"Do you not have anything else to do, Edward?" Lizzy asked with a smile.

"Not in the least," he sat back. "I find I'm free all day."

The women laughed at him.

"Would you like to accompany us to town?" Cassandra offered, certain he would say no.

"I think I'd better. I may not have a chance to witness such a spectacle ever again."

"You had to ask him," Lizzy said to her sister, but no one was very upset. No, indeed. The Misses Elizabeth and Cassandra Steele of Newcomb Park were going to be wed.

Brown Manor

"He was acting so oddly Wednesday night, Anne. I didn't know what to think. And then in today's post, the letter arrived."

"And one for Cassie too?"

"Yes! Henry sent word back to both men directly."

Anne's sigh was deep, her eyes dreamy.

"How lovely." She looked at Lizzy suddenly. "When, Lizzy? When will you be wed?"

Lizzy looked surprised. "I don't know. I didn't think about it. Cassie and I are going shopping later, but I forgot all about selecting a date."

Anne laughed at her.

"I so wish I could have witnessed this firsthand. You have plans to shop for a wedding, but you don't know the date."

Lizzy had to laugh with her, but the question of a date stayed on her mind. It would have been the only thing on her mind had she known that Morland was already at the house looking for her to discuss this very subject.

"She's gone to see Anne Weston," Cassandra told him.

"I think she mentioned doing that. I forgot all about it."

"I don't suppose I can help with anything?"

"Only if you're going to tell me what day she'll marry me."

"Of course I can," Cassandra said with a smile, shocking Morland, whose mouth was left open. "It's the same day Tate is going to marry me."

"Tate asked for your hand?"

Cassandra smiled. "Just this morning."

Morland hugged her and kissed her cheek. "Congratulations."

"And to you also."

"Thank you. Did I hear you right? We're

having a double wedding?"

Cassandra stared at him, filled with sudden doubts. She'd failed to consider what the men would want.

"Well, we thought it would be nice." Cassandra's voice had grown soft and uncertain. "I haven't asked Tate, nor has Lizzy asked you, but then you know that."

Morland smiled, just short of laughter.

Cassandra sighed. "There's more to this than I imagined."

"That's probably true for all of us, Cassie, but if Tate feels as I do, you may have any wedding you wish. What does Henry think?"

This time Morland could not stop his laugh. Cassandra's eyes had grown saucerlike, telling him that Henry had not been let in on the plan either.

"Don't panic," Morland cautioned when he could speak. "Why don't we first look at a calendar, choose some dates, and see if any of those would work for you and Lizzy. From there, you can ask Tate and gain his input. Henry probably won't care to have much opinion on any of it."

"Good!" Cassandra declared. "That's a fine plan."

When Edward wandered along not five

minutes later, he naturally wanted to know what they were doing.

"Finding a date to be wed."

Edward wondered at the fact that Morland and Cassandra were working together but only said, "Can I help?"

"No!" Cassandra replied with such panic that Edward chuckled.

"Edward, do you know what I've done?"

"No, what?"

"I've begun planning without ever once asking Tate if he minded a double wedding."

"He won't, Cassie. And as bride it's your choice."

"But it's his wedding day too."

Edward only smiled and reiterated, "He won't care, Cassie. You may trust me on this."

Cassandra only frowned in concentration and went back to the calendar.

"Let's see," Morland was saying. "The banns have to be read two weeks in church, so this Sunday and next, and we could all be married in about ten days."

"You can't be serious, Morland!" Cassandra turned to him. "There are dresses to be made and plans to settle."

"Twenty days, then?"

His face was so serious that Cassandra turned to Edward.

"Can you please make him understand?"

"Understand what?" Lizzy wished to know, coming through the doorway in the nick of time.

Cassandra and Morland began to speak at the same time, and once again, Edward sat back and watched, not sure if even the wildlife in Africa could compete with this spectacle for interest and fascination.

"Wait a minute," Lizzy cut in, "I'm not getting any of this."

Cassandra closed her mouth and let Morland explain, satisfied to see her sister's surprise when Morland suggested they marry in 20 days' time.

"I don't think that's enough time, Morland," Lizzy said gently. "Will it bother you terribly to have the wedding in August or even September when the weather has cooled?"

Waiting that long had never occurred to Morland, and he was very bothered but did not immediately answer.

"Morland?" Lizzy tried again.

"I'm just considering a few things," he said but didn't elaborate.

Lizzy looked to Cassandra, but she only shrugged.

"Did you really think it would be in just a few weeks, Morland?" Lizzy asked, not certain what he was thinking.

"I admit I did."

Lizzy didn't know what to say. Charlotte had taken several months to plan her wedding. It didn't seem overly long to any of them at the time, but maybe Barrington would disagree.

"We haven't actually chosen a date," Cassandra mentioned. "I still haven't spoken to Tate."

"Well, maybe you should do that, Cassie, and let me know what you decide." Morland's smile was normal, and his eyes were kind, but Lizzy could tell he was disappointed.

"Now, I'd best be off. I understand you were headed to do some shopping."

Lizzy was so surprised she didn't speak. Morland bid them all goodbye and made his way to the door.

He was gone before Lizzy realized she should have gone after him. Thankfully, her siblings did nothing to add to her confusion. Edward told her that he was ready to go at any time, and Cassandra said she would need only ten minutes.

Lizzy thanked them, decided to go ahead and shop, and hoped that Morland would come back that evening so they could talk.

Richmond

"Back from Lizzy's, are you?" Aunt Penelope wished to know.

"Yes."

"When are you getting married?"

"Not for some time, it would seem."

"What do you mean?"

Morland took a chair, sitting down slowly, his face distracted.

"It seems Lizzy feels she needs time."

"What kind of time?"

"To prepare."

"Well, what day have you set?" The elderly aunt was growing testy.

"Sometime in August or September."

"That's just two months away, Morland, if that! What did you expect?"

"I didn't expect two months."

"Gracious, Morland! Did you really think Lizzy could snap her fingers and put this wedding together?"

Morland had to admit that he must have thought that very thing. Either that or he was utterly unaware of what a wedding entailed.

"So tell me," Morland asked, a little testy himself. "What exactly has to be done?"

Penelope calmed in an instant. Her favorite nephew was never cross with her. Telling her about this situation had most definitely bothered him. Her voice, when she began to speak, held all the patience in the world.

"It takes some time to make dresses, Morland, especially when working in a small town like Collingbourne. If Lizzy were being married in London, it might be easier, but she's not. And the dresses can be made only after fabric and design are chosen. Indeed, Morland, you'll be needing a new suit yourself.

"And that has to happen before the wedding clothes are made. She's going to want a new wardrobe for your honeymoon. *That* event will be planned by you, incidently. And then there are flowers to prepare, wedding hats with veils to be chosen, the pastor to notify, the church spoken for, and banns read.

"Morland," she concluded. "There is simply no need to rush this. If you do, your bride is sure to be exhausted when you begin life as husband and wife."

Morland could have kicked himself. Had he only stopped and asked a few questions, he could have figured all of this out for himself. He had been at Charlotte and Barrington's wedding. It had not been an elaborate affair, but it never once occurred to him how it all happened.

"Thank you," Morland said simply.

"Is it possible that you'll be going back to Newcomb tonight?" Penelope asked, a distinct twinkle in her eye.

Morland smiled. "If Lizzy hadn't gone shopping, I'd be leaving on the spot."

Penelope smiled at him. "Never forget, Morland, she loves you. And all couples have these things to work out."

Morland nodded, rose from his chair, and went to kiss her cheek.

"Go on now," she said, shooing him away. "You'll have me in tears, and it's bad luck to cry at a wedding."

"You don't believe in luck."

"I know that, but I had to say something!"

Morland laughed as he made his exit. He checked the clock, his mind making calculations. Even if the sisters weren't back, he would head back to Newcomb in five hours and wait there. He'd speak to Lizzy the moment she returned.

"I know you want to work things out with Morland," Cassandra said sternly from her place in the carriage. "And you will work things out. If I know Morland, he'll be back this very night, but for right now we're going shopping for the most special day of our lives, and you're going to have fun!"

Edward turned in his seat to watch his younger sister. He didn't think he'd ever heard her so bold. She noticed his appraisal and turned to spear him with her eyes.

"Don't you agree, Edward?"

"Wholeheartedly."

Cassandra looked back to Lizzy, her look pointed.

"I'll work on it," Lizzy said, her own eyes sending a message.

Cassandra let the matter drop. She was sorry that Morland had left before things were settled, but she knew they would work out. There was no point in crying about it now.

That she was being selfish and unfair occurred to her just moments later. She looked across at her sister and knew she'd been in the wrong.

"Or we can go another day, Lizzy," Cassandra said softly. "I should haven't pushed you. Just say the word, and we'll go home."

"Thank you, Cassie, but I think you might be right. It won't hurt to look, even if I don't spot anything I like."

"But, Lizzy," Cassandra teased, "aren't you getting married in 20 days?"

Lizzy couldn't help but laugh.

"Poor Morland. I do hope he'll give me a chance to explain."

Edward and Cassandra wished for the same thing but made the remainder of the ride to Collingbourne in silence.

The women went directly to the dressmaker's shop. Edward did not join them but promised to meet them later. Lizzy had low expectations but did in fact spot a length of white silk that she was immediately drawn to. She fingered the fabric, smiling at the perfect texture.

"What do you think of this?" she asked Cassandra when the younger woman checked on her.

"Oh, it's lovely. It feels marvelous."

"Doesn't it, though?"

"Will you go with that?"

"Yes, I think I will. I'm just so surprised to find something so swiftly."

"What do you think about this fabric?" Cassandra brought out the bolt she'd found.

"I like it. Oh, I really like it. I want that."

Cassandra began to laugh.

"Don't start that, Lizzy. What you have picked out is perfect."

Lizzy frowned down at her sister's choice.

"But I like yours better."

"Well, the styles of our dresses are sure to be completely different, so it doesn't really matter what fabric we choose, does it?"

"No, probably not."

But it was nowhere near that simple. The typically practical-minded Lizzy altered her decision with nearly everything they found.

Cassandra stuck with her first choice, and Lizzy ended up getting the same. Both were very content. They looked at patterns, but only Cassandra found something she liked. They spoke of looking at hats and accessories, but suddenly both were tired.

"Is Tate coming for dinner?" Lizzy asked, once they were on their way home. Edward hadn't said what he had found to do.

"Yes, and then I'm invited there tomorrow night. Lizzy," she asked, changing the topic, "what will you do if Morland doesn't come this evening?"

Lizzy looked to Edward and then back to Cassandra.

"I'll ask a certain brother if he can persuade him."

This was the last word on the matter, and in the end it was of no consequence. Morland was there when they arrived, asking immediately to see Lizzy.

"Please forgive me, Lizzy," were the first words out of Morland's mouth.

"There's nothing to forgive."

Morland shook his head. "I can't think when I moved off course. My expectations were utter nonsense."

"You just didn't know."

Morland still looked contrite. "Aunt Penelope spoke to me."

"Oh, no." Lizzy laughed a little. "Was she very harsh?"

"A bit, but then she calmly explained it all to me."

"I'll have to thank her."

"So what date did you choose?"

"Tate is coming for dinner, and we'll work on it then."

Morland nodded, still getting used to the fact that things could take as long as they did.

"I found dress material."

"Did you?" Morland asked with pleasure, not having expected this.

"Yes. Cassie found material and a pattern, so she was pleased as well."

"It sounds as if you're off to a good start."

Lizzy smiled at his understanding, even as she wondered if they could marry sooner. She didn't want to exhaust herself, but in truth she was just as eager as he was.

"Tate is here," Edward opened the parlor door long enough to say.

Lizzy thanked him, and the two went out to greet him. A short time later, they all went in to dinner.

"Has a date been set?" Henry asked over the meal.

"Not quite." Morland took the question. "But we're looking at the end of August or early September. We plan to settle the matter directly after dinner."

"Will that give everyone enough time to prepare?"

There were nods all around before Henry lobbed his next question.

"Where will you and Lizzy live, Morland?"

"I'm still working on that. There are two properties in the area. I'll probably take Lizzy to see them next week."

"Tate?" Henry moved to him next.

"I've asked my aunt if we can use Pembroke for the first ten months of our marriage. I think that will give us time to decide where we want to be."

Cassandra did not know this and found herself smiling. Tate caught her eye and winked. Cassandra bent her head over her plate to cover her blush, but her grin still stretched across her face.

And she just kept smiling, even after the meal. The four of them met together around the calendar, and in short order chose August 28, 1812. They informed Henry before settling down to cards. In everyone's estimation, the evening passed much too swiftly.

"Are you still awake?"

"Yes, Cassie, come in."

Cassie climbed onto Lizzy's bed, her own gown and robe in place, and settled against the headboard with her. Lizzy set her book aside and turned to her.

"Are you pleased with the date?"

"Yes. It won't be so warm in late August, and that was my only concern. Do you think Morland is happy with it, Lizzy?"

"Yes. His aunt explained things to him, and he was very understanding."

"I'm glad."

Lizzy waited, wondering what was really on her mind. She soon found out.

"Lizzy, do you think about your wedding night very often?"

"Almost every time I climb into this bed."

"Do you truly?"

"Yes. Did you think you were the only one?"

"I guess I did. Are you at all nervous?"

"A little. It's hard to imagine after the kissing."

"I can't even imagine the kissing."

Lizzy smiled.

"Has Morland kissed you?"

"Yes."

"And?"

Lizzy laughed a little. "At first I was so surprised that I barely knew what was happening, but then I realized I enjoyed it very much."

Cassandra thought about kissing Tate and felt herself blush.

"I'm going to blush the entire service, Lizzy," Cassandra whispered, quietly outraged. "And every moment of my honeymoon. I'm certain of it."

Lizzy laughed. "I don't think you will, and besides, you won't have eyes for anyone but Tate, so you won't notice who sees your red face."

"Where will you and Morland honeymoon?"

"I haven't asked him yet. Has Tate told you?"

Cassandra nodded. "Just tonight. For a few nights we'll be at the home of friends — the owners will be in London — and then on to Weston-super-Mare."

"To the sea! How fun."

"We're going to sea bathe."

"That will be wonderful."

"I shall have to add a bathing costume to my list of clothing."

In a moment, the women were talking about their trousseaus and the fact that Lizzy still had to find a wedding dress pattern that she liked.

They did not speak on the subject of wedding nights again, but as each woman settled into her own bed for sleep, it returned as an issue in both of their minds.

Chapter Twenty-Two

Thornton Hall

"A double wedding, Mari!" her sister-in-law announced with enthusiasm. "Isn't it marvelous?"

"Yes. I can just imagine the activity at Newcomb Park."

Oliver, the youngest of the Palmer clan, came looking for his mother just then. He toddled along wanting into Lydia's lap, his cousin Catherine not far behind him. Once the little ones were comfortably ensconced in their mothers' laps, thumbs in place, the women continued to talk.

"How is Judith?" Marianne wished to know. "Has everyone in the church family figured it out?"

"They would have to have poor eyesight not to notice. She's beginning to think she's carrying twins."

"I had a dream of that sort when I was expecting Catherine. One was a baby and the other was a pig. It was the most horrific sight. I was afraid to go back to sleep for hours."

Lydia found this highly amusing, and her burst of laughter startled her young son, who had been falling asleep in her arms. This made the scene even more amusing, and both women shook with their efforts to hold in their giggles.

Marianne glanced down at Catherine, who was smiling around her thumb, finding her own amusement over her mother's shaking and laughing. Marianne's smile was very tender for her daughter, and she bent her head to press a kiss to the soft, tiny brow.

Another one like this, Lord. I hope you give me another one like this.

Richmond

"Did you see the dress?" Penelope asked her nephew three weeks before the wedding.

"Yes. It's perfect."

"I've worn it before, you know."

"Yes."

"That doesn't matter, of course, but I thought you should know. Everyone is to be looking at the bride on that day in any event, and on your wedding day they'll have two brides to stare at."

Morland only nodded, not certain why he was hearing all of this.

"I think it's wasteful to have more clothing than you need," Penelope went on, even as Morland knew she had dozens of dresses. "I don't need a new dress. I don't go out much anymore, and I can't see having a new garment for one day."

"Why are you telling me this?" Morland suddenly asked pointedly, even knowing it might upset her.

"I just thought you should know," she said, her voice becoming quiet.

"Do you know," Morland began gently, "that you are all I have? And do you know that I don't care what you wear to my wedding, as long as I have your blessing and you are there in the church with me?"

"I can't stand for very long."

"You may sit for the entire service."

"I'm going to miss you so much," the old woman admitted, her face a mask of pain.

"I'm not going far. Lizzy fell in love with Ludlow. We're staying in Collingbourne so we can be near you, Lizzy's family, and the church family."

Tears filled the old, tired eyes.

"It's bad luck to cry at weddings."

"You don't believe in luck."

The tears would not be stopped.

"Come here, Morland."

In an act much younger than his years, Morland went to her chair and knelt on the floor. Her arms went around him and held him close as she cried. Morland held her back, thanking God for this strong woman. Sometimes cross in her old age, she had been the first one to talk to him about Christ.

Morland had things to do, but he postponed as much as he could to spend most of the day with her. It was one of the most precious times he'd ever known. And in his heart he determined that he and Lizzy would visit often. As he'd reminded his aunt: Until he married Lizzy, she was all he had.

Brown Manor

Drenched with sweat and gasping for air, Anne Weston listened to the tiny cries of her very small daughter and fell back against the pillows with relief. The pain had been nearly unbearable, but the baby was alive. She was early and tiny. But she was alive.

"How is she?" Anne asked, still with very little breath to talk.

"She looks fine." Dr Smith's voice was calm. "She's no larger than a loaf of bread, but everything is there."

"Weston? Where is Weston?"

"He was looking pale. I sent him out of the room. Are you ready to see him?"

"Please."

Weston, who had also heard his daughter's cries, was frozen in the hallway. He stared at the door, his heart beating furiously, but he couldn't move.

"Robert," his mother, Lenore, asked from his side. "Are you all right?"

"The baby cried."

"Yes," she agreed with him, her heart filled with tenderness and compassion even as she realized she'd never seen him this way.

The door opened suddenly and Jenny appeared. With that Weston broke from his trance. He went forward into the room, eyes only for Anne, who was smiling at him and speaking. Lenore was close behind him, looking for a sign of the baby even as she waited and let her son go alone to his wife.

Within minutes, however, the four of them huddled together, the baby in Anne's arms, and looked in wonder at what God had given them. Already asleep, tiny and perfect, Sarah Anne Weston had come into their lives.

Charlotte and Barrington had arrived. The wedding was only two weeks away, and Charlotte showed up at the door, announcing her intentions of helping. Her sisters were delighted to see her, and between the three women, plans had shaped up nicely.

On one of her first days there, Charlotte asked her sisters to come to her room and approve her dress for the wedding.

"Try it on," Lizzy urged her, and the women chatted while she did the honors. They loved the dark plum color and the detailing on the sleeves, telling her it was just right for the season. Charlotte didn't stay in the dress but changed back into her muslin gown and joined her sisters where they'd made themselves comfortable in the chair and on the bed.

It didn't take long before conversation shifted to the wedding night.

"I wasn't afraid, but I was nervous," Charlotte told them openly. "So was Barrington."

"Barrington was nervous?" Cassandra clarified.

"Yes."

Lizzy and Cassandra exchanged surprised looks. Charlotte watched them. It was clear by her sisters' faces that it had never occurred to either of these women that their husbands might be nervous about this new experience as well.

"Charlotte." Cassandra all but whispered the next question. "Did everything work properly?"

Charlotte found the question and her sister's doubtful eyes hysterical and began to laugh.

"What did I say?" Cassandra asked.

But Charlotte was red in the face for laughing and couldn't answer. She had to put a pillow over her mouth to muffle the sound.

Cassandra looked to Lizzy.

"Why was that funny?"

"It just was, Cassie." Even Lizzy chuckled a little. "The wording. You might wonder if a carriage would work properly, but not the relationship between a husband and wife."

Cassandra laughed too, but both younger women waited until Charlotte was in control before expecting her to answer. She hadn't meant to make light of the situation, and she knew she was the perfect person to help, so she searched her mind for what would have comforted her and spoke seriously.

"I think if I could give you one word of advice, I would tell you to enjoy yourself. Ask questions if something isn't completely clear to you. If your husband doesn't know, you can figure it out together. Don't be frustrated and have high expectations of yourself or your groom. Think of it as an adventure and laugh your way through it. It's only one night among a lifetime together. Don't take it too seriously."

"Thank you," Lizzy said, now confessing that she'd been doing just that. "I've been reminding myself that God planned this very special time for husbands and wives, and we should enjoy His gift to us, but I can tell I've been seeing it as a project."

"Morland is sure to enjoy that," Charlotte teased her gently.

The women would have talked longer, but Barrington came looking for his wife not long after. Lizzy and Cassandra vacated the room, and when the door shut, Barrington's brows rose in question.

"Did I interrupt something important?"

"No, I think I put their minds at rest."

"The wedding night?"

"Yes."

Barrington smiled. "They'll be fine."

Charlotte put her arms around him.

"If Morland and Tate are half as loving as you are, they'll be more than fine."

Barrington's arms encircled her as well, their lips meeting in a kiss. There was much he could have said to that comment, but right now it was more satisfying to act out his feelings.

"Dearly beloved," Pastor Hurst said as he began the service on a sunny Friday morning. "We are gathered today in the sight of God and in the company of this assembly to unite this man and this woman, and this man and this woman, in holy matrimony."

Tate tried to hear the rest, but he was completely distracted. Cassandra stood beside him, ready to become his wife. He didn't know when his heart had felt so light.

Morland was in no better shape. He listened to Pastor Hurst, but every fiber of his being wanted to turn and look at the beautiful woman beside him: the woman who loved him, the woman who filled his heart until it threatened to overflow.

The service didn't last overly long. For all the preparation, the ceremony was rather swift work. Soon Pastor Hurst presented Mr and Mrs Morland and Mr and

Mrs Tate to the church family and towns-
folk who attended. The congregation was
quick to wish them well and send them on
their way.

The foursome shared a carriage back to
Pembroke, where Tate and Cassandra exited Morland's carriage and went their
own way.

The sisters hugged, their eyes alight with
happiness.

"I'll see you when you get back," Lizzy
said.

"Yes. We won't stay away as long as
Charlotte did."

"No, indeed."

A final hug and a wave, and the two families separated. Having sat and visited in
the coach, each couple was now alone, free
to hold each other and dream and talk
until they arrived at their destinations for
the night.

The couples gone, Walker caught up
with Henry outside the church, wanting to
offer his congratulations to him personally.

"Well, Henry, all three sisters married in
one year."

"Yes, Walker." Henry was smiling. "And
to men I count it a privilege to know."

"Do you never yearn for yourself, Henry? Do you never wish for a wife and companion of your own?"

Henry's smile grew. "Walker, you should know better. She might expect me to talk to her."

James Walker laughed and turned back to where the coach had departed. Though long out of view, he prayed for the two new families, feeling utterly content that they would be staying in the area. He hoped they would be among them for a very long time.

"That was a lovely meal," Lizzy told Morland hours later, just as he reached for her hand across the dining table they shared at the inn.

"You didn't eat very much."

"I find I'm suddenly all aflutter, Morland. We've known each other for years. Why would I feel that way?"

"This is new. This is foreign and exciting."

"But it's with you. Not some stranger, but you, my friend, and the man I love."

"I think," Morland's voice dropped, "that I would like to finish this conversation in our room."

"Do you think someone will hear us?"

"No. I think I'm going to end up chasing you around the room, and I want to increase my chances."

Lizzy's hand came to her mouth to keep from laughing, but she wasn't about to argue. When Morland rose to help her with her chair, she stood and tucked her arm in his. Rather taken with each other, that they made it up the stairway of the inn to their room above was something of a miracle.

"Do you know what my sister told me a few days ago?" Cassandra said when they were finally alone at the home they were staying in their first night.

Tate shook his head no, stepping very close to wait for her answer.

"She said to see this night as an adventure and to laugh my way through it."

Tate smiled, his hands finding hers.

"I like that idea," he whispered. "Will you go on an adventure with me, Mrs Tate?"

"Anytime you ask."

Mrs Tate went into his arms, all doubts fleeing. His first kiss sent her pulses racing, and she found herself with one final thought: *You were right, Charlotte. This is going to be a most wondrous adventure.*

Epilogue

Ludlow

"We've a letter, Lizzy," Morland said as he climbed back into bed on a lazy Saturday morning. "It's from Henry."

"Oh, please read it, Morland," she begged, snuggling close in the large bed they had shared for several weeks.

Dearest Morland and Lizzy,
We are arrived safely. It was raining when we got to the house, but nothing torrential. I can feel the heat that Edward spoke of, although I think the weather may have cooled some.

I never in my life thought to see a live elephant, but I can tell you that I have. He was huge. A bull with several females. When he trumpeted, I shook in terror but would not have missed it for the world.

Morland had to stop. His wife was gasping and laughing with such delight

425

that he had to stop and watch her.

"Can you imagine?" Lizzy exclaimed. "I almost wish we could go."

"Well, maybe someday we will. Shall I read on?"

"Yes, I shall try to remain quiet."

The nights are warm, so warm that you can hear insects moving about all night. I haven't slept deeply since arriving, but we nap in the afternoons when the heat is at its fiercest.

Edward and I speak of you often, hoping you're doing well. We shall be gone for another two months, and then I shall be more than ready to come home. Your Christmas gifts this year will all be quite exotic. Lizzy, maybe you would like a huge beetle of your own.

Love to both of you. Take care and God bless.

> *Warmly,*
> *Henry*

"How wonderful," Lizzy said, her voice dreamy.

Morland set the letter aside and slipped his arms around her.

"It was wonderful," he agreed. "But I can't say that I would switch England right now for Africa."

Lizzy snuggled against him and kissed his neck and chin.

"Why is that?"

Morland's eyes lit with little flames.

"I'll give you a hint," he said before his lips found hers. Lizzy had all she could do not to giggle, but her husband was right. His hint gave away the answer.

Pembroke

Alexander Tate had misplaced his wife of two months. He was certain she would be enjoying breakfast by now, but she was nowhere downstairs.

He glanced into the room they shared, Aunt Harriet's old room, but didn't see her. A thorough search of the upstairs did not unearth her, and Tate was headed back down the stairs when he remembered.

"I had a feeling I would find you here," Tate said, having finally gained the second-story porch from their bedroom.

He hadn't checked earlier because the days had cooled considerably.

"I did warn you," Cassandra said with a smile, "that I would want to live out here."

"Yes, you did." Tate put his hands on the

arms of her chair and bent to give her a lingering kiss.

"Are you not cold?"

"Not anymore."

Tate took a seat nearby.

"What's this?" Cassandra asked, seeing the paper in his hand.

"A letter from Ellenborough. A bill actually."

"Well worth it, I would imagine."

"Yes. Pierrepont is behind bars, and we recover a little more property all the time."

"How did he ever imagine he would get away with such a scheme?"

"I don't know. I tried to speak to him, but he wouldn't see me."

Cassandra remembered that. At the time, Tate said that his business manager had probably hated him for years. It made them both very sad.

"Would you like to go riding with me today?" Tate invited.

Cassandra looked at him.

"Do you think you should?"

"Yes."

"What brought this about?"

"I finally feel that it's time. I haven't been afraid really, just not willing to risk it again."

"So why now?"

Tate studied her. "I don't know, except that I want to do everything with you. I don't want to have a part of our life that you have to enjoy without me while I stand on the side and watch."

"Will you mind, Tate, if we go very slowly?"

"Who's worrying now?"

"I am."

Tate kissed her again.

"We won't move above a walk. We'll just ride along on this sunny, cool morning, knowing we have all the time in the world."

Cassandra liked the sound of that. She leaned and kissed him and then pulled back, getting ready to stand.

"Shall I go and dress now? Would you like to leave right away?"

Tate was already pulling her back to him, his arms possessive and strong.

"Later," he said softly. "Remember, we have all the time in the world."

About the Author

Lori Wick is one of the most versatile Christian fiction writers in the market today. Her works include pioneer fiction, a series set in Victorian England, and contemporary novels. Lori's books (3.5 million copies in print) continue to delight readers and top the Christian bestselling fiction list. Lori and her husband, Bob, live in Wisconsin with "the three coolest kids in the world."